GW00372432

30130503565900

PORTRAIT OF A MAN WITH RED HAIR

Hugh Walpole subtitled this story *A Romantic Macabre*, and it is a classic study in terror and madness. Harkness is a sophisticated yet curiously innocent American traveller, who comes to Treliss in north Cornwall for a holiday. Overhearing by chance an exchange between a young husband and wife, from which it is clear that the latter is being subjected to some strange mental cruelty, he becomes involved in a bizarre plot to rescue her. He meets her father-in-law, who is like himself a connoisseur of art, and at first finds 'the man with red hair' an ambiguous character, but soon discovers that behind the civilised veneer lurk all kinds of primal horrors. The rescue attempt is successful, until a fog descends and the party find themselves back at the house from which they have just escaped, and at its owner's mercy. It is a novel not only of suspense, but also of genuine psychological depth, a 'portrait' in a very real sense, full of tensions and contrasts.

PORTRAIT OF A MAN WITH RED HAIR

Hugh Walpole

Introduction by Rupert Hart-Davis

THE BOYDELL PRESS

Introduction © Rupert Hart-Davis

First published 1925
First published in BOOKMASTERS 1984
by The Boydell Press
an imprint of Boydell and Brewer Ltd
PO Box 9, Woodbridge, Suffolk, IP12 3DF

British Library Cataloguing in Publication Data

ISBN 0 85115 231 7

Printed in Great Britain by
St Edmundsbury Press, Bury St Edmunds, Suffolk

ESSEX COUNTY LIBRARY

*BOOKMASTER is a registered trademark of
Bowaters United Kingdom Paper Corporation Ltd and
is used with their permission*

ER9326

INTRODUCTION

On 9 February 1923, when Hugh Walpole, aged thirty-nine and already an increasingly successful novelist, was in the middle of a tumultuous lecture tour of the United States, he wrote in his diary: 'Fixed the serial-rights for the next novel with [Arthur] Vance [Editor of the *Pictorial Review*] over the telephone for 15,000 dollars—there's something.' He dashed off a synopsis of the proposed story, Vance accepted it with acclamation, and the contract was signed.

He had no time for novel-writing while he was lecturing, and on 4 March he began what he thought would be a short story called 'Red Amber', but which later grew into a full-length novel, *The Old Ladies*.

The tour ended on May 29, and on June 1, at the Waldorf-Astoria Hotel in New York, 'Began *Portrait of a Man with Red Hair*. It started easily, and I have had it so long in my head that it should not be difficult to do—intense joy at returning to writing again.' He wrote steadily while staying in New Jersey with the Fowlers (to whom he dedicated the book) and on 11 June recorded 'Finished first quarter of book—wonderful pace!'

Homeward bound on the *Empress of France* he wrote two thousand words a day, more in Edinburgh staying with his parents, and at Munich on 16 July 'finished the first half of *The Red-Haired Man*—not bad in six weeks, considering how much travelling I've been doing during that time'.

Then, staying with his parents at Champéry in Switzerland, 'August 5. I have never had anything harder to do than my dialogue between the three towards the end of the book. The slightest mistake and it slips over into silliness.' And, two days later, 'Finished *Red Hair*. June 1–August 7. Never have I written a book so fast—but it had to be written this way. It's of course a book of atmosphere and not of character.'

But on November 12 he had 'a most horrible blow'. Vance, who had expected an ordinary thriller, was appalled by what he called the 'revolting character' of the story, with its sadistic lunatic as villain, and said he could not possibly print it in his paper. Hugh immediately told his mother: 'I think I shall not publish *The Red-Haired Man* as a book. I am at present dissatisfied with it. I shall lose a good deal of money if I don't, but that is better than publishing a poor thing. I am happy about *The Old Ladies*. Never will I write anything for money again.'

The Old Ladies, written almost as fast as its predecessor, was finished on 9 January 1924 and published on October 7. By then Hugh had changed his mind about the rejected *Red-Haired Man*. The American serial-rights were taken over by the *Cosmopolitan* magazine, the English ones bought by *Nash's*, and the book was published by Macmillan on 14 October 1925. By this time he had already finished his next novel, *Harmer John*, and was well into its successor, *Wintersmoon*. From now he was always a long way ahead of his publisher, and when he died in 1941 he left two and a half unpublished novels.

The reviews of *The Red-Haired Man* were mostly favourable, the sales excellent, and the book has appeared in many editions, as well as in a Walpole omnibus-book called *Four Fantastic Tales*. It was dramatised by Benn Levy and produced at the Little Theatre in February 1928, with a terrifying performance by Charles Laughton as Crispin. It was also produced in America and made into a film.

The original manuscript, bound, as were all Hugh's manuscripts, in full morocco, is now in my library and will eventually be preserved in the University of Tulsa, Oklahoma. As ever with Hugh, there is scarcely a word altered, added, or deleted. So clear was the story in his mind that it might be automatic writing.

One curious fact I cannot with certainty explain. The manuscript is entitled *The Flight of the Duchess*, and the text begins, as in the printed version, with the opening lines of Browning's poem of that name. But if the story of the Red-Haired Man was so firmly in Hugh's mind, as it certainly was, it is hard to imagine how he thought that title suitable. Browning's poem tells of the beautiful and ill-treated wife of a mediaeval Duke who is rescued by a gipsy witch. I think Hugh happened to read the poem just then, and brought it in willy-nilly into his book. He often introduced his latest admirations into his novels. Harkness's etchings in this book are the result of Hugh's buying $8000 worth of etchings during his American tour. But he soon realised that *Portrait of a Man with Red Hair* was the right title.

The story is set in Cornwall, where Hugh had spent all his childhood holidays with his mother's family at Truro; later he had his own cottage overlooking the little harbour of Polperro. Treliss, he said, was 'a faint echo of St Ives as it used to be—not at all as it is now'. The dance through the town, which he had already described in his second novel *Maradick at Forty*, was based on the annual Floral Dance at Helston.

Hugh's greatest gift was his narrative power as a story-teller. Here, as in all his novels, however improbable the plot, the reader always wants to know what is going to happen next—a sure sign of the born novelist.

13 March 1984   RUPERT HART-DAVIS
(Hugh's hundredth birthday)

. . . Within these few restrictions, I think, every writer may be permitted to deal as much in the wonderful as he pleases ; nay, if he then keeps within the rules of credibility, the more he can surprise the reader the more he will engage his attention, and the more he will charm him.

As a genius of the highest rank observes in his fifth chapter of the Bathos, " The great art of all poetry is to mix truth with fiction, in order to join the credible with the surprising."

For though every good author will confine himself within the bounds of probability, it is by no means necessary that his characters or his incidents should be trite, common, or vulgar ; such as happen in every street, or in every house, or which may be met with in the home articles of a newspaper. Nor must he be inhibited from showing many persons and things which may possibly never have fallen within the knowledge of great part of his readers.

HENRY FIELDING.

PART I

THE SEA LIKE BRONZE . . .

PART I

I

You're my friend:
I was the man the Duke spoke to:
I helped the Duchess to cast off his yoke too:
So here's the tale from beginning to end,
My friend!

II

Ours is a great wild country;
If you climb to our castle's top,
I don't see where your eye can stop;
For when you've passed the cornfield country,
Where vineyards leave off, flocks are packed,
And sheep-range leads to cattle-tract,
And cattle-tract to open-chase,
And open-chase to the very base
Of the mountain where, at a funeral pace,
Round about, solemn and slow,
One by one, row after row,
Up and up the pine trees go,
Go, like black priests up, and so
Down the other side again
      To another greater, wilder country. . . .

' To another greater, wilder country . . .
' To another greater . . .'

I

THE soul of Charles Percy Harkness slipped, like
a neat white pocket-handkerchief, out through the

carriage window into the silver-blue air, hung there
changing into a tiny white fleck against the im-
mensity, struggling for escape above the purple-
pointed trees of the dark wood, then, realising that
escape was not yet, fluttered back into the carriage
again, was caught by Charles Percy, neatly folded
up, and put away.

The Browning lines—old-fashioned surely?—
had yielded it a moment's hope. Those and some
other lines from another outmoded book:

' But the place reasserted its spell, marshalling
once again its army, its silver-belted knights, its
castles of perilous frowning darkness, its meadows
of gold and silver streams.

' The old spell working the same purpose.
For how many times and for what intent? That
we may be reminded yet once again that there is
the step behind the door, the light beyond the
window, the rustle on the stair, and that it is for
these things only that we must watch and wait?'

For Harkness had committed the folly of having
two books open on his knee—a peck at one, a peck
at another, a long, eager glance through the window
at the summer scene, but above all a sensuous state
of slumber hovering in the hot scented afternoon
air just above him, waiting to pounce . . . to
pounce . . .

First Browning, then this other, the old book in
a faded red-brown cover, ' To Paradise: Frederick
Lester.' At the bottom of the title-page, 1892—
how long ago! How faded and pathetic the old
book was! He alone in all the British Isles at that
moment reading it—certainly no other living soul
—and he had crossed to Browning after Lester's
third page.

He swung in mid-air. The open fields came swimming up to him like vast green waves, gently to splash upon his face, hanging over him, laced about the telegraph poles, rising and falling with them. . . .

The voice of the old man with the long white beard, the only occupant of the carriage with him, broke sharply in like a steel knife cutting through blotting-paper.

'Pardon me, but there is a spider on your neck!'

Harkness started up. The two books slipped to the floor. He passed his hand, damp with the afternoon warmth, over his cool neck. He hated spiders. He shivered. His fingers were on the thing. With a shudder he flung it out of the window.

'Thank you,' he said, blushing very slightly.

'Not at all,' the old man said severely; 'you were almost asleep, and in another moment it would have been down your back.'

He was not the old man you would have expected to see in an English first-class carriage, save that now in these democratic days you may see any one anywhere. But first-class fares are so expensive. Perhaps that is why it is only the really poor who can afford them. The old man, who was thin and wiry, had large shabby boots, loose and ancient trousers, a flopping garden straw hat. His hands were gnarled like the knots of trees. He was terribly clean. He had blue eyes. On his knees was a large basket and from this he ate his massive luncheon—here an immense sandwich with pieces of ham like fragments of banners, there a colossal apple, a monstrous pear—

'Going far?' munched the old man.

'No,' said Harkness, blushing again. 'To Treliss. I change at Trewth, I believe. We should be there at 4.30.'

'*Should be*,' said the old man, dribbling through his pear. 'The train's late. . . . Another tourist,' he added suddenly.

'I beg your pardon?' said Harkness.

'Another of these damned tourists. You are, I mean. *I* lived at Treliss. Such as you drove me away.'

'I am sorry,' said Harkness, smiling faintly. 'I suppose I *am* that if by tourist you mean somebody who is travelling to a place to see what it is like and enjoy its beauty. A friend has told me of it. He says it is the most beautiful place in England.'

'Beauty,' said the old man, licking his fingers— 'a lot you tourists think about beauty—with your char-a-bangs and oranges and babies and Americans. If I had my way I'd make the Americans pay a tax, spoiling our country as they do.'

'*I* am an American,' said Harkness faintly.

The old man licked his thumb, looked at it, and licked it again. 'I wouldn't have thought it,' he said. 'Where's your accent?'

'I have lived in this country a great many years off and on,' he explained, 'and we don't all say "I guess" every moment as novelists make us do,' he added, smiling.

Smiling, yes. But how deeply he detested this unfortunate conversation! How happy he had been, and now this old man with his rudeness and violence had smashed the peace into a thousand fragments. But the old man spoke little more. He only stared at Harkness out of his blue eyes, said:

' Treliss is too beautiful a place for you.　It will
do you harm,' and fell instantly asleep.

2

Yes, Harkness thought, looking at the rise and
fall of the old man's beard, it is strange and indeed
lamentable how deeply I detest a cross word!　That
is why I am always creeping away from things,
why, too, I never make friends—not *real* friends—
why at thirty-five I am a complete failure—that is,
from the point of view of anything real.

I am filled too with self-pity, he added as he
opened *To Paradise* again and groped for page
four, and self-pity is the most despicable of all the
vices.

He was not unpleasing to the eye as he sat there
thinking.　He was dressed with exceeding neatness, but his clothes had something of the effect of
chain armour.　Was that partly because his figure
was so slight that he could never fill any suit of
clothes adequately?　That might be so.　His soft
white collar, his pale blue tie, his mild blue eyes,
his long tranquil fingers, these things were all
gentle.　His chin protruded.　He was called
' gaunt ' by undiscerning friends, but that was a
poor word for him.　He was too slight for that,
too gentle, too unobtrusive.　His hair was already
retreating deprecatingly from his forehead.　No
gaunt man would smile so timidly.　His neatness
and immaculate spotless purity of dress showed a
fastidiousness that granted his cowardice an excuse.

For I am a coward, he thought.　This is yet
another holiday that I am taking alone.　Alone

after all these years. And Pritchard or Mason, Major Stock or Henry Trenchard, Carstairs Willing or Falk Brandon—any one of these might have wished to go if I had had courage . . . or even Maradick himself might have come.

The only companions, he reflected, that he had taken with him on this journey were his etchings, kinder to him, more intimate with him, rewarding him with more affection than any human being. His seven etchings—the seven of his forty—Lepère's 'Route de St. Gilles,' Legros' 'Cabane dans les Marais,' Rembrandt's 'Flight into Egypt,' Muirhead Bone's 'Orvieto,' Whistler's 'Drury Lane,' Strang's 'Portrait of himself Etching,' and Meryon's 'Rue des Chantres.' His seven etchings—his greatest friends in the world, save of course Hetty and Jane his sisters. Yes, he reflected, you can judge a man by his friends, and in my cowardice I have given all my heart to these things because they can't answer me back, cannot fail me when I most eagerly expect something of them, are always there when I call them, do not change nor betray me. And yet it is not only cowardice. They are intimate and individual as is no other form of graphic art. They are so personal that every separate impression has a fresh character. They are so lovely in soul that they never age nor have their moods. My Aldegrevers and Penczs, he was reflecting. . . . He was a little happier now. . . . The Browning and *To Paradise* fell once more to the ground. I hope the old man does not waken, he thought, and yet perhaps he will pass his station. What a temper he will be in if he does that, and then I too shall suffer!

He read a line or two of the Browning:

Ours is a great wild country;
If you climb to our castle's top,
I don't see where your eye can stop . . .

How strange that the book should have opened again at that same place as though it were there that it wished him to read!

And then *To Paradise* a line or two, now page 376, ' And the Silver Button? Would his answer defy that too? Had he some secret magic? Was he stronger than God Himself? . . .'

And then, Harkness reflected, this business about being an American. He had felt pride when he had told the old man that that was his citizenship. He was proud, yes, and yet he spent most of his life in Europe. And now as always when he fell to thinking of America his eye travelled to his own home there—Baker at the portals of Oregon. All the big trains pass it on their way to the coast—three hundred and forty miles from Portland, fifty from Huntington. He saw himself on that eager arrival coming out by the 11.30 train from Salt Lake City steaming in at 4.30 in the afternoon, an early May afternoon perhaps with the colours violet in the sky and the mountains elephant-dusk—so quiet and so gentle. And when the train has gone on and you are left on the platform and you look about you and find everything as it was when you departed a year ago—the Columbia Café. The Antlers Hotel. The mountains still with their snow caps. The Lumber Offices. The notice on the wall of the café: ' You can EAT HERE if you have NO MONEY.' The Crabill Hotel. The fresh sweet air, three thousand five hundred feet up. The soft pause of the place. Baker did not grow very fast as did other places.

It is true that there had been but four houses when his father had first landed there, but even now as towns went it was small and quiet and unprogressive. Strange that his father with that old-cultured New England stock should have gone there, but he had fled from mankind after the death of his wife, Harkness' mother, fled with his three little children, shut himself away, there under the mountains with his books, a sad, severe man in that long, rambling, ramshackle house. Still long, still rambling, still ramshackle, although Hetty and Jane, who never moved away from it, had made it as charming as they could. They were darlings, and lived for the month every year when their brother came to visit them. But he could not live there! No, he could not! It was exile for him, exile from everything for which he most deeply cared. But Europe was exile too. That was the tragedy of it! Every morning that he waked he thought that perhaps to-day he would find that he was a true European! But no, it was not so. Away from America, how deeply he loved his country! How clearly he saw its idealism, its vitality, its marvellous promise for the future, its loving contact with his own youthful dreams. But back in America again it seemed crude and noisy and materialistic. He longed for the Past. Exile in both with his New England culture that was not enough, his half-cocked vitality that was not enough. Never enough to permit his half-gods to go! But he loved America always; he saw how little these Europeans truly knew or cared about her, how hasty their visits to her, how patronising their attitude, how weary their stale conventions against her full, bursting energy. And yet——! And yet——! He could not live there. After two weeks of Baker, even though he had with him his etchings, his diary in its dark blue cover, Frazer's *Golden Bough*, and some of the Loeb Classics, life was not enough. Hetty and Jane bored him with their goodness and little Culture Club. It was not enough for him that Hetty had read a very good paper on ' Archibald Marshall— the modern Trollope ' to the inhabitants of Baker and Haines. Nevertheless they seemed to him finer women than the women of any other country, with their cheery independence, their admirable common sense, their warm hearts, their unselfishness, but—it was not enough—no, it was not enough. . . . What he wanted . . .

3

The old man awoke with a start.

' And when you come to this Prohibition question,' he said, ' the Americans have simply become a laughing stock. . . .'

Harkness picked up the Browning firmly. ' If you don't mind,' he remarked, ' I have a piece of work here of some importance and I have but little time. Pray excuse me. . . .'

4

How had he dared? Never in all his life had he spoken to a stranger so. How often had he envied and admired those who could be rude and indifferent to people's feelings. It seemed to him that this was a crisis with him, something that he would never forget, something that might alter all his life. Perhaps already the charm of which Maradick had spoken was working. He looked out of his window and always, afterwards, he was to remember a stream that, now bright silver, now ebony dark, ran straight to him from the heart of an emerald green field like a greeting spirit. It laughed up to his window and was gone.

He had asserted himself. The old man with the beard was reading the *Hibbert Journal*. Strange old man—but defeated! Harkness felt a triumph. Could he but henceforward assert himself in this fashion, all might be easy for him. Instead of retreating he might advance, stretch out his hand and take the things and the people that he wanted as he had seen others do. He almost wished that the old man might speak to him again, that he might once more be rude.

He had had, ever since he could remember, the belief that one day, suddenly, some magic door would open, some one step before him, some magic carpet unroll at his feet, and all life would be changed. For many years he had had no doubt of this. He would call it, perhaps, the coming of romance, but as he had grown older he had come to distrust both himself and life. He had always been interested in contemporary literature. Every new book that he opened now seemed to tell him that he was extremely foolish to expect anything of life at all. He was swallowed by the modern realistic movement as a fly is swallowed by an indifferent spider. These men, he said to himself, are very clever. They know so much more about everything than I do that they must be right. They are telling the truth at last about life as no one has ever done it before. But when he had read a great many of these books (and every word of Mr. Joyce's *Ulysses*), he found that he cared much less about truth than he had supposed. He even doubted whether these writers were telling the truth any more than the naïve and sentimental Victorians; and when at last he read a story all about an American manufacturer of washing machines whose habit it was to strip himself naked on every possible occasion before his nearest and dearest relations and friends, and when the author told him that this was a typical American citizen, he, knowing his own country people very well, frankly disbelieved it. These realists, he exclaimed, are telling fairy stories quite as thoroughly as Grimm, Fouqué, and De la Mare; the difference is that the realistic fairy stories are depressing and discouraging, the others are not. He determined to desert the realists and wait until something pleasanter came along. Since it was impossible to have the truth about life any-way let us have only the pleasant hallucinations. They are quite as likely to be as true as the others.

But he was lonely and desolate. The women whom he loved never loved him, and indeed he never came sufficiently close to them to give them any encouragement. He dreamt about them and painted them as they certainly were not. He had his passions and his desires, but his Puritan descent kept him always at one remove from experience. He never, in fact, seemed to have contact with anything at all—except Baker in Oregon, his two sisters, and his forty etchings. He was so shy that he was thought to be conceited, so idealistic that he was considered cynical, so chaste that he was considered a most immoral fellow with a secret double life.

Like the hero of ' Flegeljahre,' he ' loved every dog
and wanted every dog to love him,' but the dogs
did not know enough about him to be interested;
he was so like so many other immaculately dressed,
pleasant-mannered, and wandering American cosmo-
politans that nobody had any permanent feeling for
him—fathered by Henry James, uncled by Howells,
aunted (severely) by Edith Wharton—one of a
million cultured, kindly, impersonal Americans seen
as shadows by the matter-of-fact, unimaginative
British. Who knew or cared that he was lonely,
longing for love, for home, for some one to whom
he might give his romantic devotion? He was all
these things, but no one minded.

And then he met James Maradick.

5

The meeting was of the simplest. At the
Reform Club one day he was lunching with two
men, one a novelist, Westcott, whom he knew very
slightly, the other a fellow-American. Westcott, a
dark, thick-set man of about forty, with a reputation
that without being sensational was solid and well
merited, said very little. Harkness liked him and
recognised in him a kindly shyness rather like his
own. After luncheon they moved into the big
smoking-room upstairs to drink their coffee.

A large, handsome man of between fifty and
sixty came up and spoke to Westcott. He was
obviously pleased to see him, putting his hand on
his shoulder, looking at him with kindly, smiling
eyes. Westcott also flushed with pleasure. The
big man sat down with them and Harkness was

introduced to him. His name was Maradick—
Sir James Maradick. A strange, unreal kind of
name for so real and solid a man. As he sat forward
on the sofa with his heavy shoulders, his deep chest,
his thick neck, red-brown colour, and clear open
gaze, he seemed to Harkness to be the typical,
rather naïve, friendly, but cautious British man of
business.

That impression soon passed. There was something in Maradick that almost instantly warmed his
heart. He responded—as do all American men—
immediately, even emotionally, to any friendly
contact. The reserves that were in his nature were
from his superficial cosmopolitanism; the native
warm-hearted, eager, and trusting American was as
real and active as it ever had been. It was, in five
minutes, as though he had known this large kindly
man always. His shyness dropped from him. He
was talking eagerly and with great happiness.

Maradick did not patronise, did not check that
American spontaneity with traditional caution as so
many Englishmen do; he seemed to like Harkness
as truly as Harkness liked him.

Westcott had to go. The other American also
departed, but Maradick and Harkness sat on there,
amused, and even absorbed.

'If I am keeping you——' Harkness said
suddenly, some of his shyness for a moment returning.

'Not at all,' Maradick answered. 'I have
nothing urgent this afternoon. I've got the very
place for you, I believe.'

They had been speaking of places. Maradick
had travelled, and together they found some of the
smaller places that they both knew and loved—

Dragör on the sea beyond Copenhagen, the woods
north of Helsingfors, the beaches of Ischia, the
enchantment of Girgente with the white goats
moving over carpets of flowers through the ruined
temples, the silence and mystery of Mull. He
knew America too—the places that foreigners never
knew; the teeth-shaped mountains at Las Cruces,
the lovely curve of Tacoma, the little humped-up
hills of Syracuse, the purple horizons beyond Nash-
ville, the lone lake shore of Marquette——

'And then in this country there is Treliss,' he
said softly, staring in front of him.

'Treliss?' Harkness repeated after him, liking
the name.

'Yes. In North Cornwall. A beautiful place.'
He paused—sighed.

'I was there more than ten years ago. I shall
never go back.'

'Why not?'

'I liked it too well. I daresay they've spoiled
it now as they have many others. Thanks to
wretched novelists, the railway company and char-a-
bancs, Cornwall and Glebeshire are ruined. No, I
dare not go back.'

'Was it very beautiful?' Harkness asked.

'Yes. Beautiful? Oh yes. Wonderful. But
it wasn't that. Something happened to me there.' [1]

'So that you dare not go back?'

'Yes. Dare is the word. I believe that the
same thing would happen again. And I'm too
old to stand it. In my case now it would be
ludicrous. It was nearly ludicrous then.' Harkness said nothing. 'How old are you? If it isn't
an impertinence——'

[1] See *Maradick at Forty*.

'Thirty-five? You're young enough. I was forty. Have you ever noticed about places——?' He broke off. 'I mean—— Well, you know with people. Suppose that you have been very intimate with some one and then you don't see him or her for years, and then you meet again—don't you find yourself suddenly producing the same set of thoughts, emotions, moods that have, perhaps, lain dormant for years, and that only this one person can call from you? And it is the same with places. Sometimes of course in the interval something has died in you or in them, and the second meeting produces nothing. Hands cross over a grave. But if those things haven't died, how wonderful to find them all alive again after all those years, how you had forgotten the way they breathed and spoke and had their being; how interesting to find yourself drawn back again into that old current, perilous perhaps, but deep, real after all the shams——'

He broke off. 'Places do the same, I think,' he said. 'If you have the sort of things in you that stir them they produce in their turn *their* things . . . and always will for your kind . . . a sort of secret society; I believe,' he added, suddenly turning on Harkness and looking him in the face, 'that Treliss might give you something of the same adventure that it gave me—if you want it to, that is—if you need it. Do you *want* adventure, romance, something that will pull you right out of yourself and test you, show you whether you *are* real or no, give you a crisis that will change you for ever? Do you want it?'

Then he added quietly, reflectively: 'It changed *me* more than the war ever did.'

'Do I *want* it?' Harkness was breathing deeply,

driven by some excitement that he could not stop to analyse. 'I should say so. I want nothing so much. It's just what I need, what I've been looking for——'

'Then go down there. I believe you're just the kind—but go at the right time. There's a night in August when they have a dance, when they dance all round the town. That's the time for you to go. That will liberate you if you throw yourself into it. It's in August. August the—— I'm not quite sure of the date. I'll write to you if you'll give me your address.'

Soon afterwards, with a warm clasp of the hand, they parted.

6

Two days later Harkness received a small parcel. Opening it he discovered an old brown-covered book and a letter.

The letter was as follows:

DEAR MR. HARKNESS—In all probability in the cold light of reason, and removed from the fumes of the Reform Club, our conversation of yesterday will seem to you nothing but foolishness. Perhaps it was. The merest chance led me to think of something that belongs, for me, to a life quite dead and gone; not perhaps as dead, though, as I had fancied it. In any case, I had not, until yesterday, thought directly of Treliss for years.

Let us put it on the simplest ground. If you want a beautiful place, near at hand, for a holiday, that you have not yet seen, here it is—Treliss, North Cornwall—take the morning train from Paddington and change at Trewth. If you will be advised by me you really should go down for August 6th, when they have their dance. I could see that you are interested in local customs, and here is a most enter-

taining one surviving from Druid times, I believe. Go
down on the day itself and let that be your first impression
of the place. The train gets you in between five and six.
Take your room at the 'Man-at-Arms Hotel,' ten years ago
the most picturesque inn in Great Britain. I cannot, of
course, vouch for what it may have become. I should get
out at Trewth, which you will reach soon after four, and
walk the three miles to the town. Well worth doing.

One word more. I am sending you a book. A completely forgotten novel by a completely forgotten novelist.
Had he lived he would, I think, have done work that would
have lasted, but he was killed in the first year of the war
and his earlier books are uncertain. He hadn't found
himself. This book, as you will see from the inscription,
he gave me. I was with him down there. Some things
in it seem to me to belong especially to the place. Pages
102 and 236 will show you especially what I mean. When
you are at the 'Man-at-Arms' go and look at the Minstrels'
Gallery, if it isn't pulled down or turned into a jazz dancing-
hall. That too will show you what I mean.

Or go, as perhaps after all is wiser, simply to a beautiful
place for a week's holiday, forgetting me and anything I
have said.

Or, as is perhaps wiser still, don't go at all. In any
case I am your debtor for our delightful conversation of
yesterday.—Sincerely yours,   JAMES MARADICK.

What Maradick had said occurred. As the days
passed the impression faded. Harkness hoped that
he would meet Maradick again. He did not do
so. During the first days he watched for him in
the streets and in the clubs. He devised plans
that would give him an excuse to meet him once
more; the simplest of all would have been to invite
him to luncheon. He knew that Maradick would
come. But his own distrust of himself now as
always forbade him. Why should Maradick wish
to see him again? He had been pleasant to him,
yes, but he was of the type that would be agreeable

to any one, kindly, genial, and forgetting you immediately. But Maradick had not forgotten him. He had taken the trouble to write to him and send him a book. It had been a friendly letter too. Why not ask Westcott and Maradick to dinner? But Westcott was married. Harkness had met his wife, a charming and pretty English girl, younger a good deal than her husband. Yes, all right about Mrs. Westcott, but then Harkness must ask another woman. Maradick, he understood, was a widower. The thing was becoming a party. They would have to go somewhere, to a theatre or something. The thing was becoming elaborate, complicated, and he shrank from it. So he always shrank from everything were he given time to think.

He paid all the gentle American's courtesy and attention to fine details of conduct. Englishmen often shocked him by their casual inattention, especially to ladies. He must do social things elaborately did he do them at all. He was gathering around him already some of the fussy observances of the confirmed bachelor. And therefore as Maradick became to him something of a problem, he put him out of his mind just as he had put so many other things and persons out of his mind because he was frightened of them.

Treliss too, as the days passed, lost some of the first magic of its name. He had felt a strange excitement when Maradick had first mentioned it, but soon it was the name of a beautiful but distant place, then a seaside resort, then nowhere at all. He did not read Lester's book.

Then an odd thing occurred. It was the last day in July and he was still in London. Nearly every one had gone away—every one whom he knew. There were still many millions of human beings on every side of him, but London was empty for himself and his kind. His club was closed for cleaning purposes, and the Reform Club was offering him and his fellow-clubmen temporary hospitality.

He had lunched alone, then had gone upstairs, sunk into an arm-chair and read a newspaper. Read it or seemed to read it. It was time that he went away. Where should he go? There was an uncle who had taken a shooting-box in Scotland. He did not like that uncle. He had an invitation from a kind lady who had a large house in Wiltshire. But the kind lady had asked him because she pitied him, not because she liked him. He knew that very well.

There were several men who would, if he had caught them sooner, have gone with him somewhere, but he had allowed things to drift and now they had made their own plans.

He felt terribly lonely, soused suddenly with that despicable self-pity to which he was rather too easily prone. He thought of Baker—Lord! how hot it must be there just now! He was half asleep. It was hot enough here. Only one other occupant of the room, and he was fast asleep in another arm-chair. Snoring. The room rocked with his snores. The papers laid neatly one upon another wilted under the heat. The subdued London roar came from behind the windows in rolling waves of heat. A faint iridescence hovered above the enormous chairs and sofas that lay like animals panting.

He looked across the long room. Almost opposite him was a square of wall that caught the subdued light like a pool of water. He stared at it as though it had demanded his attention. The

water seemed to move, to shift. Something was
stirring there. He looked more intently. Colours
came, shapes shifted. It was a scene, some place.
Yes, a place. Houses, sand, water. A bay. A
curving bay. A long sea-line dark like the stroke
of a pencil against faint egg-shell blue. Water.
A bay bordered by a ring of saffron sand, and behind
the sand, rising above it, a town. Tier on tier of
houses, and behind them again in the farthest
distance a fringe of dark wood. He could even
see now little figures, black spots, dotted upon the
sand. The sea now was very clear, shimmering
mother-of-pearl. A scattering of white upon the
shore as the long wave-line broke and retreated.
And the houses tier upon tier. He gazed, filled
with an overwhelming breathless excitement. He
was leaning forward, his hands pressing in upon
the arms of the chair. It stayed, trembling with
a kind of personal invitation before him. Then,
as though it had nodded and smiled farewell to him,
it vanished. Only the wall was there.

But the excitement remained, excitement quite
unaccountable.

He got up, his knees trembling. He looked
at the stout bellying occupant of the other chair,
his mouth open, his snores reverberant.

He went out. Six days later he was in the train
for Treliss.

7

Now too, of course, he had his reactions just as
he always had. He could explain the thing easily
enough; for a moment or two he had slept, or, if
he had not, a trick of light on that warm afternoon

and his own thoughts about possible places had persuaded him.

Nevertheless the picture remained strangely vivid —the sea, the shore, the rising town, the little line of darkening wood. He would go down there, and on the day that Maradick had suggested to him. Something might occur. You never could tell. He packed his etchings—his St. Gilles, Marais, his Flight into Egypt and Orvieto, his Whistler and Strang and Meryon. They would protect him and see that he did nothing foolish.

He had special confidence in his St. Gilles.

He had intended to read the Lester book all the way, but as we have seen, managed only a bare line or two; the Browning he had not intended even to have with him, but in some fashion, with the determined resolve that books so often show, it had crept into his bag and then was on his knee, he knew not whence, and soon out of self-defence against the old man he was reading 'The Flight of the Duchess,' carried away on the wings of its freedom, strength, and colour.

Nevertheless, that is the kind of man I am, he thought, even the books force me to read them when I have no wish. And soon he had forgotten the old man, the carriage, the warm weather. How many years since he had read it? No matter. Wasn't it fine and touching and true? When he came to the place:

> . . . the door opened and more than mortal
> Stood, with a face where to my mind centred
> All beauties I ever saw or shall see,
> The Duchess—I stopped as if struck by palsy.
> She was so different, happy and beautiful,
> I felt at once that all was best,
> And that I had nothing to do, for the rest

But wait her commands, obey and be dutiful.
Not that, in fact, there was any commanding,
—I saw the glory of her eye
And the brow's height and the breast's expanding,
And I was hers to live or to die.

'Hurrah!' Harkness cried.

'I beg your pardon?' the old man said, looking up.

Harkness blushed. 'I was reading something rather fine,' he said, smiling.

'You'd better look out for what you're reading, to whom you're speaking, where you're walking, what you're eating, everything, when you're in Treliss,' he remarked.

'Why? Is it so dangerous a place?' asked Harkness.

'It doesn't like tourists. I've seen it do funny things to tourists in my time.'

'I think you're hard on tourists,' Harkness said. 'They don't mean any harm. They admire places the best way they can.'

'Yes, and how long do they stay?' the old man replied. 'Do you think you can know a place in a week or a month? Do you think a real place likes the dirt and the noise and the silly talk they bring with them?'

'What do you mean by a real place?' Harkness asked.

'Places have souls just like people. Some have more soul and some have less. And some have none at all. Sometimes a place will creep away altogether, it is so disgusted with the things people are trying to do to it, and will leave a dummy instead, and only a few know the difference. Why, up in the Welsh hills there are several places that have gone up there in sheer disgust the way they've been treated, and left substitutes behind them. Parts of London, for instance. Do you think that's the real Chelsea you see in London? Not a bit of it. The real Chelsea is living—well, I mustn't tell you where it is living—but you'll never find it. However, Americans are the last to understand these things. I am wasting my breath talking.'

The train had drawn now into Drymouth. The old man was silent, looking out at the hurrying crowds on the platform. He was certainly a pessimist and a hater of his kind. He was looking out at the innocent people with a lowering brow as though he would slaughter the lot of them had he the power. 'Old Testament Moses' Harkness named him. After a while the train slowly moved on. They passed above the mean streets, the hoardings with the cheap theatres, the lines with the clothes hanging in the wind, the grimy windows. But even these things the lovely sky, shining, transmuted.

They came to the river. It lay on either side of the track, a broad sheet of lovely water spreading, on the left, to the open sea. The warships clustered in dark ebony shadows against the gold; the hills rose softly, bending in kindly peace and happy watchfulness.

'Silence! We're crossing!' the old man cried. He was sitting forward, his gnarled hands on his broad knees, staring in front of him.

The train drew in to a small wayside station, gay with flowers. The trees blew about it in whispering clusters. The old man got up, gathered his basket and lumbered out, neither looking at nor speaking to Harkness.

He was alone.   He felt an overwhelming relief. He had not liked the old man, and very obviously the old man had not liked him.   But it was not only that he was alone that pleased him.   There was something more than that.

It was indeed as though he were in a new country. The train seemed to be going now more slowly, with a more casual air, as though it too felt a relief and did not care what happened—time, engagements, schedules, all these were now forgotten as they went comfortably lumbering, the curving fields embracing them, the streams singing to them, the little houses perched on the clear-lit skyline smiling down upon them.

It would not be long now before they were in Trewth, where he must change.   He took his two books and put them away in his bag.   Should he send the bag on and walk as Maradick had advised him?   Three miles.   Not far, and it was a most lovely day.   He could smell the sea now through the windows.   It must be only over that ridge of hill.   He was strangely, oddly happy.   London seemed far, far away.   America too.   Any country that had a name, a date, a history.   This country was timeless and without a record.   How beautifully the hills dipped into valleys!   Streams seemed to be everywhere, little secret coloured streams with happy thoughts.   Everything and every one surely here was happy.   Then suddenly he saw a deserted mine tower like a gaunt and ruined temple.   Haggard and fierce it stood against the skyline, and, as Harkness looked back to it, it seemed to raise an arm to heaven in desperate protest.

The train drew into Trewth.

8

Trewth was nothing more than a long wooden platform open to all the winds of heaven, and behind it a sort of shed with a ticket collector's box in one side of it.

Harkness was annoyed to see that others beside himself climbed out and scattered about the platform waiting for the Treliss train to come in.

He resented these especially because they were grand and elegant, two men, long, thin, in baggy knickerbockers, carrying themselves as though all the world belonged to them with that indifferent assurance that only Englishmen have; a large, stout woman, quietly but admirably dressed, with a Pekinese and a maid to whom she spoke as Cleopatra to Charmian. Five boxes, gun-cases, magnificent golf-bags, these things were scattered about the naked bare platform. The wind came in from the sea and sported everywhere, flipping at the stout lady's skirts, laughing at the elegant sportsmen's thin calves, mocking at the pouting Pekinese. It was fresh and lovely: all the cornfields were waving invitation.

It was characteristic of Harkness that a fancied haughty glance from the sportsman's eye decided him. He's laughing at my clothes, Harkness thought. How was it that Englishmen wore old things so carelessly and yet were never wrong? Harkness bought his clothes from the best London tailors, but they were always finally a little hostile. They never surrendered to his personality, keeping their own proud reserve.

I'll walk, he thought suddenly. He found a young porter who, in anxious fashion, so unlike American porters who were always so superior to the luggage that they conveyed, was wheeling magnificent trunks on a very insecure barrow.

'These two boxes of mine,' Harkness said, stopping him. 'I want to walk over to Treliss. Can they be sent over?'

'Happen they can,' said the young porter doubtfully.

'They are labelled to the "Man-at-Arms Hotel,"' Harkness said.

'They'll be there as soon as you will,' said the young porter, cheered at the sight of an American tip which he put in his pocket, thinking in his heart that these foreigners were 'dam fools' to throw their money around as they did. He advanced towards the stout lady hopefully. She might also prove to be American.

Harkness plunged out of the station into the broad white road. A sign pointed 'Treliss—Three Miles.' So Maradick had been exactly right.

As he left the village behind him and strode on between the cornfields he felt a marvellous freedom. He was heading now directly for the sea. The salt tang of it struck him in the face. Larks were circling in the blue air above him, poppies scattered the corn with plashes of crimson. Here and there gaunt rocks rose from the heart of the gold. No human being was in sight.

His love of etching had given him something of an etcher's eye, and he saw here a spreading tree and a pool of dark shadow, there a distant spire on the curving hill that he thought would have caught the fancy of his beloved Lepère, or Legros. Here a wayside pool like brittle glass that would have enchanted Appian, there a cottage with a sweeping field that might have made Rembrandt happy.

He seemed to be in unison with the whole of nature, and when the road left the fields and dived into the heart of a common his happiness was complete. He stood there, his feet pressing in upon the rough springing turf. A lark, singing above him, came down as though welcoming him, then circled up and up and up. He raised his head, staring into the pale faint blue until he seemed himself to circle with the bird, the turf pressing him upwards, his hands lifting him, he swinging into spaceless ecstasy. Then his gaze fell again and swung out beyond, and—there was the sea.

The Down ran in a green wave to the blue line of the sky, but in front of him it split, breaking into brown rocky patches, and between the brown curves a pool of purple sea lay like water in a cup.

He walked forward, deserting for a moment the road. He stood at the edge of the cliff and looked down. The tide was high and the line of the sea slipped up to the feet of the cliff, splashed there its white fringe of spray, then very gently fell back. Sea-pinks starred the cliffs with colour. Sea-gulls whirled, fragments of white foam, against the blue. Just below him one bird sat, its head cocked, waiting. With a shrill cry of vigour and assurance it flashed away, curving, circling, bending, dipping, as though it were showing to Harkness what it could do.

He walked along the cliff path happier than he had been for many, many months. This was enough were there no more than this. For this at least he must thank Maradick—this peace, this air, this silence. . . .

Turning a bend of the cliff he saw the town.

9

It was absolutely the town of his vision. He saw, with a strange tightening of his heart as though he were being warned of something, that that was so. There was the curving bay with the faint fringe of white pencilling the yellow sand, there the houses rising tier on tier above the beach, there the fringe of dusky wood.

What did it mean? Why had he a clutch of terror as though some one was whispering to him that he must turn tail and run? Nothing could be more lovely than that town basking in the mellow afternoon light, and yet he was afraid at the sight of it—afraid so that his content and happiness of a moment ago were all gone and of a sudden he longed for company.

He was so well accustomed to his own reactions and so deeply despised them that he shrugged his shoulders and walked forward. Never, it seemed, was it possible for him to enjoy anything for more than a moment. Trouble and regret always came. But this was not regret, it was rather a kind of forewarning. He did not know that he had ever before looked on a place for the first time with so odd a mingling of conviction that he had already seen it, of admiration for its beauty, and of some sort of alarmed dismay. Beautiful it was, more Italian than English, with its white walls, its purple sea, and warm scented air.

So peaceful and of so happy a tranquillity. He tried to drive his fear from him, but it hung on so that he was often turning back and looking behind him over his shoulder.

He struck the road again. It curved now,

white and broad, down the hill toward the town.
At the very peak of the hill before the descent
began a man was standing watching something.

Harkness walked forward, then also stood still.
The man was so deeply absorbed that his absorption
held you. He was standing at the edge of the road
and Harkness must pass him. At the crunch of
Harkness's step on the gravel of the road the man
turned and looked at him with startled surprise.
Harkness had come across the soft turf of the
Down, and his sudden step must have been an
alarm. The fellow was broad-shouldered, medium
height, clean-shaven, tanned, young, under thirty at
least, dressed in a suit of dark blue. He had something of a naval air.

Harkness was passing, when the man said:

'Have you the right time on you, sir?' His
voice was fresh, pleasant, well-educated.

Harkness looked at his watch. 'Quarter past
five,' he said. He was moving forward when the
man, hesitating, spoke again:

'You don't see any one coming up the road?'

Harkness stared down the white, sun-bleached
expanse.

'No,' he said after a moment, 'I don't.'

They looked for a while standing side by side
silently.

After all he wasn't more than a boy—not a day
more than twenty-five—but with that grave reserved
look that so many British boys who were old enough
to have been in the war had.

'Sure you don't see anybody?' he asked again,
'coming up that farther bend?'

'No,' said Harkness, shading his eyes with his
hand against the sun; 'can't say as I do.'

'Damn nuisance,' the boy said. 'He's half an hour late now.'

The boy stood as though to attention, his figure set, his hands at his side.

'Ah, there's some one,' said Harkness. But it was only an old man with his cart. He slowly pressed up the hill past them, urging his horses with a thick guttural cry, an old man brown as a berry.

'I beg your pardon,' the boy turned to Harkness. 'You'll think it an awful impertinence—but—are you in a terrible hurry?'

'No,' said Harkness, 'not terrible. I want to be at the "Man-at-Arms" by dinner time. That's all.'

'Oh, you've got lots of time,' the boy said eagerly. 'Look here. This is desperately important for me. The man ought to have been here half an hour ago. If he doesn't come in another twenty minutes I don't know what I shall do. It's just occurred to me. There's another way up this hill—a short cut. He may have chosen that. He may not have understood where it was that I wanted him to meet me. Would you mind—would you do me the favour of just standing here while I go over the hill there to see whether he's waiting on the other side? I won't be away more than five minutes; I'd be so awfully grateful.'

'Why, of course,' said Harkness.

'He's a fisherman with a black beard. You can't mistake him. And if he comes, if you'd just ask him to wait for a moment until I'm back.'

'Certainly,' said Harkness.

'Thanks most awfully. Very decent of you, sir.'

The boy touched his cap, climbed the hill, and vanished.

Harkness was alone again—not a sound any-

where. The town shimmered below him in the
heat. He waited, absorbed by the picture spread
in front of him, then apprehensive again and
conscious that he was alone. The alarm that he
had originally felt at sight of the town had not
left him. Suppose the boy did not return? Was
playing some joke on him perhaps? No, whatever
else it was, it was not that. The boy had been
deeply serious, plunged into some crisis that was
of tremendous importance to him.

Harkness decided that he would wait until the
shadow of a solitary tree to his right reached him,
and then go. The shadow crept slowly to his feet.
At the same moment a figure turned the bend, a
man with a black beard. He was walking quickly
up the hill as though he knew that he were late.

Harkness went forward to meet him. The man
stopped as though surprised. ' I beg your pardon,'
said Harkness; ' were you expecting to meet some
one here?'

' I was—yes,' said the man.

' He will be back in a moment. He was afraid
that you might have come up the other way. He
went over the hill to see.'

' Aye,' said the man, standing, his legs apart,
quite unconcerned. He was a handsome fellow,
broad-shouldered, wearing dark blue trousers and
a knitted jersey. ' You'll be a friend of Mr.
Dunbar's, maybe?'

' No, I'm not,' Harkness explained. ' I was
passing, and he asked me to wait for a moment and
catch you if you came while he was away.'

' Aye,' said the fisherman, taking out a large
wedge of tobacco and filling his pipe, ' I'm a bit
later than I said I'd be. Wife kept me.'

' Fine evening,' said Harkness.

' Aye,' said the man.

At that moment the boy came over the hill and joined them. 'Very good of you, sir,' he said. ' You're late, Jabez!'

' Good night,' said Harkness, and moved down the hill. He could see the two in urgent conversation as he moved forward. The incident occupied his mind. Why had the matter seemed of such importance to the boy? Why a meeting so elaborately appointed out there on the hillside? The fisherman too had seemed surprised that he, a stranger, should be concerned in the matter.

Had he been in America the affair would have been at once explained—boot-legging, of course. But here in England. . . .

10

When he reached the bottom of the hill he found that he was in the environs of the town. He was walking now along a road shaded by thick trees and close to the sea-shore.

The cottages, white-washed, crooked and, many of them, thatched, ran down to the road, their gardens like little coloured carpets spreading in front of them. The evening air was thick with the scent of flowers, above all of roses. He had never smelt such roses, no, not in California.

There was a breeze from the sea, and it seemed to blow the roses into his very heart, so that they seemed to be all about him, dark crimson, burning white, scattering their petals over his head. He could hear the tune of the sea upon the sand beyond the trees.

He stood for a moment inhaling the scent—delicious, wonderful. He seemed to be crushing multitudes of the petals between his hands.

After a while the road broke away and he saw a path that led directly through the trees to the sea.

So soon as he had taken some steps across the soft sand he seemed to be alone in a world that was watching every movement that he made. It was as though he were committing some intrusion. He stopped and looked behind him: the thin line of trees had retreated, the cottages vanished. Before him was a waste of yellow sand, the deep purple of the sea rose like a wall to his right, hiding, as it were, some farther scene, the sky stretching over it a pale blue curtain tightly held.

A mist was rising, veiling the town. No living person was in sight. He reached a stretch of hard firm sand, thin rivulets of water lacing it. The air was wonderfully mild and sweet.

Never before in his life had he known such a feeling of anticipation. It was as though he knew the stretch of sand to be the last brook to cross before he would come into some mysterious country.

How commonplace this will all seem to me to-morrow, he said to himself, when, over my eggs and bacon at a prosperous modern hotel, I shall be reading my *Daily Mail* and hearing of the trippers at Eastbourne and who has taken ' shooting ' in Scotland and whether Yorkshire has beaten Surrey at cricket. He wanted to keep this moment, not to enter the town; even he had a mad impulse to walk on the sand for an hour, to see the colour fade from the sky and the sea change to a ghostly grey, then to return up the hill to Trewth and catch the night train back to London.

It would be wonderful like that; to have only
the impression of the walk from the station, the
talk with the boy on the hill, the scent of the roses
and the afternoon sky. Everything is destroyed
if you go into it too closely, or it is so for me. I
should have a memory that would last me all my
life.

But now the town was advancing towards him.
His steps made no sound so that it seemed that he
himself stood still, waiting to be seized. He took
one last look at the sea. Then he was caught up
and the houses closed about him.

II

Six was striking from some distant clock as he
started up the street. At the bottom of the hill
there were fishermen's cottages, nets spread out on
the stones to dry, some boats drawn up above a
wooden jetty. Then, as the street spread out before
him, some little shops began. Figures were passing hither and thither all transmuted in the afternoon
light. Maradick need not have feared, he thought,
this town has not been touched at all.

As he advanced yet further the houses delighted
him with their broad doorways, their overhanging
eaves, crooked roof and worn flights of steps. He
came to a place where wooden stairs led to an upper
path that ran before a higher row of houses and
under the steps there were shops.

He could feel a stir and bustle in the place as
though this were a night of festivity. Groups
were gathered at corners, women stood in doorways
laughing and whispering, a group of children was

marching, wearing cocked hats of paper, beating on a wooden box and blowing on penny trumpets.

Then on coming into the Square he paused in sheer delighted wonder. This stands on a raised plateau above the sea, and the town hall, solid and virtuous above its flight of wide grey steps, is its great glory. Streets seemed to tumble in and out of the Square on every side. On a far corner there was a merry-go-round and there were booths and wooden trestles, some tents and flags waving above them. But just now it was almost deserted, only a man or two, some children playing in and out of the tents, a dog hunting among the scraps of paper that littered the cobbles.

A church of Norman architecture filled the right side of the Square, and squeezed between its grey walls and the modern town hall was a tall old tower of infinite age, with thin slits of windows and iron bars that pushed out against the pale blue sky like pointing fingers.

There were houses in the Square that were charming, houses with queer bow-windows and protruding doors like pepper-pots, little balconies, and here and there old carved figures on the walls, houses that Whistler would have loved to etch. Harkness stopped a man.

' Can you tell me where I shall find " The Man-at-Arms Hotel "?' he asked.

' Why, yes,' the man answered as though he were surprised that Harkness should not know. ' Straight up that street in front of you. You'll find it at the top.'

And he did find it at the top, after what seemed to him an endless climb. The houses fell away. An iron gate was in front of him as though he were entering some private residence. Going up a long drive he passed beautiful lawns that shone like silk, to the right the grass fell away to a pond fringed with trees. Flowers were around him on every side, and again in his nostrils was the heavy scent of innumerable roses.

The drive swept a wide circle before the great eighteenth-century house that now confronted him. But it is not a hotel at all, he thought, and he would have turned back had not, at that moment, a large hotel omnibus swept up to the door and discharged a chattering heap of men and women, who scattered over the steps screaming about their luggage, collecting children. The spell was broken. He had not realised how alone he had been during the last hour and with what domination his imagination had been working, creating for him a world of his own, encouraging in him what hopes, fears, and anticipations!

He slipped in after the rest, and stood shyly in the hall while the others made their wants triumphantly felt. A man of about forty, stout and round like an egg, but very shinily dressed, came forward and, bending and bowing, smiled at the women and spoke deferentially to the men.

This must be Mr. Bannister—' the King of the Castle' Maradick had told him in the Club. Not the original Mr. Bannister who has made the place what it is. He is, alas, dead and gone. Had he been still there and you had mentioned my name he would have done wonders for you. I don't know this fellow, and for all I know he may have ruined the place.

However, the original Bannister could not have been politer. Harkness was always afraid of hotel

officials, and it was only when the invasion had
broken up and begun to scatter that he came
forward. But Mr. Bannister knew all about him
—indeed was expecting him. His luggage had
already arrived. He should be shown his room,
and Mr. Bannister did hope that it would be. . . .
If anything in the least wasn't . . .

Harkness started upstairs. There is a lift here,
but if the gentleman doesn't mind. . . . His room
is only on the second floor and instead of waiting.
. . . Of course the gentleman doesn't mind. And
still less does he mind when he sees his room.

This is mine absolutely, Harkness said, as
though it had been waiting for me for years and
years with its curved bow-window, its view over that
enchanting garden and the line of sea beyond, its
white wall unbroken by those coloured prints that
hotel managers in my own country find it so necessary
always to provide. Those chintz curtains with the
roses are delicious. Just enough furniture. There
is no private bath, of course?

'The bathroom is just across the passage. Very
convenient,' said the man.

'Yes, in England we haven't reached the private
bathroom yet, although we are supposed to be so
fond of bathing.'

'No, sir,' said the man. 'Anything else I can
do for you?'

'No, thank you,' said Harkness, smiling, as he
looked on the white sunlit walls, and checking the
tip that, American fashion, he was about to give.
'How strong the smell of the roses. It is very
late for them, isn't it?'

'They are just about over, sir.'

'So I should have thought.'

Left alone he slowly unpacked. He liked un-
packing and putting things away. It was packing
that he detested. He had a few things with him
that he always carried when he travelled—a red
leather writing-case, a little Japanese fisherman in
coloured ivory, two figures in red amber, photo-
graphs of his sisters in a silver frame. He put out
these little things on a table of white wood near his
bed, not from any affectation, but because when they
were there the room seemed to understand him,
to settle about him with a little sigh as though it
granted him citizenship—for so long as he wished
to stay. Then there were his prints. He took
out four, the Lepère ' St. Gilles,' Strang's ' Etcher,'
the Rembrandt ' Flight into Egypt,' and the
Whistler ' Drury Lane.' The Strang he had on one
side of the looking-glass, the ' Drury Lane ' on the
other, the ' Flight into Egypt ' at the back of the
writing-table, whither he might glance across the
room at it as he lay in bed, the ' St. Gilles ' close to
him near to the red writing-case and the ivory
fisherman.

He sighed with satisfaction as, sitting down on
his bed, he looked at them. He felt that he needed
them to-night as he had never needed them before.
The sense of excited anticipation that had increased
with him all day was now surely approaching its
climax. That excitement had in it the strangest
mixture of delight, sensuous thrill, and something
that was nothing but panicky terror. Yes, he was
frightened. Of what? Of whom? He could not
tell. But only as he looked across the room at
those familiar scenes, at the massive dark tree of
the ' St. Gilles ' with the hot road, the high comfortable hedge, the happy figures, at the adorable

face of the donkey in the Rembrandt, at the little beings so marvellously placed under the dancing butterfly in the Whistler, at the strong, homely, friendly countenance of Strang himself, he felt as he had so often felt before, that those beautiful things were trying themselves to reassure him, to tell him that they did not change nor alter, and that where he would be there they would be too.

He took Maradick's letter from his pocket and read it again. Here he was—now what must happen next? He would dress now at once for dinner, and then walk in the garden before the light began to fail. Or no. Wasn't he to go down into the town after dinner and to see this dance, to share in it even? Hadn't Maradick said that that was what, above all else, he must do?

And then what was this about a Minstrels' Gallery somewhere? He would have a bath, change his linen, and then begin his explorations. He undressed, found the bathroom, enjoyed himself for twenty minutes or more, then slipped back across the passage into his room again. It was now nearly seven o'clock. As he was dressing, the sun was getting low in the sky. A beam of sunshine caught the intent gaze of Strang, who seemed to lean across his etching board as though to tell him, to reassure him, to warn him. . . .

He slipped out of his room and began his explorations.

12

For a while he wandered, lost in a maze of passages. He understood that the Minstrels' Gallery was at the top of the house. He did not use the lift, but climbed the stairs, meeting no one; then he was on a floor that must, he thought, be servants' quarters. It had another air, something less arranged, less handsome, old-fashioned, as though it were even now as it had been two hundred years ago—a survival, as the old grey tower in the market-place was a survival.

For a little while he stood hesitating. The passage was dark and he did not wish to plunge into a servant's room. Strange that up here there was no sound at all—an absolute deathly stillness!

He walked down to the end of the passage, then, turning, came to a door that was larger than the others. He could see as he looked at it more closely that there was some faint carving on the woodwork above it. He turned the handle, entered the room, then stopped with a little cry of surprise and pleasure.

Truly Maradick had been right. Here was a room that, if there was nothing more to come, made the journey sufficiently of value. An enchanting room! On the left side of it were broad bright windows, and at the farther end, under the Minstrels' Gallery, windows again. There were no curtains to the windows—the whole room had an empty, deserted air—but the more for that reason the place was illuminated with the glow of the evening light. The first thing that he realised was the view—and what a view!

The windows were deep set and hung forward, it seemed, over the hill, so that town, gardens, trees, were all lost and you saw only the sea.

At this hour you seemed to swing in space; the division lost between sea and sky in the now nearly horizontal rays of the sun—only a golden glow covering the blue with a dazzling blaze of colour. He stood there drinking it in, then sat in one of the window-seats, his hands clasped, lost in happiness.

After a while he turned back to the room. Flecks of dust, changed into gold by the evening light, floated in mid-air. The room was disregarded indeed. The walls were panelled. The little Minstrels' Gallery was supported on two heavy pillars. The floor was bare of carpet and had even a faint waxen sheen, as though, in spite of the room's general neglect, it was used, once and again, for dances.

But what pathos the room had! He did not know that, almost fifteen years before, Maradick had felt that same thing. How vastly now that pathos was increased, how greatly since Maradick's day the world's history had relentlessly cut away those earlier years. He saw that round the platform of the gallery was intricate carving, and, going forward more closely to examine, saw that in every square was set the head of a grinning lion. Some high-backed, quaintly-shaped chairs, that looked as though they might be of great age, were ranged against the wall.

Being now right under the gallery he saw some little wooden steps. He climbed up them, and then from the gallery's shadow looked down across the room. How clearly he could picture that old scene, something straight from Jane Austen with Miss Bates and Mrs. Norris, stiff-backed, against the wall, and Anne Elliot and Elizabeth Bennet, Mr. Collins and the rest. The fiddlers scraping, the negus for refreshment, the night darkening, the carriages with their lights gathering. . . .

The door at the far end of the room closed with a gentle click. He started, not imagining that any one would choose that room at such an hour.

Two figures were there in the shadow beyond the end room. The light fell on the man's face—Harkness could see it very clearly. The other was a woman wearing a white dress. He could not see her face.

For an instant they were silent, then the man said something that Harkness could not hear.

The girl at once broke out: ' No, no. Oh, please, Herrick.'

She must be a very young girl. The voice was that of a child. It had in it a desperate note that held Harkness's attention instantly.

The man said something again, very low.

' But if you don't care,' the girl's voice pleaded, then let me go back. Oh, Herrick, let me go! Let me go!'

' My father does not wish it.'

' But I am not married to your father. It is to you.'

' My father and I are the same. What he says I must do, I do.'

' But you can't be the same.' Her voice now was trembling in its urgency. ' No one could love their father more than I do and yet we are not the same.'

' Nevertheless you did what your father asked you to do. So must I.'

' But I didn't know. I didn't know. And he didn't know. He has never seen me frightened of anything, and now I am frightened. . . . I've never said I was to any one before, but now . . . now . . .'

She was crying, softly, terribly, with the terrified crying of real and desperate fear.

Harkness had been about to move. He did not, unseen and his presence unrealised, wish to overhear, but her tears checked him. Although he could not see her he had detected in her voice a note of pride. He fancied that she would wish anything rather than to be thus seen by a stranger. He stayed where he was. He could see the man's face, thin, white, the nose long pointed, a dark, almost grotesque shadow.

' Why are you frightened?'

' I don't know. I can't tell. I have never been frightened before.'

' Have I been unkind to you?'

' No, but you don't love me.'

' Did I ever pretend to love you? Didn't you know from the very first that no one in the world matters to me except my father?'

' It is of your father that I am afraid. . . . These last three days in that terrible house. . . . I'm so frightened, Herrick. I want to go home only for a little while. Just for a week before we go abroad.'

' All our plans are made now. You know that we are sailing to-morrow evening.'

' Yes, but I could come afterwards. Forgive me, Herrick. You may do anything to me if I can only go home for just some days. . . . You may do anything. . . .'

' I don't want to do anything, Hesther. No one wishes to do you any harm. But whatever my father wishes, that every one must do. It has always been so.'

She seemed to be seized by an absolute frenzy

of fear; Harkness could see her white shadow
quivering. It appeared to him as though she
caught the man by the arm. Her voice came in
little breathless stifled cries, infinitely pitiful to
hear.

'Please, please, Herrick. I dare not speak to
your father. I don't dare. I don't dare. But
you—let me go—Oh! let me go—just this once,
Herrick. Only this once. I'll only be home for a
few days and then I'll come back. Truly I'll come
back. I'll just see father and Bobby and then I'll
come back. They'll be missing me. I know they
will. And I'll be going to a foreign country—such
a long way. And they'll be wanting me. Bobby's
so young, Herrick, only a baby. He's never had
any one do anything for him but me. . . .'

'You should have thought of that before you
married me, you cannot leave me now.'

'I won't leave you. I've never broken my
word to any one. I won't break it now. It's only
for a few days.'

'How can you be so selfish, Hesther, as to want
to upset every one's plans just for a whim of your
own? For myself I don't care. You could go
home for ever, for all I care. I didn't want to marry
any one. But what my father wished had to be.'

She clung to him then, crying again and again
between her sobs:

'Oh, let me go home! Let me go home! Let
me go home!'

Harkness fancied that the man put his hands on
her shoulders. His voice, cold, lifeless, impersonal,
crossed the room.

'That is enough. He is waiting for us downstairs. He will be wondering where we are.'

The little white shadow seemed to turn to the
window, towards the limitless expanse of sunlit sea.
Then a voice, small, proud, empty of emotion, said:
' Father wished me——'
Harkness was once more alone in the room.

13

They had gone but the girl's fear remained. It
was there as truly as the two figures had been and
its reality was stronger than their reality.

Harkness had the sense of having been caught,
and it was exactly as though now, as he stood alone
there in the gallery staring down into the room,
some Imp had touched him on the shoulder, crying,
' Now you're in for it! Now you're in for it!
The situation has got you now!'

He was, of course, not ' in for it ' at all. How
many such conversations between human beings
there were; it simply was that he had happened
against his will to overhear a fragment of one of
them. Yes, ' against his will.' How desperately
he wished that he hadn't been there. What induced
them to choose that room and that time for their
secret confidences? He felt still in the echo of
their voices the effect of their urgency.

They had chosen that room because there was
some one watching their every movement and they
had had only a few moments. The child—for
surely she could not be more—had almost driven
her companion into that two minutes' conversation,
and Harkness could realise how desperate she must
have been to have taken such a course.

But after all it *was* no business of his! Girls

married every day men whom they did not love, and
although apparently in this case the man also did
not love her and they were both of them in evil
plight, still that too had happened before and nothing
very terrible had come of it.

It *was* no business of his, and yet he did wish,
all the same, that he could get the ring of the girl's
voice out of his ears.   He had never been able to
bear the sight, sound, or even inference of any sort
of cruelty to helpless humans or to animals.   Perhaps
because he was so frantic a coward himself about
physical pain!   And yet not altogether that.   He
had on several occasions taken risks of pretty savage
pain to himself in order to save a horse a beating
or a dog a kicking.   Nevertheless, those had been
spontaneous emotions roused at the instant; there
was something lingering, a sad and tragic echo, in
the voice that was still with him.

The very pathos of the room that he was in—
the lingering of so many old notes that had been
rung and rung again, notes of anticipation, triumph,
disappointment, resignation, made this fresh, living
sound the harder to escape.

By Jupiter, the child *was* frightened—that was
the final ringing of it upon Harkness's heart and
soul.   But he was going to have his life sufficiently
full were he to step in and rescue every girl frightened
by matrimony!   Rescue!   No, there was no question of rescue.   It wasn't, once again, his affair.
But he did wish that he could just take her hand
and tell her not to worry, that it would all come
right in the end.   But would it?   He hadn't at
all cared for the fragment of countenance that
fellow had shown to him, and he had liked still less
the tone of his voice, cold, unfeeling, hard.   Poor

child! And suddenly the thought of his Browning's
' Duchess ' came to him:

> I was the man the Duke spoke to:
> I helped the Duchess to cast off his yoke too;
> So, here's the tale from beginning to end,
> My friend!

Well, here was a tale with which he had definitely
nothing to do. Let him remember that. He was
here in a most beautiful place for a holiday—that
was his purpose, that his intention—what were
these people to him or he to them?

Nevertheless the voice lingered in his ear, and to
be rid of it he left the room. He stepped carefully
down the wooden steps, and then at the bottom of
them, under the dark lee of the gallery, he paused.
He was so foolishly frightened that he could not
move a step.

He waited. At last he whispered ' Is any one
there?'

There was no answer. He pushed his way then
out of the shadow, his heart drumming against his
shirt. There was no one there. Of course there
was not.

In his room once more with his friend Strang
and the Rembrandt Donkey to take him home he
sat on his bed holding his hands between his
knees.

He was positively afraid of going down to dinner.
Afraid of what? Afraid of being drawn in.
Drawn into what? That was precisely what he
did not know, but something that ever since his
first glimpse of Maradick at the Reform Club had
been preparing. It was that he saw, as he sat there
thinking of it, that he feared—this Something that

was piling up outside him and with which he had
nothing to do at all.

Why should he mind because he had heard a
girl say that she was frightened and wanted to go
home? And yet he did mind—minded terribly
and with increasing violence from every moment
that passed. The thought of that child without a
friend and on the very edge of an experience that
might indeed be fatal for her, the thought of it
was more than he could endure.

He was clever at escaping things did they only
give him a moment's pause, but in this case the
longer he thought about it the harder it was to
escape from. It was as though the girl had made
her personal appeal to himself.

But what an old scamp her father must be,
Harkness thought, to give her up like this to a
man for whom she has no love, who doesn't love
her. Why did she do it? And what kind of a
man is the father-in-law of whom she is so afraid
and who dominates his son so absolutely? In any
case I must go down to dinner. I must just take
what comes. . . .

Yes, but his prudence whispered, don't meddle
in this affair actively. It isn't the kind of thing
in which you are likely to distinguish yourself.

'No, by Jove, it isn't.'

'Well, then, be careful.'

'I mean to be.' Then suddenly the girl's voice
came sharp and clear. 'Damn it, I'll do anything
I can,' he cried aloud, jumped from the bed and
went downstairs.

14

As he went downstairs he felt a tremendous sense of liberation. It was as though he had, after many hesitations and fears, passed through the first room successfully and closed the door behind him. Now there was the second room to be confronted.

What he immediately confronted was the garden of the hotel. The sun was slowly setting in the west, and great amber clouds, spreading out in swathes of colour, ate up the blue.

The amber flung out arms as though it would embrace the whole world. The deep blue ebbed from the sea, was pale crystal, then from length to length a vast bronze shield. The amber receded as though it had done its work, and myriads of little flecks of gold ran up into the pale blue-white, thousands of scattered fragments like coins flung in some God-like largesse.

The bronze sea was held rigid as though it were truly of metal. The town caught the gold and all the windows flashed. In the fresh evening light the grass of the lawn seemed to shine with a fresh iridescence—the farther hills were coldly dark.

Several people were walking up and down the gravel paths, pausing, before going in to dinner. In the golden haze only those things stood out that were more important for the scene, nature, as always, being more theatrical than any man-contrived theatre. The stage being set, the principal actor made his entrance.

A window running to the gravel path caught the level rays of the setting sun. A man stepped before this, stopping to light a cigarette, and then, being there, stayed like an oriental image staring out into the garden.

Harkness looked casually, then looked again, then, fascinated, remained watching. He had never before seen such red hair nor so white a face, nor so large a stone as the green one that shone in a ring on the finger of his raised hand. He was lighting his cigarette—it was after this that he fell into rigid immobility—and the fire of the match caught the ring until, like a great eye, it seemed to open, wink at Harkness, and then regard him with a contemptuous stare.

The man's hair was *en brosse*, standing straight on end as Loge's used to do in the old pre-war Bayreuth 'Ring.' It was, like Loge's, a flaming red, short, harsh, instantly arresting. Evening dress. One small black pearl in his shirt. Very small feet in shining shoes.

There had stuck in Harkness's mind a phrase that he had encountered once in George Moore's description of Verlaine in *Memories and Opinions*— ' I shall not forget the glare of the bald prominent forehead (*une tête glabre*). . . .' That was the phrase now, *une tête glabre*—the forehead glaring like a challenge, the red hair springing from it like something alive of its own independence. For the rest, this interesting figure had a body round, short, and fat like a ball. Over his protruding stomach stretched a white waistcoat with three little plain black buttons.

The colour of his face had an unnatural pallor, something theatrical like the clown in *Pagliacci*, or again, like one of Benda's masks. Yes, this was the truer comparison, because through the mask the eyes were alive and beautiful, dark, tender, eloquent, but spoilt because above them the eyebrows were so faint as to be scarcely visible. The mouth in the white of the face was a thin, hard, red scratch. The eyes stared into the garden. The body soon became painted into the window behind it, the round short limbs, the shining shoes, the little black pearl in the gleaming shirt.

Harkness, from the shadow where he stood, looked and looked again. Then, fearing that he might be perceived and his stare be held offensive, he moved forward. The man saw him and, to Harkness's surprise, stepped forward and spoke to him.

'I beg your pardon,' he said; 'but do you happen to have a light? My cigarette did not catch properly and I have used my last match.'

Here was another surprise for Harkness. The voice was the most beautiful that he had ever heard from man. Soft, exquisitely melodious, with an inflection in it of friendliness, courtesy, and culture that was enchanting. Absolutely without affectation.

'Why, yes. Certainly,' said Harkness.

He felt for his little gold matchbox, found it, produced a match and, guarding it with his hand, struck it. In the light the other's forehead suddenly sprang up again like a live thing. For an instant two of his fingers rested on Harkness's hand. They seemed to be so soft as to be quite boneless.

'Thank you. What an exquisite evening!'

'Yes,' said Harkness. 'This is a very beautiful place.'

'Yes,' said the other, 'is it not? And this is incidentally the best hotel in England.'

The voice was so beautiful to Harkness, who was exceedingly sensitive to sound, that his only desire was that by some means he should prolong the conversation so that he might indulge himself in the luxury of it.

' I have only just arrived,' he said; ' I came only an hour ago, and it is my first visit.'

' Is that so? Then you have a great treat in store for you. This is splendid country round here, and although every one has been doing their best to spoil it, there are still some lovely places. Treliss is the only town in Southern England where the place is still triumphant over modern improvements.'

There was a pause, then the man said:

' Will you be here for long?'

' I have made no plans,' Harkness replied.

' I wish I could show you around a little. I know this country very well. There is nothing I enjoy more than showing off some of our beauties. But, unfortunately, I leave for abroad early to-morrow morning.'

Harkness thanked him. They were soon talking very freely, walking up and down the gravel path. The exquisite modulation of the man's voice, its rhythm, gentleness, gave Harkness such delight that he could listen for ever. They spoke of foreign countries. Harkness had travelled much and remembered what he had seen. This man had been apparently everywhere.

Suddenly a gong sounded. ' Ah, there's dinner.' They paused. The stranger said: ' I beg your pardon. You tell me that you are American, and I know therefore that you are not hampered by ridiculous conventionalities. Are you alone?'

' I am,' said Harkness.

' Well, then——why not dine with us? There is

myself, my son and a charming girl to whom he
has lately been married. Do me that pleasure.
Or, if people are a bore to you, be quite frank and
say so.'

'I shall be delighted,' said Harkness.

'Good.   My name is Crispin.'

'Harkness is mine.'

They walked in together.

15

He had, as he walked into the hall, an overwhelming sense that everything that was occurring
to him had happened to him before, and it was only
part of this dream-conviction that Crispin should
pause and say: 'Here they are, waiting for us,' and
lead him up to the girl who, half an hour before, had
been with him in the little gallery. He had even a
moment of protesting panic crying to the little imp
whose voice he had already heard that evening:
'Let me out of this. I am not so passive as you
fancy. It is a holiday I am here for. There is no
knight errantry in me—you have caught the wrong
man for that.'

But the girl's face stopped him. She was beautiful. He had from the first instant of seeing her
no doubt of that, and it was as though her voice
had already built her up for him in that dim
room.

Straight and dark, her face had child-like purity
in its rounded cheeks, its large brow and wondering
eyes, its mouth set now in proud determination, but
trembling a little behind that pride, its cheeks very
soft and faintly coloured. Her hair was piled up

as though it were only recently that it had come to that distinction. She was wearing a very simple white frock that looked as though it had been made by some little local dressmaker of her own place. She had been proud of it, delighted with it, Harkness could be sure, perhaps only a week or two ago. Now experiences were coming to her thick and fast. She was clutching them all to her, determined to face them whatever they might be, finding them, as Harkness knew from what he had overheard, more terrible than she had ever conceived.

She had been crying, as he knew, only half an hour ago, but now there were no traces of tears, only a faint shell-like flush on her cheeks.

The man standing beside her was not much more than a boy, but Harkness thought that he had seldom perceived an uglier countenance. A large broad nose, a long thin face like a hatchet, grey colourless eyes and a bony body upon which the evening clothes sat awkwardly, here was ugliness itself, but the true unpleasantness came from the cold aloofness that lay in the unblinking eyes, the hard straight mouth.

'He might be walking in his sleep,' Harkness thought, 'for all the life he's showing. What a pair for the girl to be in the hands of!' Harkness was introduced.

'Hesther, my dear, this is Mr. Harkness, who is going to give us the pleasure of dining with us. Mr. Harkness, this is my boy Herrick.'

The little man led the way, and it was interesting to perceive the authoritative dignity with which he moved. He had a walk that admirably surmounted the indignities that the short legs and stumpy body would, in a less clever performer, have inevitably

entailed. He did not strut, nor trot, nor push out
his stomach and follow it with proud resolve.

His dignity was real, almost regal, and yet not
absurd. He walked slowly, looking about him as
he went. He stopped at the entrance of the dining-
hall, now crowded with people, spoke to the head
waiter, a stout pompous-looking fellow, who was at
once obsequious, and started down the room to a
reserved table.

The diners looked up and watched their progress,
but Harkness noticed that no one smiled. When
they came to their table in the middle of the room
Mr. Crispin objected to it, and they were at once
shown to another one beside the window and looking
out to the sea.

' It will amuse you to see the room, Hesther.
You sit there. You can look out of the window
too when you are bored with people. Will you sit
here, Mr. Harkness, on my right?'

Harkness was now opposite the girl and looking
out to the sea that was lit with a bronze flame that
played on the air like a searchlight. The window
was slightly open, and he could hear the sounds from
the town, the merry-go-round, a harsh trumpet, and
once and again a bell.

' Do you mind that window?' Crispin asked him.
' I think it is rather pleasant. You don't mind it,
Hesther dear? They are having festivities down
there this evening. The night of their annual
ceremony when they dance round the town—something as old as the hill on which the town is built, I
fancy. You ought to go down and look at them,
Mr. Harkness.'

' I think I shall,' Harkness replied, smiling.

He noticed that now that the man was seated

he did not look small. His neck was thick, his shoulders broad, that forehead in the brilliantly-lit room absolutely gleamed, the red hair springing up from it like a challenge. The mention of the dance led Crispin to talk of other strange customs that he had known in many parts of the world, especially in the East. Yes, he had been in the East very often and especially in China. The old China was going. You would have to hurry up if you were to see it with any colour left. It was too bad that the West could not leave the East alone.

'The matter with the West, Mr. Harkness, is that it always must be improving everything and everybody. It can't leave well alone. It must be thrusting its morals and customs on people who have very nice ones of their own—only they are not Western, that's all. We have too many conventional ideas over here. Superstitious observances that are just as foolish as any in the South Seas —more foolish indeed. Now I'm shocking you, Hesther, I'm afraid. Hesther,' he explained to Harkness, 'is the daughter of an English country doctor—a very fine fellow. But she hasn't travelled much yet. She only married my son a month ago. This is their honeymoon, and it is very nice of them to take their old father along with them. He appreciates it, my dear.'

He raised his glass and bowed to her. She smiled very faintly, staring at him for an instant with her large brown eyes, then looking down at her plate.

'I have been driven,' Crispin explained, 'into the East by my collector's passions as much as anything. You know, perhaps, what it is to be a collector, not of anything especial, but a collector.

Something in the blood worse than drugs or drink. Something that only death can cure. I don't know whether you care for pretty things, Mr. Harkness, but I have some pieces of jade and amber that would please you, I think. I have, I think, one of the best collections of jade in Europe.'

Harkness said something polite.

'The trouble with the collector is that he is always so much more deeply interested in his collection than any one else is, and he is not so interested in a thing when he owns it as he was when he was wondering whether he could afford it.

'However, women like my jade. Their fingers itch. It is pleasant to see them. Have you ever felt the collector's passion yourself?'

'In a tiny way only,' said Harkness. 'I have always loved prints very dearly, etchings especially. But I have so small and unimportant a collection that I never dream of showing it to anybody. I have not the means to make a real collection, but if I were a millionaire it is in that direction that I think I would go. Etchings are so marvellously human, unaccountably personal.'

'Why, Herrick, listen to that! Mr. Harkness cares about etchings! We must show him some of ours. I have a " Hundred Guilders " and a " De Jonghe " that are truly superb. Do you know my favourite etcher in the world? I am sure that you will never guess.'

'There is a large field to choose from,' said Harkness, smiling.

'There is indeed. But Samuel Palmer is the man for me. You will say that he goes oddly enough with my jade, but whenever I travel abroad " The Bellman " and " The Ruined Tower " go with me. And then Lepère—what a glorious artist! and Legros' woolly trees, and our old friend Callot —yes, we have an enthusiasm in common there.'

For the first time Harkness addressed the girl directly:

'Do you also care about etchings, Mrs. Crispin?'

She flushed as she answered him: 'I am afraid that I know nothing about them. Our things at home were not very valuable, I am afraid—except to us,' she added.

She spoke so softly that Harkness scarcely caught her words. 'Ah, but Hesther will learn,' Crispin said. 'She has a fine taste already. It needs only some more experience. You are learning already, are you not, Hesther?'

'Yes,' she answered almost in a whisper, then looked up directly at Harkness. He could not mistake her glance. It was an appeal absolutely for help. He could see that she was at the end of her control. Her hand was trembling against the cloth. She had been drinking some of her Burgundy, and he guessed that this was a desperate measure. He divined that she was urging herself to some act from which, during all these weeks, she had been shuddering.

His own heart was beating furiously. The food, the wine, the lights, Crispin's strange and beautiful voice were accompaniments to some act that he saw now hanging in front of him, or rather waiting, as a carriage waits, into which now of his own free-will he is about to step to be whirled to some terrific destination.

He tried to put purpose into his glance back to her, as though he would say 'Let me be of some use to you. I am here for that. You can trust me.'

He felt that she knew that she could. She might,
such was her case, trust any one at this crisis, but
she had been watching him, he felt sure, throughout
the meal, listening to his voice, studying his movements, wondering, perhaps, whether he too were
in this conspiracy against her.

He had the sudden conviction that on an instant
she had resolved that she could trust him, and had
he had time to do as was usual with him, to step
back and regard himself, he would have been amazed
at his own happiness.

They had come to the dessert. Crispin, as
though he had no purpose in life but to make every
one happy, was cracking walnuts for his daughter-in-
law and talking about a thousand things. There
was nothing apparently that he did not know and
nothing that he did not wish to hand over to his
dear friends.

' It is too bad that I can't show you my " Hundred
Guilders." '   He cracked a walnut, and his soft
boneless fingers seemed suddenly to be endued
with an amazing strength.   ' But why shouldn't I?
What are you doing this evening?'

' I have no plans,' said Harkness; ' I thought
I would go perhaps down to the market and look
at the fun.'

' Yes—well. . . . Let me see.   But that will
fit splendidly.   We have an engagement for an
hour or two—to say good-bye to an old friend.
Why not join us here at—say—half-past ten?   I
have my car here.   It is only half an hour's drive.
Come out for an hour or two and see my things.
It will give me so much pleasure to show you what
I have.   I can offer you a good cigar too and some
brandy that should please you.   What do you say?'

Harkness looked across at the girl. ' Thank you,' he said gravely, ' I shall be delighted.'

' That's splendid. Very good of you. The house also should interest you. Very old and curious. It has a history too. I have rented it for the last year. I shall be quite sorry to leave it.'

Then, smiling, he leant across—' What do you say, Hesther? Shall we have our coffee outside?'

' Yes, thank you,' she answered, with a curious childish inflection as though she were repeating some lesson that was only half remembered.

She rose and started down the room. Harkness followed her. Half-way to the door Crispin was stopped for a moment by the head waiter and stayed with his son.

Harkness spoke rapidly. ' There is no time at all, but I want you to know that I was in the room at the top of the house just now when you were there. I heard everything. I apologise for over-hearing. I could not escape, but I want you to know that if there's anything I can do—anything in the world—I will do it. Tell me if there is. We have only a moment.'

On looking back afterwards he thought it marvellous of her that, realising who was behind them, she scarcely turned her head, showed no emotion, but speaking swiftly, answered:

' Yes, I am in great trouble—desperate trouble. I am sure you are kind. There is a thing you can do.'

' Tell me,' he urged. They were now nearly by the door and the two men were coming up.

' I have a friend. I told him that if I would agree to his plan I would send a message to him to-night. I did not mean to agree, but now—

I'm not brave enough to go on. He is to be at
half-past nine at a little hotel—" The Feathered
Duck "—on the sea-front. Any one will tell you
where it is. His name is Dunbar. He is young,
short, you can't mistake him He will be waiting
there. Go to him. Tell him I agree. I'll never
forget . . .'

Crispin's forehead confronted them. ' What do
you say to this? Here is a sheltered corner.'

Dunbar? Dunbar? Where had he heard the
name before?

They all sat down.

PART II

THE DANCE ROUND THE TOWN

PART II

THE DANCE ROUND THE TOWN

I

QUARTER of an hour later he left them, making his excuses, promising to return at half-past ten. He could not have stayed another moment, sitting there quietly in his wicker arm-chair looking out on the darkening garden, listening to Crispin's pleasure in Peter Breughel, without giving some kind of vent to his excitement.

He must get away and be by himself. Because —yes, he knew it, and nothing could alter the vehement pulsating truth of it—he was in love for the first time in his life.

As he threaded his way along the garden paths that was at first all that he could see—that he was in love with that child in the shabby frock who was married to that odious creature, that bag-of-bones, who had not opened his mouth the whole evening long—that child terrified out of her life and appealing to him, a stranger, in her despair, to help her.

In love with a married woman, he, Charles Percy Harkness? What would his two sisters, nay, what would the whole of Baker, Oregon, say, did they know?

But, bless you, he was not in love with her like that—no hero of a modern realistic novel he! He had no thought in that first ecstatic glow, of any thought for himself at all—only his eyes were upon her, of how he could help her, how serve her, now—at once—before it was too late.

He was deeply touched that she should trust him, but he also realised that at that particular moment she would have trusted anybody. And yet she had waited, watching him through all the first part of that meal, making up her mind—there was some tribute to him at least in that!

It was a considerable time before he could fight his way behind his own singing happiness into any detailed consideration of the facts.

He was in touch with real life at last, had it in both hands like a magic ball of crystal, after which for so long he had been searching.

Where had he been all his life, fancying that this was love and that? That ridiculous touching of hands over a tea-cup, that fancied glance at a crowded party, that half-uttered suggested exchange of gimcrack phrases? And this! Why, he could not have stopped himself had he wished! None of the old considered caution to which he had now grown so accustomed that it had seemed like part of his very soul, could have any say in this. He was committed up to his very boots in the thing, and he was glad, glad, glad!

Meanwhile he had lost his way. He pulled himself up short. He had been walking just in any direction. He was in a far part of the garden. A lawn in the twilight, like dark glass beneath whose surface green water played, stretched between scattered trees and beds of flowers now grey and shadowy. Sparks of fire were already scattered across a sky that was smoky with coils of mist as though some giant train had but now thundered through on its journey to Paradise. Little whistles of wind stole about the garden making secret appointments among the trees. Somewhere near to him a fountain was splashing, and behind the lingering liquid sound of it he could hear the merry-go-round and the drum. He cared little about the dance now, but in some fashion he must pass the time until nine-thirty, when he would see her friend and learn what he might do.

Her friend? A sudden agitation held him. Her friend? Had she a lover? Was that all that there was behind this—that she had married in haste, for money, luxury, to see the world, perhaps, and now that she had had a month of it with that miserable bag-of-bones and his painted, talkative father, discovered that she could not endure it and called to her aid some earlier lover? Was that all that his fine knight-errantry came to, that he should assist in some vulgar ordinary intrigue? He stopped, standing beside a small white gate that led out from the garden into the road. It was as though the gate held him from the outer world and he would never pass through it until this was decided for him. Her face came before him as she had sat there on the other side of the table, as it had been when their glances met. No, he did not doubt her for an instant.

Whatever her experiences of the last month she was pure in heart and soul as some child at her mother's knee. She had her pride, her pluck, her resolve, but also, above all else, her innocent simplicity, her ignorance of all the evil in the

world. And as though the most urgent problem
of all his life had been solved, he gave the little
white gate a push and stepped through it into the
open road.

2

He was now in the country to the left of, and
above, the town. He could see its lights clustered,
like gold coins thrown into some capacious lap,
there below him in the valley.

He struck off along a path that led between
deeply scented fields and that led straight down the
hill. He began now more soberly to consider the
facts of the case, and a certain depression stole
about him. He didn't after all see very well what
he would be able to do. They were going, on
the following morning, the three of them, abroad,
and once there how was he to effect any sort of
rescue?

The girl was apparently quite legally married,
and, although the horrible young Crispin had been
silent and sinister, there were no signs that he was
positively cruel. The deeper Harkness looked into
it the more he was certain that the secret of the
whole mystery lay in the older Crispin—it was of
him that the girl was terrified rather than the son.
Harkness did not know how he was sure of this,
he could trace no actual words or looks, but there
—yes, there the centre of the plot lay.

The man was strange and queer enough to look
at, but a more charming companion you could not
find. He had been nothing but amiable, friendly,
and courteous. His attitude to his daughter-in-
law had been everything that any one could wish.

He had seemed to consider her in every possible way.

Harkness, with his American naïveté of conduct, was fond of the word ' wholesome,' or rather, had he not spent so much of his life in Europe, would have found it his highest term of praise to call his fellow-man ' a regular feller!' Crispin Senior was *not* ' a regular feller ' whatever else he might be. There had, too, been one moment towards the end of dinner when a waiter, passing, had jolted the little man's chair. There had been for an instant a glance that Harkness now, in his general survey of the situation, was glad to have caught—a glance that seemed to tear the pale powdered mask away for the moment and to show a living moving visage, something quite other, something the more alive in contrast with its earlier immobility. Once, years before, Harkness had seen in the Naples Aquarium two octopi. They lay like grey slimy stones at the bottom of the shining sun-lit tank. An attendant had let down through the water a small frog at the end of a string. The frog had nearly reached the bottom of the tank when in one flashing instant the pile of shiny stone had been a whirling sickening monster, tentacles, thousands of them it seemed, curving, two loathsome eyes glowing. In one moment of time the frog was gone and in another moment the muddy pile was immobile once again. An unpleasant sight. Were the etchings of Samuel Palmer Crispin's only appetite? Harkness fancied not.

3

Plunging almost recklessly down the hill he was soon in the town, and, pushing his way through two or three narrow little streets, found himself in the market-place.

He caught his breath at the strange transformation of the place since his last view of it more than three hours before. He learnt later that this dance was held always as the Grand Finale of the Three Days' Annual Fair, and on the last of the days there is an old custom that, from four-thirty to six-thirty no trading shall be done, but that every one shall entertain or be entertained within their homes. This pause had its origin, I should fancy, in some kind of religious ceremony, to ask the Good God's blessing on the trading of the three days, but it had become by now a most convenient interval for the purpose of drinking healths, so that when, at seven o'clock, all the citizens of the town poured out of their doors once again, they were truly and happily primed for the fun of the evening.

Harkness found, therefore, what at first seemed to be naked pandemonium, and, stepping into it, crossed into the third room of his house of delivery.

The old buildings—the town hall, the church, the old grey tower—were lit up as though by some supernatural splendour, all the lights of the booths, the hanging clusters of fairy lamps, and, in the very middle of the place, a huge bonfire flinging arms of flame to heaven.

In one corner there was the merry-go-round, a twisting, heaving, gesticulating monster screaming out ' Coal Black Mammy of Mine,' and suddenly

whooping with its own excitement, showing so
much emotion that it would not have been surprising to find it, at any moment, leap its bearings
and come hurtling down into the middle of the
crowd.

The booths were thick with buyers and sellers,
and every one, to Harkness's excited fancy, seemed
to be screaming at the highest pitch of his or her
strident voice.

Here was everything for sale—hats, feathers,
coats, skirts, dolls, wooden dolls, rag dolls, china
dolls, monkeys on sticks, ribbons, gloves, shoes,
umbrellas, pies, puddings, cakes, jams, oranges,
apples, melons, cucumbers, potatoes, cabbages,
cauliflowers, brooches, diamonds (glass), rubies
(glass), emeralds (glass), prayer books, bibles,
pictures (King George, Queen Mary), cups, plates,
tea-pots, coffee-pots, rabbits, white mice, dogs,
sheep, pigs, one grey horse, tables, chairs, beds,
and one wooden house on wheels. More than
these, much more. And around them, about them,
in and out of them, before them and beside them
and behind them men, women, children, singing,
crying, shouting, sneezing, laughing, hiccuping,
quarrelling, kissing, arguing, denying, confirming,
whistling, and snoring. Men of the sea bronzed
with dark hair, flashing eyes, rings on their fingers
and bells on their toes; men of the fields, the soil
interpenetrated with the very soul of their being,
bearded to the eyes, broad-shouldered, broad-
buttocked, their Sunday coats flapping over their
corduroy thighs, their rough thick necks moving
restlessly in their unaccustomed collars; women of
the fair with eyes like black coals; gipsy women
straight from the tents with crimson kerchiefs and

black hair piled high under feathered hats; women of the town with soft voices, sidling eyes, and creeping hands; women of the farm with gaze wondering and adrift, hands like leather, children at their skirts; women householders with their purses carefully clutched, their hands feeling the cabbages, pinching the cauliflowers, estimating the chairs and tables, stroking the china; young boys and girls, confidence in their gaze, timidity in their hearts, suddenly catching hands, suddenly embracing, suddenly triumphant on their merry-go-round, suddenly everything, conscious of the last penny burning deep down in the pocket, conscious of love, conscious of appetite, conscious of possible remorse, conscious of blood pounding in their veins. And the magicians, the wonder workers, the steal-a-pennies, the old men with white beards and trays of coloured treasures, the bold bad men with their thimble and their penny, the little stumpy fellow with his cards, the long thin melancholy fellow with his medicines, the thick jolly drunken fellow with his tales of the sea, the twisty turn-his-head-both-ways fellow with his gold watches and silver chains, the red wizard with his fortunes in envelopes, his magic on strings of coloured paper, his mysterious signs and countersigns whispered into blushing ears. And then the children that should have been in bed hours ago—little children, large children, young children, old children, fat children, thin children, children clinging to mother's skirts, children running in and out, like mice, between legs and trousers, children riding on father's shoulder, children sticky with sweets and sucking their thumbs, children screaming with pleasure, shrieking with terror, howling with weariness—and one child all by itself on the steps of the town hall, curled up and fast asleep.

Away, to one side of the place, just as he had been there fifteen years ago when Maradick had been present, was a preacher, aloft on an over-turned box, singing with hand raised, his thin earnest face illumined with the lights, his scant hair blowing in the breeze. Around him a thin scattering of people singing just as fifteen years ago they had sung:

> So like little candles
> We shall shine,
> You in your small corner
> And I in mine.

The same recipe, the same cure, the same key offered to the unlocking of the same mysterious door—and so it will be to the end of created life—Amen!

The hymn was over. The preacher's voice was raised. Children step to the edge of the circle, looking up with wondering eyes, their fingers in their mouths.

'And so, dear friends, we have offered to us here the Blood of the Lamb for our salvation. Can we refuse it? What right have we to disregard our salvation? I tell you, my dear friends, that Judgement is upon us even now. There cometh the night when no man may work. How shall we be found? Sleeping? With our sins heavy upon us? There is yet time. The hour is not yet. Let us remember that God is merciful—there is still time given us for repentance——'

The Town Hall clock stridently, with clanging verberation, heard clearly above all the din, struck nine.

4

Even as the strokes sounded in the air the wide
doors of the Town Hall unfolded and a tall stout
man, dressed in the cocked hat and the cape and
cloak of a Dickensian beadle, appeared. Flaming
red they were, and very fine and important he looked
as he stood there on the steps, his legs spread,
holding his gold staff in his hands. He was
attended by several other gentlemen who looked
down with benignant approval upon the crowd,
and by a drum, a trumpet, and a flute, these last
being instruments rather than men.

A crowd began to gather at the foot of the steps
and the beadle to address them at the top of his voice,
but unlike his rival, the preacher, his voice did not
carry very far.

And now the Fair, having only five minutes more
of life before it, lifted itself into a final screaming
manifestation. Now was the time for which the
wise and the cautious had been waiting throughout
the three days of the Fair—the moment when all
the prices would tumble down with a rush because
it was now or never. The merry-go-round shrieked;
the animals bellowed, lowed, mooed, and grunted;
the purchasers argued, quarrelled, shouted, and
triumphed; the preacher and his followers sang and
sang again; the bells clanged, the gas-jets flared,
the bonfire rose furiously to heaven. But meanwhile
the crowd was growing larger and larger around the
Town Hall steps ; they came with penny whistles
and horns and hand-bells and even tea-trays. Then
suddenly, strong above the babel, carried by men's
stout voices, the song began:

Now, gentles all, attend this song,
 Tra-*la*, la-la, Tra-*la*,
It is but short, it can't be long,
 Tra-*la*-la-la, Tra-*la*,
How Farmer Brown one summer day
Was in his field a-gathering hay,
When by there came a pretty maid
Who smiling sweetly to him said,
 Tra-*la*-la-la-Tra-*la*.

Then Farmer Brown, though forty year,
 Tra-*la*, la-la, Tra-*la*,
When he that pretty voice did hear,
 Tra-*la*-la-la, Tra-*la*,
He threw his fork the nearest ditch
And caught the maiden tightly, which
Was what she wanted him to do,
And so the same would all of you,
 Tra-*la*-la-la-Tra-*la*.

But she withdrew from his embrace,
 Tra-*la*, la-la, Tra-*la*,
And mocked poor Farmer to his face,
 Tra-*la*-la-la, Tra-*la*,
And danced away along the lane,
And cried, ' Before I'm here again,
Poor Farmer Brown, you'll dance with Pain,'
 Tra-*la*-la-la-Tra-*la*.

And that was true, as you shall hear,
 Tra-*la*-la-la, Tra-*la* ;
Poor Farmer Brown danced many a year,
 Tra-*la*-la-la, Tra-*la*,
But never once that maid did see,
He grew as aged as aged could be,
And danced in*to* Eterni-tee,
 Tra-*la*-la-la-Tra-*la*.

The red-flaming beadle moved down the steps, and behind him came the drum, the trumpet, and the flute. The drum, a stout fellow with wide-spreading legs, had from the practice of many a year, and his father and grandfather having been

drummers before him, caught the exact measure of
the tune.   Along the market-place went the beadle,
the drum, the trumpet, and the flute.

For a moment a marvellous silence fell.

To Harkness this silence was exquisite.   The
myriad stars, the high buildings, their façades
ruby-coloured with the leaping light, the dark piled
background, the crowd humming now with quiet,
like water on the boil, the glow of rich suffused
colour sheltering everything with its beautiful cloak,
the rich voices tossing into the air the jolly song,
the sense of well-being and the tradition of the
lasting old time and the spirit of England eternally
fresh and sturdy and strong; all this sank into his
very soul and seemed to give him some hint of the
deliverance that was, very soon, to come to him.

Then the procession definitely formed.   All
the voices—men's, women's, and children's alike
—caught it up.   One—two—three, one—two—
three.   The drum, the trumpet, and the flute came
to them through the air:

> How Farmer Brown one summer day
> Was in his field a-gathering hay,
> When by there came a pretty maid
> Who smiling sweetly to him said,
>   Tra-*la*-la-la-Tra-*la*.

He was never to be sure whether or no he had
intended to join in the dance.   He was not aware
of more than the colour, the lights, the rhythm of
the tune, when a man like a mountain caught him
by the arm, shouting, ' Now we're off, brother—
now we're off,' and he was carried along.

There had always been a superstition about the
dance that to join in it, to be in it from the beginning
to the end, meant the best of good luck, and to miss

it was misfortune. There was, therefore, now a
flinging from all sides of eager bodies into the
fray. No one must be left out, and as the path
between the line of bodies and houses was a narrow
one, every one was pressed close together, and as
there had been much friendly swilling of beer and
ale, every one was in the highest humour, shouting,
laughing, singing, ringing their bells, and blowing
their whistles.

Harkness was crushed in upon his enormous
friend so completely that he had no other impression
for the moment but of a vast expanse of heaving,
leaping, corduroy waistcoat, of a hard brass button
in his eye, and of himself clutching with both hands
to a shiny trouser that must hold himself from
falling. But they were off indeed! Four of them
now in a row and the song was swinging fine and
strong. One—two—three, one—two—three. Forward bend one leg in air, backward bend, t'other
leg in air, forward bend again, down the market-
place and round the corner, voices raised in one
tremendous song.

He was easier now and able more clearly to
realise his position. One arm was tightly wedged
in that of his companion, and he could feel the thick
welling muscles taut through the stuff of the shirt.
On the other side of him was a girl, and he could
feel her hand pressing on his sleeve. On her side,
again, was a young man—her lover. He said so, and
shouted it to the world.

He leaned across her and cried out her beauties
as they moved, and she threw her head back and
sang.

The giant on the hither side seemed to have
taken Harkness into his especial protection. He

had been drinking well, but it had done him no order of harm. Only he loved the world and especially Harkness. He felt, he knew, that Harkness was a stranger from ' up-along.' On an average day he would have resented him, been suspicious of him, and tried ' to do him out of some of his blasted money.' But to-night he would be his friend and protect him from the world.

He would rather have had a girl crooked there under his arm, but the girl he had intended to have had somehow missed him when the fun began—but it didn't matter—the beer made everything glorious for him—and after all he had two daughters ' nigh grown up,' and his old missus was around somewhere, and it was just as good he didn't slip into any sort of mischief, which it was easy to do on a night like this—and his name was Gideon. All this he confided to Harkness while the procession halted, for a minute or two, at the corner of the market-place to pull itself straight before it started down the hill.

He had his arm around Harkness's neck and words poured from him. Gideon what or something Gideon? It didn't matter. Gideon it was and Gideon it would be so long as Harkness's memory remained.

All the soil of the English country, all the deep lanes with their high dark hedges, the russet corn-fields with their sudden dips to the sea, the high ridges with the white cottages perched like birds resting against the sky, the smell of the earth, the savour of the leaves wet after rain, the thick smoke and damp of the closed-in rooms, the mud, the clay, the running streams, the wind through the thick-sheltering trees—all these were in Gideon's speech as he stood, close pressed, thigh to thigh with Harkness.

He was happy although he knew not why, and Harkness was happy because he was in love for the first time in his life and tingled from head to foot with that knowledge. And up and down and all around it was the same. This was the night of all the nights of the year when enmities were forgotten and new friendships made. As Maradick once had felt the current of love running strong and true through a thousand souls, so Harkness felt it now, and, as with Maradick once, so with Harkness now, it seemed strange that life might not be simply run, that the lion might not lie down with the lamb, that nations might not be for ever at peace the one with another, and that the Grand Millennium might not immediately be at hand.

All beer you say? Maybe, and yet not altogether so. Something anxious and longing in the human heart was rising, free and strong, that night, and would never again entirely leave some of the hearts that knew it.

Harkness for one. There were to be many years in the future when he was to feel again the beating of Gideon's heart under his arm. Something of Gideon's was his, and something of his was Gideon's for evermore, though they would never meet again.

5

And now the procession was arranged. Harkness, looking back, could see how it stretched, a winding serpent black in the shadows of the leaping bonfire, through the square. They were off again.

The drum had started.   Down the hill they went, all packed together, all swinging with the tune.   A kind of divine frenzy united them all.   Young and old, men and women, married and single, good and evil, vicious and virtuous, all were together bound in one chain.   Harkness was with them.   For the first time in all his life, restraint was flung aside. He did not smell the beer, nor did the sweat of the perspiring bodies offend his sensitive nostrils, nor the dung from the fields, nor the fishy odours of the sea.   With Gideon on one side and a young man's girl on the other, he swung through the town.

Details for a time eluded him.   He was singing the song at the top of his voice, but what words he was singing he could not have told you ; he was dancing to the measure, but for the life of him he could not have afterwards repeated the rhythm.

They swung down into the heart of the town. The doors of all the houses were crowded with the very aged and the very young, who stood laughing and crying out, pointing to their friends and acquaintances, laughing at this and cheering at that.

And always more were joining in, pushing their way, dancing the more energetically because they had missed the first five minutes.   Now they were down on the fish-market all sprinkled with silver under the little moon and the cloth of stars.   Here the wind from the sea came to meet them, and through the music and the singing and the laughter and the press-press of the dancing crowd could be heard the faint breath of the tide on the shore ' seep-seep-sough-sough,' wistful and powerful, remaining for ever when they all were gone.   The sheds of the fish - market were gaunt and dark and deserted. For one moment all the naked place was filled with

colour and movement. Then up the hill they all
pressed.

It was difficult up the hill. There were breaths
and pants and ' Eh, sirs,' and ' Oh, the poor worm,'
and ' But my heart's beating,' and ' I cannot! I
cannot! ' One woman fell, was picked up and
planted by the side of the road, a young man staying
with melancholy kindness beside her. The rest
passed on.

Soon they were at the top of the hill before they
turned to the left again back into the town. And
this was Harkness's greatest moment. For an
instant the dance paused, and just then it happened
that Harkness was at the highest point of the
climb.

Catching his breath, his hand to his heart, for
he was out of training and the going had been hard,
he looked about him. Below him to the right and
to the left and to the farthest horizon the sea, a
grey silk shadow, hung, so soft, so gentle, that the
stars that crackled above it seemed to be taunting
it with its lethargy. On the other side of the hill
was all the clustered town, and before him and
behind him the dark multitudes of human beings.

He was happy, ecstatically happy. Pressed close
to Gideon, who was drinking something out of a
bottle, he was unconscious of any personality—
only that time had found for him, it seemed, a
solution to the whole problem of life. The sea-
wind fanning his temples, the salt snap of the sea,
the pounding of his own heart in union with that
other heart of his companion who was with him—
all these things together made of him, who had been
always afraid and timorous and edged with caution,
a triumphant soul.

And it was good that it was so, because of all that he would be called upon to do that night.

Gideon put his arm around him, pressing him close to him, and pushed the bottle up to his lips. 'Drink, brother,' he said.   'Drink, then, my dear.' And Harkness drank.

Now they were starting down the hill into the town once more, and the dance reached the height of its madness.

> He threw his fork the nearest ditch
> And caught the maiden tightly, which
> Was what she wanted him to do,
> And so the same would all of you,
>   Tra-*la*-la-la-Tra-*la*.

They screamed, they shrieked, they tumbled on to one another, they held on where they could, they swung from side to side.   The red beadle himself caught the frenzy, flinging his fat body now here, now there.   The very houses and the cobbles of the streets seemed to swing and sway as the lights flashed and flared.   All the bells of the town were pealing.   In the market-place they were setting off the fireworks, and the rockets, green and red and gold, streaked the purple sky and fought for rivalry with the stars.   All the sky now was scattered with sparks of gold.   From the highest heaven to the lowest of man's ditches the world crackled and split and sang.

Now was the moment when all enmities were truly forgotten, when love was declared without fear, when lips sought lips and hands clasped hands, and heaven opened and all the human souls marched in.

> Tra-*la*-la-la-Tra-*la*
> Tra-*la*-la-la-Tra-*la*.

Back into the market-place they all tumbled; then, standing in a serried mass as the beadle and his followers mounted the Town Hall steps, they shouted:

'All together: One—two—three.
One—Two—Three.
ONE. TWO. THREE.
HURRAY! HURRAY! HURRAY!'

The dance of all the hearts was, for one more year, at an end.

6

Every one was splitting up into little groups, some to look at the fireworks, some to have a last drink together, some to creep off into the dark shadows and there confirm their vows, some to drive home on their carts and waggons to their distant farms, some to sit in their homes for a last chatting about all the news, some to go straight to their beds—the common impulse was over although it would not be forgotten.

Harkness looked around to find Gideon, but that giant was gone nor was he ever to see him again. He paused there panting, happy, forgetting for an instant everything but the fun and freedom that he had just passed through. Then, as though it would forcibly remind him, the Town Hall clock struck half-past nine.

He spoke to a man standing near him:

'Can you kindly tell me where a hotel called "The Feathered Duck" is?' he asked.

'Certainly,' said the man, wiping the sweat from the hair matted on his forehead. 'It's out on the

sea front.   Go down High Street—that'll take you
to the sea front.   Then walk to your right and it's
about five houses down.'

Harkness thanked him and hurried away.   He
had no difficulty in finding the High Street, but
there how strange to walk so quietly down it, hearing
your own foot tread, watched by all the silent houses,
when only five minutes ago you had been whirling
in Dionysian frenzy!   He was on the sea front
and two steps afterwards was looking up at the
quiet and modest exterior of 'The Feathered
Duck.'

The long road stretched shining and sleek.
Not a living soul about.   The little hotel offered a
discreet welcome with plants in large green pots,
one on either side of the door, a light warm enough
to greet you and not too startling to frighten you,
and the knob gleaming like an inviting eye.

Harkness pushed open the door and entered.
The hall was anæmic and dark, with the trap to
catch visitors some way down on the right.   There
seemed to be no one about.   Harkness pushed
open a door and at once found himself in one of
those little hotel drawing-rooms that are so peculiarly
British, compounded as they are of ferns and dis-
cretion, convention and an untuned piano.   In
this little room a young man was sitting alone.
Harkness knew at once that his search was over.
He knew where it was that he had heard the name
Dunbar before—this was his young man of the
high road, the wandering seaman and the serious
appointment, the young man of his expectant
charge.

There was yet, however, room for mistake, and
so he waited standing in the doorway.   The young

man was bending forward in a red plush armchair, eagerly watching. He recognised Harkness at once as his friend of the afternoon.

'Hullo!' he said, and then hurriedly, 'why, what *has* been happening to you?'

Harkness stepped forward into the room. 'To me?' he said.

'Why, yes. You're sweating. Your collar's undone. You look as though you had run a mile.'

'Oh that!' Harkness blushed, fingering his collar, that had broken from its stud. 'I've been dancing.'

'Dancing?'

'Yes. All round the town. Like the lion and the unicorn.'

'Oh, I heard you. On any other night——' He broke off. During this time he had been watching Harkness with a curious expression, something between eagerness, distrust, and an impatience which he was finding very difficult to conceal. He said nothing more. Harkness also was silent. They stared the one at the other, and could hear beyond the door the noises of the little hotel, a shrill female voice, the rattle of plates, some man's laughter.

At last Harkness said: 'Your name is Dunbar, isn't it?'

The young man, instead of answering, asked his own question. 'Look here, what the devil are you after? I don't say that it is or it isn't, but anyway why do *you* want to know?'

'It's only this,' said Harkness slowly, 'that if your name *is* Dunbar, then I have a message for you.'

'You *have*?'

He started out of his chair, standing up in front of Harkness as though challenging him.

' Yes, a friend of yours asked me to come here, to meet you at half-past nine and tell you that she agrees to your proposal——'

' She does? . . . At last!'

Then his voice changed to suspicion. ' You seem to be a lot in this. Forgive my curiosity. I don't want to seem rude, but meeting me on the hill this afternoon and now this. . . . I've got to be so *damn* careful——'

' My name is Harkness. It was quite by chance that I was walking down the hill this afternoon and met you. As I told you then, I was on my way to " The Man-at-Arms." This evening I offered my help to a lady there who seemed to be in distress, and asked her whether there was anything that I could do. She asked me to bring you that message. There was no one else for her to ask.'

Dunbar stared at Harkness, then suddenly held out his hand. ' Jolly decent of you. I won't forget it. My name is Dunbar, as you know, David Dunbar.'

' And mine Harkness, Charles Harkness.'

' I can't tell you what you've done for me by bringing me that message. Here, don't go for a minute. Have something, won't you?'

' Yes, I think I will,' said Harkness, conscious of a sudden weariness.

' What shall it be? Whisky? Small soda?'

They sat down. Dunbar touched a bell and then, in silence, they waited. Harkness was humorously conscious that he seemed to be the younger of the two. The boy had taken complete command of the situation.

The older man was also aware that there was some very actual and positive situation here that was developing under his eyes. As he sat there, sticking to the plush of his chair, listening to the ridiculous chatter of the marble clock, staring into the Wardour Street Puritans of ' When did you see father last?' he felt urgency beating in upon them both. A shabby waiter looked in upon them, received his order, and departed.

Dunbar suddenly plunged. ' Look here, I know I can trust you, I'm sure of it. And *she* trusted you, so that should be enough for me. But— would you mind—telling me exactly how it happened that you got this message?'

' Certainly,' Harkness said. ' I——'

' Wait,' Dunbar interrupted; ' forgive me, but drop your voice, will you? One doesn't know who's hanging round here.'

They drew their chairs closer together, and Harkness, sitting forward, continued. ' I had dressed for dinner early. A friend of mine in London had told me that there was a little old room at the top of the hotel that was well worth seeing. I guess, like most Americans, I care for old-fashioned things, so I got to the top of the house and found the room. I was up in a little gallery at the back when two people came in, a man and a girl. They began to talk before I could move or let them know I was there. It was all too quick for me to do anything. The girl begged the man, to whom she was apparently married, to let her go home for a week before they went abroad, and the man refused. That was all there was, but the girl's terror struck me as extreme——'

' My God!' Dunbar broke in, 'if you only knew!'

'Well, I was touched by that, and I didn't like the man's face either. They went out. I came down to dinner. While I was waiting in the garden an extraordinary man spoke to me—extraordinary to look at, I mean—short, fat, red hair——'

'You needn't describe him,' Dunbar interrupted, 'I know him.'

'He came and asked me for a match. He was very polite, and finally invited me to dine with him, his son, and daughter-in-law. I accepted. Of course the son and daughter-in-law were the two that I had overheard upstairs. I saw that throughout dinner she was in great distress, and at the end as we were leaving the room I let her know that I had overheard her inadvertently before dinner, and that I was eager to help her if there was any way in which I could do so. We had only a moment, Crispin and his son were close upon us. She was, I suppose, at the end of her endurance and snatched at any chance, so she told me to do this—to find you here and give you that message—that's all—absolutely all.'

The door opened, making both men turn apprehensively. It was only the shabby little waiter with his tray and the whiskies. He set down the glasses, split the soda, and stared at them both as Dunbar paid him.

'Will that be all, gentlemen?' he asked, scratching his ear.

'Everything,' said Dunbar abruptly.

'Gentlemen sleeping here?'

'No, we're not. Good night.'

'Good night, sir.' With a little sigh the waiter withdrew. The door closed, and instantly the ferns

in the pots, the plush chairs and sofa closed round
as though they also wanted to hear.

'It's an extraordinary piece of luck,' Dunbar
began. Then he hesitated. 'But I don't want to
bother you with any more of this. It isn't your
affair. You've come into it, after all, only by
accident——'

He hesitated as though he were making an
invitation to Harkness. And Harkness hesitated.
He saw that this was his last opportunity of with-
drawal. Once again he could hear the voice of the
imp behind his shoulder: 'Well, clear out if you
want to. You have still plenty of time. And this
is positively the last chance I give you——'

He drank his whisky and, drinking, crossed his
Rubicon.

'No, no, I am interested, tremendously interested. Tell me anything you care to, and if I can
be of any help——'

'No, no,' Dunbar assured him, 'I'm not going
to drag you into it. You needn't be afraid of that.'

'But I *am* in it!' Harkness answered, smiling;
'I'm going back with Crispin to his house this
evening!'

7

The effect of that upon Dunbar was fantastic.
The young man jumped from his chair crying:

'You're going back?'

'Yes.'

'To the house?'

'Why, yes!'

'And to-night!'

He stared down at him as though he could not

believe the evidence of his ears nor of his eyes nor
of anything that was his. Then he finished his
whisky with a desperate gulp.

'But what's pushing you into this anyway?' he
cried at last. 'You don't look like the kind of
man—— And yet there you were on the hill this
afternoon, and then at the hotel and overhearing
what Hesther said, and then dining with the man
and his asking you—— He did ask you, didn't
he?'

'Of course he asked me,' Harkness answered.
'You don't suppose I'd have gone if he didn't.'

'No, I don't suppose you would,' agreed Dunbar.
'I bet he offered to show you his jewels and his
pictures, his collections.'

'Yes,' said Harkness, 'he did.'

'Well, that's just a miracle of good luck for me,
that's all. You can help me to-night, help me
marvellously. But I don't like to ask you. Things
might turn out all wrong and then we'd all be in for
a bad time and that wouldn't be fair to you.' He
paused, thinking, then he went on. 'I'll tell you
what I'll do. You saw that girl to-night and talked
to her, didn't you?'

Harkness nodded his head.

'You saw that she was a damned fine girl?'

Harkness nodded again.

'Worth doing a lot for. Well, I'll put the whole
story to you—let you have it all. We've got nearly
three-quarters of an hour. I can tell you most of
it in that time, and then you can make up your
mind. If, when I've told you everything, you
decide to have nothing whatever to do with it,
that's all right. There's no obligation on you at
all, of course. But if you *did* help me, being in the

house at that very time, it would make the whole
difference. My God, yes!' he ended with a sigh
of eagerness, staring at Harkness.

Harkness sat there, thinking only of the girl.
His own personal history, the town, the dance,
Crispin and his son, all these things had faded away
from his mind; he saw only her—as she had been
when turning her head for a moment she had spoken
to him with such marvellous self-control.

He loved her just as she stood there granting
him permission to help her. His own prayer was
that it might not be long before he was allowed to
help her again. He was recalled to the immediate
moment by Dunbar's voice:

' You'll forgive me if I go back to the beginning
of things—it's the only way really to explain. Have
you ever heard of Polchester, a town in Glebeshire,
north of this? There's a rather famous cathedral
there.'

' Yes,' said Harkness, ' I thought I might go
there from here.'

' Well,' Dunbar went on, ' out of Polchester
about ten miles there's a village—Milton Haxt.
I was born there and so was Hesther. Her name
was Hesther Tobin, and she was the only daughter
of the doctor of the place—she had two brothers
younger than herself. We've known one another
all our lives.'

' Wait a moment,' Harkness interrupted; ' are
you and she the same age?'

' No. I'm thirty, she's only twenty.'

' You look younger than that, or you did this
afternoon, I'm not so sure now.' Indeed the boy
seemed to have acquired some new weight and
responsibility as he sat there.

'No,' he went on. 'When I said that we'd known one another always I mean that she's always known about me. I used to take her on my knee and toss her up and down. That was where all the trouble began. If she hadn't been always used to me and fancied that I was years older than she—a kind of grandfather—she'd have married me.'

'Married you!' Harkness brought out.

'Yes. I can't remember a time when I wasn't in love with her. I always was, and she never was with me. She liked me—she likes me now—but she's always been so used to the idea of me. I've always been David Dunbar—and that's all,—a friend who was always there, but nothing more. There was just a moment when I was missing for six months in the middle of the war, I think she really cared then—but soon they heard that I was safe in Germany and it was all as it had been before.'

'Were her father and mother living?' Harkness asked.

'Her father. Her mother died when her youngest brother was born, when she was only six years old. The mother's death upset the father and he took to drink. He'd always been inclined that way I expect. He was too brilliant a doctor to have landed in that small village without there being some reason. Well, after Mrs. Tobin's death there was simply one trouble after another. Tobin's patients deserted him. The big house on the hill had to be sold and they moved into a small one in the village. He had been a big, jolly, laughing, generous man before; now he was always quarrelling with everybody, insulting the few

patients left to him, and so on. Hesther was
wonderful. How she kept the house together all
those years nobody knew. There was very little
she didn't know about life by the time she was ten
years old——ordinary life, I mean, not this damned
Crispin monstrosity. She always had the pluck
and courage of the devil, and you can fancy what I
felt just now when you told me about her asking
young Crispin to let her off. That *swine!*'

He paused for a moment, then went on hurriedly:

'But we haven't much time. I must buck
ahead. I was quite an ordinary sort of fellow, of
course, but there was nothing I wouldn't do for her
if I got a chance. I helped her sometimes, but
not so much as I'd have liked. She was always
terribly proud. All the things that happened at
home made her hold up her head in a kind of
defiance.

'The odd thing was that she loved her father,
and the worse he got the more she loved him. But
she loved her young brothers still more. She was
mother, sister, nurse, everything to them, and would
be still if she'd been let alone. They were nice
little chaps too, only a lot younger, of course——one
three years, one six. One's in the Navy——very
decent fellow——and if he'd been home he'd never
have allowed any of this to happen.

'Well, the war came when she was quite a kid.
I was away most of that time. Then in 1918 my
father died and left me a bit of property there in
Milton. I came home and asked her to marry me.
She thought I was pitying her, and anyway she
didn't love me. And I hadn't enough of this
world's goods to make the old man keen about
me.

' Then this devil came along.'   Dunbar stopped
for a moment.   They both listened.   There was
not a sound in the whole house.

' What brought him to a village like yours?'
asked Harkness, lowering his voice.   ' I shouldn't
have thought that a man like that——'

' No, you wouldn't,' said Dunbar.   ' But that's
one of his passions apparently, suddenly landing
on some small village where there's a big house
and bossing every one around him. . . . I shall
never forget the day I first saw him.   It was just
about a year ago.

' I had heard that some foreigner had taken
Haxt, that was the big house in Milton that the
Dombeys, the owners, were too poor to keep up.
Soon all the village was talking.   Furniture arrived,
then lots of servants, Japs and all sorts.   Then
one evening going up the hill I saw him leaning
over one of the Haxt gates looking into the road.

' It was a lovely July evening and he was without
a hat.   You've spoken of his hair.   I tell you that
evening it was just flaming in the sun.   It looked
for a moment like some strange sort of red flower
growing on the top of the gate.   He stopped me
as I was passing and asked me for a match.'

' That's what he asked me for,' murmured
Harkness.

' Yes, his opening gambits are all the same.   He
offered me a cigarette and I took one.   We talked
for a little.   I didn't like him at first, of course,
with his hair, white face, painted lips; but—did you
notice what a beautiful voice he has?'

' I should think I did,' said Harkness.

' And then he can make himself perfectly charming.   The beginning of your acquaintance with him

is exactly like your introduction to the villain of
any melodrama—painted face, charming voice,
cosmopolitan, delightful information. The change
comes afterwards. But I must hurry on, I'll never
be done. I'm as bad as Conrad's Marlowe. Have
another whisky, won't you?'

' No thanks,' said Harkness.

' Well, it wasn't long before he was the talk of
the whole place. At first every one liked him.
Odd though he looked, you can just fancy how a
man with his wealth and knowledge of the world
would fascinate a country-side if he chose to make
himself agreeable, and he *did* choose. He gave
parties, he went round to people's houses, sent
his motors to give old ladies a ride, allowed people
to pick flowers in his garden, adored showing people
his collections. I happened to be in Milton during
the rest of that year looking after my little property,
and he seemed to take to me. I was up at Haxt a
good deal.

' Looking back now I can see that I never really
liked him. I was aware of my caution and laughed
at myself for it. I like pretty things, you know,
and I loved his jade and emeralds, and still more his
prints. And he knew so much and was never tired
of telling me and never seemed to laugh at one's
ignorance.

' He was, as I have said, all the talk that summer.
It was " Mr. Crispin " this and " Mr. Crispin "
that—Mr. Crispin everything. The men didn't
take to him much, but of course they wouldn't!
They had always thought *me* a bit queer because I
liked reading and played the piano. The first
thing that people didn't like about him was his
son. That beauty arrived at Haxt somewhere in

September, and everybody hated him. I ask you,
could you help it? And he was the exact opposite
of his father. *He* didn't try to make himself
agreeable to anybody—simply went about scowling
and frowning. But it wasn't that that people disliked—it was his relation to his father. He was
absolutely in his father's power—that is the only
way to put it—and there was something despicable,
something almost obscene, you know, almost as
though he were hypnotised, the way he obeyed him,
listened to his voice, slaved away for him.'

'I noticed something of that myself this evening,'
said Harkness.

'You couldn't help it if you saw them together.
Somehow the son turning up beside the father made
the *father* look queer—as though the son showed
him up. People round Milton are not very per-
ceptive, you know, but they soon smelt a rat, several
rats in fact. For one thing the people in the village
didn't like the Jap servants, then one or two maids
that Crispin had hired abruptly left. They wouldn't
say anything except that they didn't like the place,
that old Crispin walked in his sleep or something
of the kind.

'It was just about this time, early in October
or so, that Crispin became friendly with the Tobins.
Young Crispin had a cold or something and Tobin
came up and doctored him. Crispin gave him the
best liquor he'd ever had in his life, so he came
again, and then again. That was the beginning of
my dislike of Crispin. It seemed to me rotten of
him, when Tobin was already going as fast down-
hill as he could, to give him an extra push. And
Crispin liked doing that. One could see it at a
glance. I hated him from the moment when I

caught him watching with an amused smile Tobin
fuddled in his chair. You can imagine that Tobin's
drunkenness, having cared for Hesther as I had
for so long, was a matter of some importance
for me. I had tried to pull him up, without any
sort of success, of course, and it simply maddened
me to see what Crispin was doing. So I lost my
temper and spoke out. I told him what I thought
of him. He listened to me very quietly, then he
suddenly threw his head up at me like a snake
hissing. He said a lot of things. That was the
first time I heard all his nonsensical stuff about
sensations. We haven't time now, and anyway it
wasn't very new——the philosophy that as this was
our only existence we had better make the most of
it, that we had been given our senses to use, not to
stifle, and the rest of it. Omar put it better than
Crispin.

' He had also a lot of talk about Power, that if
he liked he could have any one in his power, and so
could I if I liked. You had only to know other
people's weaknesses enough. And more than that.
Some stuff about its being good for people to suffer.
That the thing that made life interesting and worth
while was its intensity, and that life was never so
intense as when we were suffering. That, after all,
God liked us to suffer. Why shouldn't *we* be
gods? We might be if we only had courage
enough.

' It was then, that morning, that it first entered
my head that there was something wrong with him
——something wrong with his brain. It had never
occurred to me during all those months because he
had always been so logical, but now——he seemed
to step across the little bridge that separates the

sane from the insane. You know how small that bridge is?' Harkness nodded his head.

'Then all in a moment he took my arm and twisted it. I can't give you any sort of idea how queer and nasty that was. As he did it he peered into my face as though he didn't want to miss the slightest shadow of an expression. Then—I don't know if you noticed when he shook hands with you —his fingers haven't any bones in them, and yet they are beastly powerful. He ought to be soft all over and he *isn't*. He twisted my arm once and smiled. It was all I could do to keep from knocking him down. But I broke away, told him to go to hell and left the house. From that moment I hated him.

'It was directly after this that I noticed for the first time that he had his eye on Hesther, and he had his eye upon her exactly because she hated him and wouldn't go near him if she could possibly help it. I must stop for a moment and tell you something about her. You've seen her, but you cannot have any kind of idea how wonderful she really is.

'She has the most honourable loyal character you've ever seen in woman. And she's never been in love—she doesn't know what love is. Those are the two most important things about her. That doesn't mean that she's ignorant of life. There's nothing mean or sordid or disgusting that hasn't come into her experience through her beauty of a father, but she's stood up to it all—until this, this Crispin marriage. The first thing in her life she's funked.

'She's been saved all along by her devotion to one thing, her family—her father and two brothers.

She must have given her father up pretty completely
by now, seen that it was hopeless; but her small
brothers—why, they are the key to the whole thing!
If it weren't for them she wouldn't be where she is
to-night, and, as I have said, if the elder one had
known anything about it he wouldn't have allowed
it, but he's away on a foreign station and Bobby's
too young to understand.

'She was always very independent in the village,
keeping to herself. Not being rude to people, you
understand, but making no real friends. She simply
lived for those two boys, and she had to work so
hard that she had no time for friends. She knew
that I loved her—I had told her often enough.
She saw more of me than of any one else, and she
would allow me to do things for her sometimes,
but even with me she kept her independence.
To-night is the very first time in both our lives that
she has begged me to do anything!'

He stopped for a moment. 'By God!' he
cried, 'if I can't help her to-night I'll finish myself;
there'll be nothing left in life for me!'

'We *will* help her,' Harkness said. 'Both of
us. But go on. Time's advancing. I mustn't
miss my appointment.'

'No, by Jove, you mustn't,' said Dunbar.
'Everything hangs on that. Well, to get on. It
didn't take me very long to see what Crispin was
doing to her father, and one day she went up to
see him alone and begged him to be merciful. She
says that he was charming to her and that she hated
him worse than ever.

'He promised her that he would stop her father's
drinking, and, of course, he didn't keep his promise,
but made Tobin drink more than ever.

' It was round about Christmas that these things happened, and just about this time all sorts of stories began to circulate about him. He suddenly left, came over to Treliss, and took the White Tower where you're going to-night. After he had gone the stories grew in volume—the most ridiculous things you ever heard, about his catching rabbits and skinning them alive and holding witches' Sabbaths with his Japs—every kind of fantastic thing. And all the women who had gone to see his pretty things and raved about him when he first came said they didn't know how they " ever could have seen anything in him," and that he deserved imprisonment and worse.

' It was now that I discovered that Hesther was desperately worried. I had known her all my life and had never seen her worried like this before. She lost her colour, was always thinking about other things when one spoke to her, and, several times, had been crying when I came upon her. Naturally I couldn't stand this, and I bullied her until I got the truth out of her. And what do you think that was? Why, of all the horrible things, that the younger Crispin had asked her to marry him, and that all the time her blackguard of a father was pressing her to do it.

' You can imagine what I felt like when I heard this! I cursed and swore and blasphemed, and still couldn't believe that she was in any way taking it seriously until, when I pressed her, I found that she was!

' She was always as obstinate as sin, had her own way of looking at things, made up her own mind and stuck to it. She didn't hate the son as she hated the father, although she disliked the little she'd seen of him well enough ; but, remember, she knew very little about marriage. All her thoughts were on those two boys, her brothers.

'I found out that old Crispin had offered Tobin any amount of money if he'd give his daughter up, and that Tobin had put this to Hesther, telling her that he was desperately in debt, that he'd be put in prison if the money didn't turn up from somewhere, and, above all, that the boys would be ruined if she didn't agree, that he'd have to take the younger boy away from school and so on.

'I did everything I could. I went and saw Tobin and told him what I thought of him, and he was drunk as usual and we had a scuffle, in the course of which I unfortunately tumbled him over. Hesther came in and saw him on the floor, turned on me, and then said she'd marry young Crispin.

'I begged, I implored her. I said that if she would marry me I'd give her everything that I had in the world, that we'd manage so that Bobby shouldn't have to be taken away from school, and the rest of it. Then Father Tobin got up from the floor and asked me with a sneer how much I'd got, and I tried to bluster it out, but of course they both of them knew that I hadn't got very much.

'Anyway Hesther was angry with me—ashamed, I think, that I'd seen her father in such a state, and her pride hurt that I should know how badly they were placed. She accepted young Crispin by the next mail. If the Crispins had actually been there in the flesh I don't think she would have done it, but some weeks' absence had softened her horror of them, and she could only think how wonderful

it was going to be to do all the marvellous things
for the boys that she was planning.

'I'm sure that when young Crispin did turn up
with his long body and cadaverous face she repented
and was frightened, but her pride wouldn't let her
then back out of it.

'I had one last talk with her before her marriage.
I begged her to forgive me for anything that I had
done that might seem casual or insulting, that she
must put me out of her mind altogether, but just
consider in a general way whether this wasn't a
horrible thing that she was doing, marrying a man
that she didn't love, taking on a father-in-law whom
she hated.

'She was very sweet to me, sweeter than she
had ever been before. She just shook her head
and let me kiss her. And I knew that this was a
final good-bye.'

8

'She married Crispin and came to Treliss. I
wasn't at the wedding. I heard nothing from her.
And then a story came to my ears that, after I had
once heard it, gave me no peace.

'It was an old woman—a Mrs. Martin. She
had, months before, been up at Haxt doing some
kind of extra help. She was an old mottled woman
like a strawberry—I'd known her all my life—and
a grandmother. She suddenly left, and it was only
weeks after Crispin went that I found out why.
She was very shy about it, and to this day I've never
discovered exactly what happened. Something one
evening when she was alone in the kitchen preparing
to go home. The elder Crispin came in followed

by one of his Japs.   He made her sit down in one
of the kitchen chairs, sat down beside her, and began
to talk to her in his soft beautiful voice.   What it
was all about to this day she doesn't know—some
of his fine stuff about Sensation, I dare say, and the
benefit of suffering so that you could touch life at
its fullest!   I shouldn't wonder — anyway an old
woman like Mrs. Martin, who had borne eight or
nine children of her husband who beat her, knew
plenty about suffering without Crispin trying to
teach her.   Anyway he went on in his soft beautiful
voice, and she sat there bewildered, fascinated a bit
by his red hair which she told me " she never could
get out of her mind like," and the Jap standing
silent beside her.

'Suddenly Crispin took hold of her old wrinkled
neck and began stroking it, putting his face close
to hers, talking, talking, talking all the time.   Then
the Jap stepped behind her, caught the back of her
head and pulled it.

'What would have happened next I don't know
had not the younger Crispin come in, and at the sight
of him the older man instantly got up, the Jap
disappeared—it was as though nothing had been.
Old Mrs. Martin got out of the house, then tumbled
to pieces in the shrubbery.   She was ill for days
afterwards, but she kept the whole thing quiet
with a kind of villager's pride, you know—" she
wasn't going to have other folks talking as they
did anyway when they saw how quickly she had
left."

'But she told one of her daughters and the
daughter told me.   There was almost nothing in
the actual incident, but it told me two things, one,
that the older Crispin really is mad—definitely,

positively insane, the other that the son, in spite of his seeming so submissive, has some sort of hold over him. There is something between the two that I don't understand.

'Well, that decided me. I went to Treliss to find out what I could. I had to hang about for quite a time before I could learn anything at all. Crispin was going on at Treliss just as he had done at Milton. He's taken this strange house outside the town which you'll see to-night. Quite a famous place in a way, built on the sea-cliff with a tangled overgrown wood behind it and a high white tower that you can see for miles over the country-side. At first the people liked him just as they had done at Milton and were interested in him. Then there were stories and more stories. Suddenly, only a week ago he said he was going abroad, and to-morrow he's going.

'Now the point I want to make clear to you is that the man's mad. I'm not a clever chap. I don't know any of your medical theories. I've never had any leaning that way, but I take it that the moment that any one crosses the division between sanity and insanity it means that they can control their brain no longer, that they are dominated by some desire or ambition or lust or terror that nothing can stop, no fear of the law, of public shame, of losing social caste. Crispin is mad, and Hesther, whom I love more than anything in this world and the next, is in his hands completely and absolutely. They go abroad to-morrow morning where no one can touch them.

'The time's been so short, and I've not been sufficiently clever to give you any clear idea of the man himself. I've got practically no facts. You can't say that his stroking an old woman's neck is a fact that proves anything. All the same I believe you've seen enough yourself to know that it isn't all imagination, and that the girl is in terrible peril. My God, sir,' the boy's voice was shaking, ' before the war there were all sorts of things that didn't seem possible, we knew that they couldn't exist outside the books of the story-tellers. But the war's changed all that. There's nothing too horrible, nothing too beastly, nothing too bad to be true—yes, and nothing too fine, nothing too sporting.

' And this thing is quite simple. There are those two madmen and my girl in their hands, and only to-night to get her out of them.

' I must tell you something more,' he went on more quietly. ' I've been making desperate attempts to see her, and at the same time to prevent either of those devils from seeing *me*. I saw her twice, once in the grounds of the White Tower, once on the beach below the house. Neither time would she listen to me. I could see that she was miserable, altogether changed, but all that she would say was that she was married and that she must go through with what she had begun.

' She begged me to go away and leave Treliss. Her one fear seemed to be lest Crispin should find out I was there and do something to me.

' Her terror of him was dreadful to witness— but she would tell me nothing. I hung about the place and made a friend of a fisherman he had up there working on the place—Jabez Marriot—you saw him on the hill to-day.

' He's a fine fellow. He's only been working on the grounds, had nothing to do with inside the

house, but he didn't love the Crispins any better
than I did, and he had lost his heart to Hesther.
She spoke to him once or twice, and he would do
anything for her. I sent letters to her through
him: she replied to me in the same way, but they were
all to the same effect, that I was to go away quickly
lest Crispin should do something to me, that she
wasn't being badly treated and that there was nothing
to be done.

'Then, about a week ago, Crispin saw me. It
was in one of the Treliss lanes, and we met face to
face. He just gave me one look and passed on,
but since then I've had to be terribly careful. All
the same I've made my plans. All that was needed
was her consent to them, and that, until to-night,
she has steadily refused to give. However, something worse than usual has broken her down. What
he has been doing to her I don't know, I dare not
think—but to-night I've got to get her out. I've
got to, or never show my face anywhere again.
Now I've told you this as quickly as I could. Will
you help me?'

Harkness stood up holding out his hand: ' Yes,'
he said, ' I will.'

' It can be beastly, you know.'

' That's all right.'

' You don't mind what happens?'

' I don't mind what happens.'

' Sportsman.'

The two men shook hands. They sat down
again. Dunbar spread out a paper on the little
green-topped table.

' This is a rough plan of the house,' he said.
' I can't draw, but I think you can make this
out.'

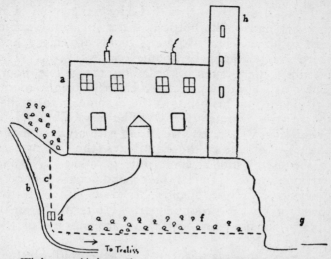

a Window over kitchen garden.
b High road to Treliss.
c Wall enclosing garden.
d Gate in wall.
e Wood behind house.
f Wood at bottom of garden.
g Sea.
h White Tower.

'Please forgive this childish drawing,' he said
again. 'It's the best I can do. I think it makes the
main things plain. Here's the house, the tower
over the sea, the wood, the garden, the high road.
Now look at this other plan of the second floor.

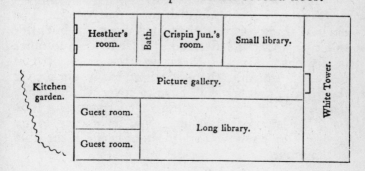

' You'll see from this that Hesther's room is at
the very end of the house and her husband's room
next to hers.   The two guest rooms are empty, and
there are no other bedrooms on that floor.   The
picture gallery runs right along the whole floor.
The small library is a rather cheerful bright room.
Crispin has put his prints in there, some on the walls,
the rest in solander boxes.   The large library is a
gaunt, dusty, deserted place hung with heads of many
animals that one of the Pontifexes (the real owners
of the place) shot at some time or other.   No one
ever goes there.   In fact this second floor is generally
deserted.   Crispin spends his time either in the
tower or on the ground floor.   He is in the small
library playing about with his prints some of the
time though.

' Now, my plan is this.   I have told Hesther
everything to the very tiniest detail, and all that
she had to do was to send word at any moment
that she agreed to it.   That she has now done.

' To-night at one o'clock I am going to be up
the high road under the shadow of the wood at the
back of the kitchen garden with a jingle and
pony——'

' A jingle?' asked Harkness.

' Yes, a jingle is Cornish for a pony trap.   The
obvious thing for me to have had was a car, but after
thinking about it I decided against it for a number
of reasons.   One of them was the noise that it
makes in starting, then it might easily stick over
the ground that we shall have to cover, then I fancy
that it will be the first thing that Crispin will look
for if he starts in pursuit.   We have only to go
three miles anyway, and most of it over the turf
of the moor.'

' Only three miles?' Harkness asked.

' Yes, I'll tell you about that in a moment. Crispin Senior is pretty regular in his movements, and just about one o'clock he goes up to his bedroom at the top of the tower with his two Japs in attendance. That is the only time of the day or night that one or another of those Japs isn't hanging about somewhere. They are up there with him on exactly the opposite side of the house from Hesther's room at just that time. That leaves only young Crispin. We shall have to chance him, but, according to Jabez, he has the habit of going to bed between eleven and twelve, and by one o'clock he ought to be sound asleep.

' However, that is one of the things we ought to look out for, one of the things indeed that I want your help about. Meanwhile Jabez is patrolling in the grounds outside.'

' Jabez!' Harkness cried, startled.

' Yes, that is our great piece of luck. Crispin has had some fellow of his own in the grounds all this time, but three nights ago he sent him up to London on some job and Jabez has taken his place. I don't think he trusts Jabez altogether, but he trusts the others still less. He is always cursing the Cornishmen, and they don't love him any the better for it.'

' Well, when you've got safely to your pony cart what happens next?'

' We drive up Shepherd's Lane, down across the moor until we reach the cliff just above Starling Cove. Here I've got a boat waiting, and we'll row across that corner of the bay to another cove —Selton—and just above Selton is Selton Minor where there's a station. At four in the morning there's the first train, local, to Truro, and at Truro we can catch the six o'clock to Drymouth. In Drymouth there are an uncle and aunt of hers— the Bresdins—who have long been fond of her and wanted her often to stay with them. Stephen Bresdin is a good fellow and will stand up for her, I know, once she's in his hands. Then we can get the law to work.'

' Won't Crispin be after you before you reach the Truro train?'

' Well, I'm reckoning first that he doesn't discover anything at all until he wakes in the morning. They are making an early start for London that day, but he shouldn't be aware of anything until six at least. But secondly, if he does, I'm calculating that first he'll think she's catching the three o'clock Treliss to Drymouth, or that she's motored straight into Truro. If he goes into Truro after her or sends young Crispin I'm reckoning that he won't have the patience to wait for that six o'clock or won't imagine that we have, and will be sure that we will have motored direct into Drymouth.

' He'll post after us there. I don't think he knows about the Bresdins in Drymouth. He may, but I don't think so. Of course it's all chance, but I figure that it is the best we can do.'

' And what's my part in this?' asked Harkness.

' Of course you're not to do a thing more than you want to,' said Dunbar. ' But this is where you could be of use. The thing that we're mainly afraid of is young Crispin. Hesther can get out of her room easily enough. It is only a short drop on to an outhouse roof, and then a short drop from there again, but if young Crispin is moving about, coming into her room and so on, it may be very difficult. What I suggest is that you stay with the older Crispin looking at his collections and the rest until half-past twelve or so, then bid him a fond good-night and go. Wait for a quarter of an hour in the grounds. Jabez will be there, and then at about a quarter to one he will let you into the house again. Crispin Senior should be up in the tower by then, but if he isn't, you can pretend that you have lost something, take him back into the small library where the prints are, and keep him well occupied until after one. If he *has* gone up to his tower, Hesther will leave a small piece of white paper under her door *if* Crispin Junior is in the way and hanging about. In that case I should knock on his door, apologise, say that you lost your gold match-box, had to come back for it as they are all leaving early the next day, think it must be in the small library ; he goes back with you to look for it and—you keep him there. Do you think you could manage that?'

'I will,' said Harkness.

'There's more than that. One of the principal reasons that Hesther refused to consider any of this was—well, running off alone with me in the middle of the night. But if you are with us—some one, if I may say so, so entirely——'

'Respectable,' Harkness suggested as Dunbar hesitated.

'Well, yes—if you don't mind that word. It alters everything, don't you see. Especially as you've never seen me before, aren't in love with her or anything.'

'Exactly,' said Harkness gravely.

'There you are. The thing's full of holes. It can fall down in all sorts of places, and if Crispin

catches us and knows what we are up to, it won't
be pleasant. But there's nothing else. No other
plan that seems any less dangerous. Are you for
it, sir?'

'I'm for it,' said Harkness. At that moment
the little marble clock struck the half-hour.

'My God!' Harkness cried, 'I should be at
the hotel this very minute. If I miss them there's
our plan spoiled.'

He gripped Dunbar's hand once and was off.

9

He went racing through the darkness, the two
thoughts changing, mingling, changing incessantly
over and over in his brain—that he must catch
them at the hotel before they left it, and that he
loved, he loved her, he loved her with an intensity
that seemed to increase with every step that he
ran.

In some way, although Dunbar had said so little
about her, his picture of her was infinitely clearer
and stronger than it had been before. He saw her
in that small village of hers struggling with that
drunken father, with insufficient means, with the
individualities and rebellions of her two brothers,
who, however deeply they loved her (and normal
boys are not conscious of their deep emotions), must
have kicked often enough against the limitations
of their conditions, sneering servants, spying neigh-
bours, jesting and scornful relations, the father in
his cups abusing her, insulting her, and for ever
complaining—and yet she, through all of this,
showing a spirit, a hardihood, a pluck and, he

suspected, a humour that only this last fatal intercourse with the Crispin family had broken down.

Harkness was the American man at his simplest and most idealistic, and than this there is nothing simpler and more idealistic in the whole of modern civilisation. The Englishman has too much common sense and too little imagination, the Frenchman is too mercenary, the Southern peoples too sensuous to provide the modern Quixote. In the United States of America to-day there are as many Quixotes as there are builders of windmills to be tilted at— and that is saying much.

So that, with his idealism, his hatred of cruelty and abnormality, Harkness saw far beyond any personal aggrandisement in this pursuit. He was not thinking now of himself at all, he had danced himself that night into a new world.

In the market-place he had to pause for breath. He had run all the way down the High Street, meeting no one as he went; he had already had considerable exercise that evening, and he was in no very fine condition of training. The market-place was quiet enough, only a few stragglers about; the Town Hall clock told him it was twenty-eight minutes to eleven.

He started up the hill, he arrived breathless at the hotel gates, the sweat pouring down his face. He stopped and tried to arrange himself a little. It would be a funny thing coming in upon them all with his tie undone and lines of sweat running down his face. But, after all, he could make the dance account for a good deal. He pushed his stud through the two ends of his collar and pulled his tie up, finding it difficult to use his hands because they were so hot, wiped his face with his handkerchief, pushed his cap straight on his head.

His face wore an expression of grim seriousness as though he were indeed St. George off to rescue his Princess from the Dragon.

His heart gave a jump of relief when he saw that the Dragon was still there, standing quite unconcernedly in the main hall of the hotel, his son and daughter-in-law quietly beside him. Harkness's first thought at view of him was that Dunbar's story was built up of imagination. The little man was standing, a soft felt hat tilted a little on one side of his head, a dark thin overcoat covering his evening clothes. Because his hair was covered and his face shaded there was nothing about him that was at all startling or highly coloured. He simply looked to be a nice plump little English gentleman who was waiting, a smile on his face, for his car to arrive that it might take him home. Nor was there anything in the least exceptional in the pair that stood beside him, the man, thin, dark, immobile; the girl, her head a little bent, a soft white wrap over her shoulders, her hands at her side. At once it flashed into Harkness's brain that all the scene with Dunbar had been imagined; there had been no 'Feathered Duck,' no melodramatic story of madness and tyranny, no twopence-coloured plan for a midnight rescue.

He was about to drive a mile or two to see some beautiful things, to smoke a good cigar and drink some admirable brandy—then to retire and sleep the sleep of the divinely worthy.

The girl raised her head. Her eyes met his, and he knew that whatever else was true or false his love for her was certain and resolved.

Crispin looked extremely pleased to see him. He came towards him smiling and holding out his hand:

'Why, Mr. Harkness, this is splendid,' he said. 'We were just wondering what we should do about you. We were giving you up.'

Harkness was conscious that, in spite of his attempts outside, he was still in considerable disorder. He fingered his collar nervously.

'I'm sorry,' he began. 'But I'm so glad that I've caught you after all.'

'Were the revels in the town amusing?' Crispin asked.

Harkness had a sudden impulse, whence he knew not, to make the younger Crispin speak.

'Why didn't you come down?' he asked. 'You'd have enjoyed it.'

The man was astonished at being addressed. He sprang into sudden life like any Jack-in-the-Box.

'Oh I,' he said, 'I had to go with my father, you know—yes, to see some old friends.'

He was looking at Harkness as though he were wondering why, exactly, he had done that.

'Are you still willing to come and see my few things?' Crispin asked. 'It's only half-an-hour's drive and my car will bring you back.'

'I shall be delighted to come,' Harkness said quickly. 'I would have been deeply disappointed if I had missed you. But you must not think of sending me back. I shall enjoy the walk greatly.'

'Why, of course not!' said Crispin. 'Walk back at that time of the night! I couldn't allow it for a moment.'

'But I assure you,' Harkness pressed, laughing, 'I infinitely prefer it. You probably imagine that

Americans never move a step unless they have a car
to carry them. Not in my case. I won't come
if I feel that during every minute that I am with
you I am keeping your chauffeur up.'

'Well, well—all right,' said Crispin, laughing.
'Have it your own way. You're a very obstinate
fellow. Perhaps you will change your mind when
the time really arrives.'

They moved out to the doorway, then into the car.

Mrs. Crispin sat in one corner. Harkness was
about to pull up the seat opposite, but Crispin said:

'No, no. Plenty of room on the back for three
of us. Herrick doesn't mind the other seat. He's
used to it.'

They sat down, Harkness between the elder
Crispin and the girl. The night was black beyond
their windows. Crispin pressed the button. The
interior of the car was at once in darkness, and
instantly the night was no longer black but purple
and threaded with wisps of grey lavender that seemed
to hold in their spider filigree all the loaded scent
of the summer evening. Again, as the car turned
into the long ribbon of the dark road, Harkness was
conscious through the open window of the smell of
innumerable roses, the late evening smell when the
heat of the day is over and the flowers are grateful.

Then a curious thing happened. Through the
darkness, Harkness felt one of the fingers of
Crispin's left hand creeping like an insect about
his knee. They were sitting very closely together
inside the car's enclosure. Harkness was conscious
that Hesther Crispin was pressed, almost crouch-
ing, against the corner of the car, and although the
stuff of her dress touched him he was aware that
she was striving desperately that he should not be

aware of her proximity, and then directly after that, of why she was so striving—it was because she was shivering—shivering in little spasms and tremors that shook her from head to foot—and she was wishing that he should not realise this.

And even as he caught from her the conscious-ness of her trembling, at the same moment he was aware of the pressing of Crispin's finger upon his knee. He was so close to Crispin, and his leg was pushed so firmly against Crispin's leg, that this movement might have been accidental had Crispin's whole hand rested there. But there was only the finger, and soon it began its movement, staying for an instant, pressing through the cloth on to the bone of the knee, then moving very slowly up the thigh, the sharp finger-nail suddenly pushing more firmly into the flesh, then the finger relaxing again and making only a faint, tickling, creeping suggestion of a pressure. Half-way up the thigh it stopped; for an instant the whole hand, soft, warm, and boneless, rested on the stuff of Harkness's trousers, then withdrew, and the fingers, like a cautious animal, moved on.

When Harkness was first conscious of this he tried to move his knee, but he was so tightly wedged in that he could not stir. Then he could not move for another reason, that he was trans-fixed with apprehension. It was exactly as though a gigantic hand had slipped forward and enclosed him in its grasp, congealing him there, stiffening him into helpless clay—and this was the appre-hension of immediate physical pain.

He had known all his days that he was a coward about physical pain, and that was always the form of human experience that he had shrunk from

observing, compelling himself sometimes, because
he so deeply hated his cowardice, to notice, to listen,
but suffering after these contacts acute physical
reactions. Only once or twice in his life had pain
actually come to him. He did not mind it so deeply
were it part of illness or natural causes, but the
deliberate anticipation of it—the doctor's ' Now
look out; I am going to hurt,' the dentist's ' I may
give you a twinge for a moment,' these things
froze him with terror. During the war, when he
had offered his service, this was the thing that
from the clammy darkness of the night leapt out
upon him. He had done his utmost to serve at
the front, and it was in no way his own fault when
he was given clerical work at home. He had tried
again and again, but his poor sight, his absurd
inside that was always wrong in one fashion or
another, these things had held him back—and
behind it all was there not a faint ring of relief,
something that he dared not face lest it should reveal
itself as cowardice? There had been times at the
dentist's and one operation. That operation had
been a slight one, but it had involved for several
weeks the withdrawing of tubes and the probing
with bright shining instruments. Every morning
for several hours before this withdrawing and probing he lay panting in bed, the beads of sweat gathering on his forehead, his hands clutching and un-
clutching, saying to himself that he did not care,
that he was above it, beyond it . . . but closer and
closer and closer the animal came, and soon he was
at his bedside, and soon bending over him, and soon
his claws were upon his flesh and the pain would
swoop down, like a cry of a discoverer, and the
voice would be sharper and sharper, the determina-

tion not to listen, not to hear, not to feel weaker and weaker, until at length out it would come, the defeat, the submission, the scream for pity.

The creeping finger upon his knee had the same sudden warning of imminent physical peril. The swiftly moving car, the silence, these things seemed to bear in upon him the urgency of the other— that it was no longer any game that he was playing but something of the deadliest earnest. Once again the soft hand closed upon his thigh, then the finger once more like a creeping animal felt its way. His body was responsive from head to foot. He was all tingling with apprehension. His hand resting firmly on his other knee began to tremble. Why was he in this affair at all? If Crispin were mad, as Dunbar declared, what was to stop him from taking any revenge he pleased on those who interfered with him?

The tale was no longer one of pleasant romantic colour, the rescuing of a distressed damsel from an enchanted castle, but rather something quite real and definite, as real as the car in which they were sitting or the clothes that they were wearing. He, suddenly feeling that he could endure it no longer— in another moment he would have cried out aloud— jerked his knee upwards. The hand vanished, and at the same moment Crispin's voice said: 'We are almost there. We are going through the gates now.'

Lamps flashed upon their faces and Crispin's eyes seemed to have vanished into his fat white face. He had, in that sudden illumination, the most curious effect of blindness. His lids were closed over his eyes, lying like little pieces of pale yellow parchment under the faint red eyelashes.

'Here we are!' he cried. 'Out you get,
Herrick.' And as Harkness stepped out of the car
something deep within him whispered: 'I am
going to be hurt. Pain is coming——'

Before him swung a cavern of light. It swung
because on his stepping from the car he was dizzy,
dizzy with a kind of poignant thick scent in the
soul's nostrils, deep deep down as though he were
at the edge of being spiritually anæsthetised. He
paused for a moment looking back into the night
piled up behind him.

Then he walked in.

10

It was an old house. The long hall was panelled
and hung with the heads of animals. A torn banner
of faded red and yellow with long tassels of gold
hung above the stone fireplace. The floor was of
stone, and some dim rugs of uncertain colour lay
like splashes of damp here and there. The first
thing of which he was aware was that a strong cold
draught blew through the hall. It seemed to come
from a wide oak staircase on his right. There
were no portraits on the panelled walls. The
house gave a deep sense of emptiness. Two
Japanese servants, short, slim, immobile, their hair
gleaming black, their faces impassive, waited. The
outer door closed. The banner fluttered, the only
movement in the house.

'Come in here, Mr. Harkness,' Crispin said.
'It is more comfortable.'

His little figure moved forward. Harkness
followed him, but he had had one moment with the
girl as he entered the hall. The two Crispins had

been for an instant back by the car. He had said, his lips scarcely moving:

'I gave him the message. He is coming,' and she had answered without turning her head or looking at him: 'Thank you.'

Only as he walked after Crispin he wondered whether the Japanese could have understood. No. He was sure that no one could have heard those words, but he turned before leaving the hall, and he had a strange impression of the bare, empty, faded place, the staircase running darkly up into mystery, and the four figures, the two servants, Hesther and the younger Crispin, at that moment immobile, waiting as though they were listening— and for what?

The room into which Crispin led him was even shabbier than the hall. It was a large ugly place with dim cherry-coloured paper, and a great glass candelabra suspended from the ceiling. The walls had, it seemed, once been covered with pictures of all shapes and sizes, because the wall-paper showed everywhere pale yellow squares and ovals and lozenges of colour where the frames had been. The wall-paper had indeed leprosy, and although there were still some pictures—a large Landseer, an engraving of a Millais, a shabby oil painting of a green and windy sea—it was these strange sea-sick evidences of a vanished hand that invaded the air.

There was very little furniture in the place, two shabby arm-chairs, a round shining table, a green sofa. The draught that had swept the hall crept here, now come now gone, stealing on hands and feet from corner to corner.

'You see,' said Crispin, standing beside the empty fireplace, 'I am here but little. I have pulled down the pictures from the walls and then left it all shabby. I enjoy the contrast.' At the far end of the room were long oak cupboards. Crispin went to them and pulled back the heavy doors, and instantly in the shabby place there were blazing such treasures as Harkness had never set eyes on before.

Not very many as numbers went—some dozen shelves in all—but gleaming, glittering, shining, flinging out their flashes of purple and amber and gold, here crystalline, now deeply wine-coloured, pink with the petals of the rose, white with the purity of the rising moon. There was jewelry here that seemed to move with its own independent life before Harkness's eyes—Jaipur enamel of transparent red and green, lovely patterns with thick long strips of enamel on a ground of bright gold, over which, while still soft from the furnace, an open-work pattern of gold had been pressed; large rough turquoises set in silver; Chinese work of carved ivory and jade, cap ornaments exquisitely worked, a cap of a Chinese emperor with its embroidered gold dragon and its crown of pearls. Then the inlaid Chinese feather work, and at the sight of these tears of pleasure came into Harkness's eyes; cells made as though for cloisonné enamel, and into these are daintily affixed tiny fragments of king-fisher feather. Colours of blue, green, and mauve here blend and tone one into another miraculously, and the effect of all is a glittering sheen of gold and blue. There was one tiny fish, barely half an inch long, and here there were thirty cells on the body, each with its separate piece of feather. Chinese enamel buttons and clasps, nail-guards beautifully ornamented, Japanese hair combs marvellously wrought in lacquer, horn, gold lac on wood, wood with ivory appliqués, and stained ivory.

Then the Netsukes! Had any one in the world such lovely things! With the ivory and its colour richly toned with age, the metal ones showing a glorious patina. The sword guards—made of various metals and alloys and gold and silver, the metal so beautifully finished that it had the rich texture of old lace.

There was then the Renaissance jewelry, pieces lying like fragments of sky, of peach tree in bloom, of cherry and apple, a lovely pendant parrot enamelled in natural colours, a beautiful ship pendant of Venetian workmanship, an Italian earring formed of a large irregular pear-shaped pearl in a gold setting, a Cinquecento jewel—an emerald lizard set with a baroque pearl holding an emerald in its mouth.

Eighteenth-century glory. Gold studs with little skeletons on silk, covered with glass and set in gold. Initials of fine gold with a ground of plaited hair, this edged with blue and covered with faceted glass on crystal and the border of garnets. A pair of earrings, paintings in gusaille mounted in gold. A brooch set with garnets. A French vinaigrette enamelled in panels of green on a gold and white ground.

Loveliest of anything yet seen, a sixteenth-century cameo portrait of Lucius Verius cut in a dark onyx. The enamel was green, with little white ' peas,' and small diamonds were set in each pod.

' Ah this!' said Harkness, holding it in his hand. ' This is exquisite!'

But Crispin was restless. The eyes closed, the short body moved to another part of the room, leaving all the treasures carelessly exposed behind him. 'That is enough,' he said—'enough of those, I bore you. And now,' turning aside with a deprecatory child-like smile, as though he had been exhibiting his doll's house, 'you must see the prints.'

Harkness turning back to the room saw it as even shabbier than before. It was lit by candle-light, and in the centre of the round shining table there were four tall amber-coloured candlesticks that threw around them a flickering colour as the draught ruffled their power. To this table Crispin drew two chairs. Then he went to a handsome old oak cabinet carved stiffly with flowers and fruit. He stayed looking with a long lingering glance at the drawers, then sharply up at Harkness. Seen there in the mellow light, with the coloured glory of the open cabinets dimly shining in the far room, with the pleasant timid smile that a collector wears when he is approaching his beloved friends, he might have stood to Rembrandt for another 'Jan Six,' short and stumpy though he be.

'Now what will you have? Durer, Whistlers, Little Masters, Meryons, Dutch seventeenth century, Callot, Hollar? What you will. . . . No, you shall have only a few, and those not the most celebrated but perhaps the best loved. Now, here's for your pleasure. . . .'

He came to the table bearing carefully, reverenti-ally, his treasures. He set them down. From one after another he withdrew the paper; there gleaming between the stiff white shining mats they breathed, they lived, they smiled. There was the Rembrandt 'Landscape with a flock of sheep,' there the Muir-head Bone 'Orvieto,' the Hollar 'Seasons,' Callot's 'Passion,' Meryon's 'College Henry Quatre,' Paul

Potter's 'Two Horses,' a seascape of Zeeman, Cotman's 'Windmill,' Bracquemond's 'Teal Alighting,' a seascape of Moreau, and Aldegrever's 'Labour of Hercules' to close the list. Not more than thirty in all, but living there on the table with their personal glow and spontaneity. He bent over them caressing them, fondling them, smiling at them. Harkness drew near and, looking at the tender wistfulness of the two old Potter's horses, bravely living out there the last days of their broken forgotten lives, he felt a sudden friendliness to all the world, a reassurance, a comfort.

Those glittering jewelled things had had at their heart a warning, an alarm; but no one, he was suddenly aware, who cared for these prints could be bad. There are no things in the world so kindly, so simple, so warm in their humanity. . . .

The little man was near to him. He put his hand on his knee.

'They are fine, eh? They know you, recognise you. They are alive, eh?'

'Yes,' said Harkness, smiling. 'They are the most friendly things in art.'

The door opened and one of the Japanese servants came in with liqueurs. They were put on the table close to Harkness, and soon he was drinking the most wonderful brandy that it had ever been his happy fortune to encounter.

He was warm, cosy, quite unalarmed. The prints smiled at him, the dim room received him as a friend.

Crispin was talking, leaning back now from the table, his fat body hugged up like a cushion into his chair.

His red hair stood, flaming, on end. Harkness

was, at first, only vaguely conscious that Crispin
was speaking, then the words began to gather
about him, to force their way in upon his brain;
then, as the monologue continued, his comfort, his
cosiness, his sense of security slowly slipped from
him.   His eyes passed from the 'Two Horses' to
the high sharp cliffs of the 'Orvieto,' to the thick
naked Hercules of the Aldegrever.   Then, he was
aware that he was frightened, as he had been on
the road, in the hotel, in the car.   Then, with a
flash of awareness, like the sharp contact with
unexpected steel, he was on his guard as though
he were standing alone with his back to the wall
against an army of terrors.

'. . . And so as I like you so much, dear Mr.
Harkness, I feel that I can talk to you freely about
these things and that you will understand.   That
has always been my trouble—that I have not been
understood sufficiently, and if now I go my own
way and have my own fashion of dealing with life I
am sure that it is comprehensible enough.

' I was a very lonely child, Mr. Harkness, and
mocked at by every one who saw me.   No, I have
not been understood sufficiently.   The colour of
my hair has been a barrier.   I realise that I am,
and always have been, absurd in appearance, and
from the very earliest age I was aware that I was
different from other human beings and must pursue
another course from theirs.   I make no complaint
about that, but it justifies, I think, my later conduct.'

Here, as though some wire had sprung taut
inside him, he sat forward upright in his chair,
staring with his little pale eyes at Harkness, and it
was now that Harkness was abruptly aware of his
conversation.

'I am not boring you, I trust, but I have taken a sympathetic liking to you, and it may interest you to understand my somewhat unusual philosophy of life.

'My mother died when I was very young. My father was a surgeon, a very wealthy man, money inherited from an uncle. He was a strange man, peculiar, odd. Cruel to me. Very cruel to me. He hated the sight of me, and told me once that it was a continual temptation to him to lay hands on me and cut my heart out—to see, in fact, whether I had a heart. He liked to torment and tease me, as indeed did every one else. I am not telling you these things, Mr. Harkness, to rouse your pity, but rather that you should understand exactly the point at which I have arrived.'

'Yes,' said Harkness, dragging his eyes with strange difficulty from the pursed white face, the red hair, and glancing about the dim faded room and the farther spaces where the jewels flashed in the candle-light.

'Many people would have called my father insane, did not hesitate to do so. He was a large, extremely powerful man, given to violent tempers. But, after all, what is insanity? There are cases— many, I suppose—where the brain breaks down and is unable to perform any longer its ordinary functions, but in most cases insanity is only the name given by envious persons to those who have strength of character enough to realise their own ideas regardless of public opinion. Such was my father. He cared nothing for public opinion. We led a strange life, he and I, in a big black house in Bloomsbury. Yes, black, that's how it was. I went to Westminster School, and they all mocked me, my hair, my body,

my difference. Yes, my difference. I was different
from them all, different from my father, different
from all the world. And I was glad that I was
different. I hugged my difference. Different. . . .'

He lent forward, tapped Harkness's knee with
his hand, staring into his face.

'Different, Mr. Harkness, different. Different. . . .'

And the long draughty room echoed 'Different
. . . different . . . different.'

'My father beat me one night terribly, beat me
so that I could not move for pain. For no reason,
simply because, he said, he wished that I should
understand life, and first to understand life one
must learn to suffer pain, and that then, if one
could suffer pain enough, one could be as God—
perhaps greater than God.

'It was to that night in the Bloomsbury house
that I owe everything. I was fifteen years of age.
He stripped me naked and made me bleed. It
was terribly cold, and I came in that bare room
right into the very heart of life, into the heart of
the heart, where the true meaning is at last revealed
—and the true meaning——'

He broke off suddenly, then whispered:

'Do you believe in God, Mr. Harkness?' and
the draught went whispering on hands and feet
round the room, 'Do you believe in God, Mr.
Harkness?'

'Yes,' said Harkness.

'Yes,' said Crispin, in his lovely, melodious
voice; 'but in a good God, a sweet God, a kind,
beneficent God. That is no God. God is first
cruel, terrible, lashing, punishing. Then when He
has punished enough, and the victim is in His

power, bleeding at His feet, owning Him as Lord and Master, then He bends down and lifts the wounded brow and kisses the torn mouth, and in His heart there is a great and mighty triumph. . . . Even so will I do, even so will I be . . . and greater than God Himself!'

There was silence in the room. Then he curled up in his chair as he had done before, and went on with his friendly air:

' Dear Mr. Harkness, it is good indeed of you to listen to me so patiently. Tell me at once when I bore you. My father died when I was seventeen and left me all his wealth. He died in a Turkish bath very suddenly—ill-temper with some casual masseur, I fancy.

' I realised that I had a power. The realisation was very satisfactory to me. I married, and during the three years of my married life I collected most of the things that I have shown you this evening. I married a woman whom I was unfortunately unable to make happy. She could have been happy, I am sure, could she have only understood, a little, the philosophy that my father had taught me. My father was a very remarkable man, Mr. Harkness, as perhaps you have perceived, and he had, as I have told you, shown me the real meaning of this strange life in which we are forced, against our wills, to take part. It was foolish of my wife not to benefit by this knowledge. But she did not, and died sooner than I had anticipated, leaving me one child.

' A widower's life is not a happy one, and you will have undoubtedly perceived how many widowers marry again.'

He paused as though he expected some comment,

so Harkness said yes, that he had perceived it. Crispin sat forward looking at him inquisitively, and making, with his fingers, a kind of pattern in the air as though he were tracing there a bar of music.

'Yes. I did not marry again, but rather gave myself up to the continuation of my father's philosophy. The philosophy of pain as related to power one might perhaps term it. God—of whose existence no thinking man can truly permit himself to doubt—have you ever thought, Mr. Harkness, that the whole of His power is derived from the pain that He inflicts upon those less powerful than Himself? We conceive of Him as a beneficent Being, and from that it follows that He must have determined that pain is, from Him, our greatest beneficence. It is plainly for our good that He torments us. Should not then we, in our turn, realising that pain is our greatest happiness, seek ourselves for more pain, and also teach our fellow human beings that it is only *through* pain that we can reach the true heart and meaning of life? Through Pain we reach Power.

'I test you with pain, and as you overcome the pain so do you climb up beside me, who have also overcome it, and we are in time as gods knowing good and evil. . . . A concrete case, Mr. Harkness. I slash your face with a knife. You are so powerful that you take the pain, twist it in your hand and throw it away. You rise up to me, and suddenly I, who have inflicted the pain on you, love you because you have taken my power over you and used it for your soul's advantage.'

'And do I love you because you have slashed my face?' asked Harkness.

Crispin's eyes narrowed. He put out his hand and laid it on Harkness's knee.

'We would have to see,' Crispin murmured. 'We would have to see. I wonder—I wonder. . . .'

They were silent. Harkness's body was cold, but the room was very hot. The candles seemed to throw out a metallic radiant heat. Harkness moved his knee.

'It would not do to prove your theory too frequently,' he said at last.

'No, no, of course it would not. It is, you understand, only a theory that I have inherited from my father. Yes. But I will confess that when an individuality comes close to me and remains entirely outside my influence I am tempted to wonder. . . . Well, to speculate. . . . I like to see how far one personality *will* surrender to another. It is interesting—simply as a speculation. For instance, you have noticed my daughter-in-law?'

'Yes,' said Harkness, 'I have. A charming girl.'

'Charming. Exactly. But independent, refusing to make the most of the advantages that are open to her. Like my poor late wife, for instance. Unfortunate, because she is young and might benefit so much from my older and more experienced brain.

'But she refuses to come under my influence, remains severely outside it. Now, my son is almost too willing to understand my meaning. Were I to plunge a knife into his arm no blood would flow. I am speaking metaphorically, of course. After a very slight training in his early youth he was all that I could wish. But too submissive—oh yes, altogether too submissive.

' His wife's independence, however, is quite of another kind. It might almost seem as though during these last weeks she had taken a dislike both to myself and my son. However, she is very young and a little time will alter that, I have no doubt— especially as we shall be in foreign countries and to some extent alone by ourselves.'

Harkness pressed his hands tightly together. A little shiver ran, as though it responded to the draught that blew through the room, up and down his body. He was anxious that Crispin should not notice that he was shivering.

' Have you any idea where you will go?' he asked—and his voice sounded strangely unlike his own, as though some third person were in the room and speaking just behind him.

' We have no idea,' said Crispin, smiling. ' That will depend on many things — on Mrs. Crispin herself, of course, amongst others. A young wife must not show too complete an independence. After all, there are others whose feelings must be considered——' He was smiling as it were to himself and as though his thoughts were pleasant ones.

Suddenly he sprang up and began to walk the room. The effect on Harkness was strange—it was as though he were suddenly shut in there with an animal. So often in zoological gardens he had seen that haunting monotonous movement, that encounter with the bars of the cage and the indifferent acceptance of their inevitability, in- different only because of endless repetition. Crispin, padding now up and down the long room, reminded Harkness of one of the smaller animals, the little jaguars, the half-wolf, half-fox; his head forward, his hands crossed behind his short thick back; his eyes, restless now, moving here, there about the room; his movements soft, almost furtive; every instinct towards escape. As he moved in the room half-clouded with light, the soft resolute step pervaded Harkness's sense, and soon the thick confined scent of a caged animal seemed to creep up to his nostrils and linger there.

Furry—captive—danger hanging behind the plodding step, so that if a sudden release were to come . . . And he sat there fixed in his seat as though nailed to it while the sweet voice continued: 'And so, my dear Mr. Harkness, I have devoted my later years to the solution of this problem.

'I feel, if I may say so without too much arrogance, that I am intending to help poor human nature along the road to a better understanding of life. Poor, muddled human nature. Defeated always by Fear. Yes, Fear. And if they have surmounted Pain and stand with their foot on its body, what remains? It is gone, vanished. I myself am increasing my power every day. First one, then another. First through Pain. Then through Love. I love all the world, yes, everything in it, but first it must be taught, and it is so reluctant—so strangely reluctant—to receive its teaching. And I myself suffer because I am too tender-hearted. I should myself be superior to the suffering of others, because I know how good it is for them to suffer. But I am not. Alas, no. It is only where my indignation is aroused, and aroused justly, that I can conquer my tenderness, and then—well then . . . I can make my important experiments. My daughter-in-law, for instance. . . .'

He paused, not far from Harkness, and once again his hands made a curious motion in the air as though he were transcribing a bar of music.   He stepped close to Harkness.   His breath, scented curiously with a faint odour of orange, was in Harkness's face.   He leaned forward, his hands were on Harkness's shoulders.

'For instance, I have taken a fancy to you, my friend—a real fancy.   I liked you from the first moment that I saw you.   I don't know when so suddenly I have taken a fancy to any one.   But to care for you deeply, first—yes, first—I would show you the meaning of pain. . . .'   Here his body suddenly quivered from the feet to the head. '. . . And I could not, liking you so much, do that unless you were seriously to annoy me, interfere in any way with my simple plans'—the hands pressed deeply into the shoulders—'yes, only then could we come really to know one another . . . after such a crisis what friends we might be, sharing our power together!   What friends!   Dear me!   Dear me!'

He moved away, turning to the table, looking down on the prints that were spread out there.

'Yes, yes, I could show you then my power.' His voice vibrated with sudden excitement.   'You think me absurd.   Yes, yes, you do.   You do. Don't deny it now.   As though I couldn't perceive it.   Do you think me so stupid?   Absurd, with my ridiculous hair, my ugly body?   Oh!   I know! You can't hide it from me.   You laugh like the rest. Secretly, you laugh.   You are smiling behind your hand.   Well, smile then, but how foolish of you to be so taken in by physical appearances.   Do you know my power?   Do you know what I could do to you now by merely clapping my hands?

' If my fingers were at your throat, at your breast, and you could not move but must wait my wish, my plan for you, would you think me then so absurd—my figure, my hair, ridiculous? You would be as though in the hands of a god. I should be as a god to you to do with you what I wished. . . .

' What is there that is so beautiful that I, ugly as I am, cannot do as I wish with it? This——' Suddenly he took up the ' Orvieto ' and held it forward under the candle-light. ' This is one of the most beautiful things of its kind that man has ever made, and I—am I not one of the ugliest human beings at whom men laugh?—well, would you see my power over it? I have it in my hands. It is mine. It is mine. I can destroy it in one instant——'

The beautiful thing shook in his hand. To Harkness it seemed suddenly to be endued with a human vitality. He saw it—the high, sharp, razor-edged rocks, the town so confidingly resting on that strength, all the daily life at the foot, the oxen, the peasants, the lovely flame-like trees, the shining reaches of valley beyond, all radiating the heat of that Italian summer.

He sprang to his feet. ' Don't touch it!' he cried. ' Leave it! Leave it!'

Crispin tore it into a thousand pieces, wrenching it, snapping at it with his fingers like an animal. The pieces flaked the air. A white shower circled in the candle-light, then scattered about the table, about the floor.

Something died.

A clock somewhere struck half-past twelve.

Crispin moved from the table. Very gently, almost beseechingly, he looked into Harkness's face.

' Forgive me my little game,' he said. ' It is

all part of my theory,—to be above these things, you know. What would happen to me if I surrendered to all that beauty?'

The eyes that looked into Harkness's face were pathetic, caged, wistful, longing. And they were mad. Somewhere deep within him his soul, caught in the wreckage of his bodily life like a human being pinned beneath a ruined train, besought— yes, besought—Harkness for deliverance.

But he had no thought at that moment of anything but his own escape. To flee from that room —from that room at any cost! He said something. Crispin did not try to keep him. They moved together into the hall.

' And you won't allow my chauffeur to drive you back?'

' No, no, thank you, I shall love the walk.'

' Well, well. It has been delightful. We shall meet some day again, I have no doubt. . . .'

Silence flooded the house. Once more Harkness's hand touched that other soft one. The door was open. The lovely night air brushed his face, and he had stepped into the dim star-drenched garden. The door closed.

PART III

SEA-FOG

PART III

SEA-FOG

I

I~n~ the garden the silence was like a warning, as though the night had her finger to her lips holding back a multitude of breathing, deeply interested spectators.

Harkness, slipping from the path on to the lawn, felt a relief, as though with the touch of his foot on the cool turf there had come a freedom from imprisonment.

The garden was so friendly, so safe, so homely in its welcome. The scent of roses that had seemed to follow him throughout the adventures of that queer evening came to him now as though crowding up to reassure him. The night sky was pieced with stars, but they were thick and dim, seen through a veil of mist. The trees of the garden, like serried ranks of giants in black armour, seemed to stand, in silent attention, on every side of him, waiting his orders. The voice of all this world was the sea stirring, with a sigh and a whisper, below the wall of rock.

His first impulse as he stood on the lawn was to go away as far as he could from that house,—yes,

as far as ever he could—miles and miles and miles—
China if you like.   Ah, no!   That was just where
that man would be!

He was trembling and shaking and wiping his
forehead with his handkerchief; the breeze stroked
him with cool fingers.   He must run for ever to
be clear of that house—and then suddenly remembered that he must not run, because he had his
duty to do—and even as he remembered that a
figure stepped up to him out of the trees.   He
would have called out—so wild and trembling were
his nerves—had he not at once recognised from his
great size that this was Jabez the fisherman.

He might have been an incarnation of the night,
with his deep black beard, his grave kindly face,
and his simple, natural quiet.   He was dressed in
his fisherman's jersey and blue trousers, and had
no covering on his head.

'Good evening, sir,' he said.   'Mr. Dunbar
told me as how you'd be wanting to be back in
the house for a moment to fetch something you'd
forgotten.

'We'd best be just stepping off the lawn, sir,
if you don't mind.   They foreigners are always
nosing around.'

They turned quietly off the grass and stood
closely together under the dark shadow of the
house.

'I must go back at once,' said Harkness.
'There's no time to lose.   It struck half-past
twelve some time ago.'

'I don't know nothing about that, sir,' said
Jabez; 'I only know as how you must be going
back into the house for something you'd forgotten
and I was to let you in.'

'Yes,' said Harkness, his teeth chattering,
'that's right.'

He wasn't made, in any kind of way at all, for
this sort of adventure. He had never before realised how utterly inefficient he was. And of all
absurdities to go back into the house when he was
now safely out of it! Of all Dunbar's mad plan
this was the maddest part. What could he do
but be seen or heard, and then rouse suspicion when
it might so easily have been undisturbed?

Let Crispin find him groping among those dark
passages and what was his fate likely to be? There
flashed into his consciousness then a sudden suspicion
of Dunbar. It might suit the boy's plans only too
well that he should be found, and so turn attention
to another part of the house, leaving the girl free.
But no! There was Dunbar's own steady clear
gaze to answer him, and beyond that the certainty
that Crispin's suspicions, roused by the discovery
of himself, would proceed immediately to the girl.

No, did he return at once, the plan was quite
feasible. Seeing him there so soon after his de-
parture, they could do nothing but accept his reasons,
and that especially if he returned quite openly with
no thought of concealment.

But oh how he hated to go back! He put his
hand on the rough stuff of Jabez's jersey, listened
for a moment to the regular, consoling breathing of
the sea, sniffed the roses and the cool, gentle night
air, then said:

'Well, come along, Jabez; show me how to
get back.'

As they moved round to the door the thought
came to him as to whether he had given the elder
Crispin and his two nasty servants time enough to

retire up to their part of the house. A difficult thing that, to hit the precise medium between too lengthy a wait and too short. He could not remember exactly what Dunbar had said as to that.

'Do you think I've waited long enough, Jabez?' he asked.

'Well, if you'd forgotten something, sir,' said Jabez, 'you'd want to be sure of finding it before the house is sleeping. They don't bolt this door, sir,' he continued in a whisper, 'because Mr. Crispin don't like to be bolted in. His fancy. After half-past one or so one of they Japs is around. It's just their hour like from half-past twelve to half-past one that I have to watch this part of the house extra careful. Yes, sir,' he added as he turned the key in the lock and pushed the door quietly open.

2

The hall was very dark. From half-way up the staircase some of the starlit evening scattered mistily through a narrow window, splintering the boards with spars of pale, milky shadow.

A clock chattered cluck-cluck-spin-spin-cluck close to Harkness's ear. Otherwise there was not a sound anywhere. He reflected that several things had been forgotten in his talk with Dunbar; one that there would, in all probability, be no light in the upper passage. How was he then to find the younger Crispin's door, or to see whether or no there were that piece of paper under Mrs. Crispin's? Secondly, it would be in the room on the ground floor where he had had his strange interview with the elder Crispin that he must see the younger, because, of course, that gloomy creature, dumb though he appeared to be, would be at least aware that Harkness had never ventured into the upper floor at all and could not therefore have left his gold match-box there. On the whole, this would be the better for Dunbar's plan, because it would lead the younger Crispin all the farther from his wife's door. But there were, at this point, so many dangers and difficulties, so many opportunities of disaster, that in absolute desperation he must perforce go forward.

He was aware that for himself now the easiest fashion would be to persuade himself that he had indeed lost his match-box and was returning to secure it. He hesitated on the bottom step of the stairs as though he were wondering what he ought to do, how he might find the tiresome thing without rousing the whole house.

He climbed the staircase slowly, walking softly, but not too softly, accompanied all the way by the clock that attended him like a faithful coughing dog. At the turn of the stairs he found the passage that Dunbar had described to him, and he was instantly relieved to find that a wide and deep window at the far end had no curtain, and that through it the long stretch was suffused with a pale, ghostly light turning the heavy old frames, the faded green paper, into shadow opaque.

He hesitated, looking about him, then clearly saw the two doors that must be those of Crispin and his wife; from under one of them, quite clearly, a small piece of white paper obtruded.

He waited an instant, then moved boldly forward, not trying to walk softly, and knocked on the nearer of the two doors. There was a moment's pause, during which the wild beating of his own heart and the friendly chatter of the clock from downstairs seemed to strive together to break the silence.

The door opened abruptly, and the younger Crispin, his white horse-face unmoved above his dark evening clothes, appeared there.

'I really must beg your pardon,' Harkness said, smiling. 'A most ridiculous thing has happened. I left the house some ten minutes ago after wishing your father good night, and it was only after going a little way that I discovered that I had lost a gold match-box of mine that was of very great value to me. I hesitated as to what I ought to do. I guess I should have gone straight back to my hotel, but it worried me to think of losing it. It has some very intimate connections for me. And I knew, you see, that you were leaving early to-morrow morning—or *this* morning as it is by this time, I fancy. So that it was now or never for my match-box. I came back very reluctantly, I can assure you, Mr. Crispin. I do feel this to be an intrusion. I had hoped that your father would still be about, and that I should simply ask him to give me a light in the room where we were sitting. In a moment I am sure that we would find the thing. Your night porter very kindly let me in, but although I had only been gone ten minutes the house was dark and there was no one about. I would have left again, but I tell you frankly I couldn't bear to leave the thing. I saw a light behind your door, and knew that some one at any rate had not gone to bed. The whole thing has been unpardonable. But just lend me a candle, and in five minutes I shall have found it.'

'I will go down with you myself,' said Crispin,

staring at Harkness as though he had never seen
him before.

'That's mighty fine of you. Thank you.'

But still Crispin did not move, his eyes fixed
on Harkness's face. The eyes moved. They fell,
and it seemed to Harkness that they were staring
at the small piece of paper underneath the next door.
Crispin looked, then without another word went back
into his room, closing the door behind him.

Harkness's heart stopped; the floor pitched and
heaved beneath his feet. It was all over already,
then: young Crispin was now in his wife's room,
had discovered her, in all probability, in the very
act of escaping. In another moment the house
would be aroused.

He prepared himself for what might come,
standing back against the wall, his hands spread
palm-wise against the paper as though he would
hold himself up.

Truly he was shaking at the knees: he could see
nothing, only that possibility of being once again
in the presence of the elder Crispin, of hearing again
that sweet voice, of feeling once more the touch of
those boneless fingers, of seeing for another time
those mad beseeching eyes. His tongue was dry
in his throat. Yes, he was afraid, more utterly
afraid than he would have fancied it possible for a
grown man ever to be. . . .

The door opened. Crispin appeared holding in
his hand a lighted candle.

'Now, let us go down,' he said quietly.

The relief was so great that Harkness began to
babble, 'You have no idea . . . the trouble I am
causing you. . . . At this late hour. . . . What
must you think . . .?'

The young man said nothing.   Harkness meekly followed, the candle-light splashing the walls and floor with its wavering shadows.   Their heads were gigantic on the faded wall-paper, and Harkness had a sudden fancy that the shadows here were the realities and he a mist.   The younger Crispin gave that sense of unreality.

A kind of weariness went with him as though he were the personification of a strangled yawn. And yet beneath the weariness and indifference there was a flame burning.   One realised it in that strange, absorbed stare of the eyes, in a kind of determination in the movements, in a concentrated indifference to any motive of life but the intended one.   Harkness was to realise this with a start of alarmed surprise when, once more in the long shabby room lit now only by the light of one uncertain candle, young Crispin turned upon him and shot out at him in his harsh, rasping voice:

'What are you here for?'

They were standing one on either side of the table, and between them on the floor were the white scattered fragments of the torn 'Orvieto.'

'I told you,' said Harkness.   'I left my match-box.   I won't keep you a moment if you'll allow me to take that candle——'

'No, no,' said the other impatiently, 'I don't mean that.   What do I care for your match-box? You are worrying my father.   I must beg you, very seriously, never to come near him again.'

'Indeed,' said Harkness, laughing, 'I don't understand you.   How could I worry your father? I have never seen him in my life before this evening. He invited me out here for an hour's chat.   I am going now.   He is leaving for abroad to-morrow.

I don't suppose that we shall ever meet again. Please allow me just to find my match-box and go.'

But Crispin had apparently heard nothing. He stood, his hand tapping the table.

' I don't wish to appear rude, Mr.—Mr.——'

' Harkness is my name,' Harkness said.

' I beg your pardon. I didn't catch it when my father introduced me this evening. I don't want to seem offensive in any way. I simply thought this a good opportunity for a few words that may help you to understand the situation.

' My father is my chief care, Mr. Harkness. He is everything to me in the world. He has no one to look after him but myself. He is, as you must have seen, very nervous and susceptible to different personalities. I could see at once to-night that your personality is one that would have a very disturbing effect on him. He does not recognise these things himself, and so I have to protect him. I beg you to leave him alone.'

' But really,' Harkness cried, ' the boot's on the other leg. Your father has been very charming in showing me his lovely things, but it was he who sought me out, not I him. I haven't the least desire to push my acquaintance with him, or indeed with yourself, any further.'

Crispin's cold eyes regarded Harkness steadily, then he moved round the table until he was close beside him.

' I will tell you something, Mr.—ah—Harkness —something that probably you do not know. There have been one or two persons as foolish and interfering as to suggest that my father is not in complete control of his faculties, even that he is dangerous to the public peace. My father is an original mind.   There is no one like him in this whole world, no one who has the good of the human race at heart as he has.   He goes his own way, and at times has pursued certain experiments that were necessary for the development of his general plan. He was the judge of their true necessity and he has had the courage of his opinions—hence the inquisitive meddlesomeness of certain people.'   He paused, then added:

'If you have come here with any idea, Mr.— Mr.—Harkness, of interfering with my father's liberty, I warn you that one visit is enough.   It will be dangerous for you to make another.'

Harkness's temper, so seldom at his command when he needed it, now happily flamed up.

'Are you trying to insult me, Mr. Crispin?' he asked.   'It looks mighty like it.   Let me tell you once again, and really now for the last time, that I am an American travelling for pleasure in Cornwall, that I had never heard of your father before this evening, that he spoke to me first and asked me to dine with him, and that he invited me here.   I am not in the habit of spying on anybody.   I would be greatly obliged if you would allow me to look for my match-box and depart.   I am not likely to disturb you again.'

But this show of force did not disturb young Crispin in the least.   He stood there as though he were a wax model for evening clothes in a tailor's window, his black hair had just that wig-like sleekness, his face that waxen pallor, his body that wooden patience.

'My father is everything to me,' he said simply. 'If my father died I should die too.   Life would simply come to an end for me.   I am of no import-

ance to my father. He is frequently irritated by
my stupidity. That is natural—but I am there to
protect him, and protect him I will. We have been
really driven from place to place, Mr. Harkness,
during the last year by the ridiculous ignorant
superstitions of local gossip. Great men always
seem odd to their inferiors, and my father seems
odd to a number of people, but I warn them
all that any spying, asking of questions, and
the like, is dangerous. We know how to protect
ourselves.'

His eyes suddenly fell on the fragments of the
' Orvieto.' He bent down and picked some of
them up. A look of true human anxiety and distress
crept into his queer fish-like eyes that gave him a
new air and colour.

' Oh dear! oh dear!' he said. ' Did he do this
while you were with him?'

' Yes,' said Harkness, ' he did.'

' Ah! it was one of his favourites. He must
have been in great distress. This only confirms
what I said to you just now about disturbing him.
I beg you to go—now, at once, immediately—and
never, never return. It is so bad for my father to
be disturbed. He has so excitable a temperament.
Please, please leave at once——'

' But my match-box,' said Harkness.

' Give me your London address. I promise you
that it shall be forwarded to you.' He held the
candle high and swept the room with it, the sudden
shadows playing on the walls, like a troop of dancing
scarecrows. ' You don't see it anywhere?'

Harkness looked about him, then up at the face
of the chattering clock. Time enough had elapsed.
She was safe away by now.

'Very well, then,' he said. 'I will give you my address. Here is my card.'

Young Crispin, who seemed in great agitation and, under this emotion, a new and different human being from anything that Harkness had believed to be possible, took the card, and with the candle moved into the hall.

He turned the key, opened the door, and the night air rushed in, blowing the flame.

'I wish you good night,' he said, holding out his hand.

Harkness touched it—it was cold and hard—bowed, said: 'I must apologise again for disturbing you. I would only reassure you that it is for the last time.'

Both bowed. The door closed, and Harkness was once again in the garden.

3

Jabez was waiting for him. They were both in the shadow; beyond them the lawn was scattered with star-dust mist as though sown with immortal daisies; the stars above were veiled. The world was so still that it seemed to march forward with the rhythm of the sea, that could be heard stamping now like a whole army of marching men.

'They are waiting for you, sir,' Jabez whispered. 'I was terrible feared you'd be too long in there.'

They moved, keeping to the shadows, and reached the path that led to the door in the wall. Here their feet crunched on the gravel, and every step was an agony of anticipated alarm. It seemed to Harkness that the house sprang into life, that

lights jumped in the windows, figures passed to
and fro, but he dared not look back, and then
Jabez's hand was on the door, he was through and
out safely in the wide free road.

Then, for an instant, he did look back, and there
the house was, dark, motionless, rising out of the
trees like part of the rock on which it was built,
the high tower climbing pale in the mist above it.

Only an instant's glimpse, because there was
the jingle, the pony, Dunbar, and the girl. An
absurd emotion took possession of him at the sight
of them. He had been through a good deal that
evening, and the picture of them, safe, honest, sane,
after the house and the company that he had left,
came with the breeze from the sea reassuring him
of normality and youth.

Jabez, too, standing over them like a protective
deity. His whole heart warmed to the man, and he
vowed that in the morning he would do something
for him that would give him security for the rest
of his days. There was something in the patient,
statuesque simplicity of that giant figure that he
was never afterwards to forget.

But he had little time to think of anything. He
had climbed into the jingle, and without a word
exchanged between any of them they were off,
turning at once away from the road to the right
over a turfy path that led to the Downs.

Dunbar, who had the reins, spoke at last.

'My God,' he said, 'I thought you were never
coming.'

'I had a queer time,' Harkness answered,
whispering because he was still under the obsession
of his escape from the house. 'You must remember
that I'm not accustomed to such adventures. I've

never had such an odd two hours before, and I shouldn't think that I'm ever likely to have such another again.'

They all clustered together as though to assure one another of their happiness at their escape. The strong tang now of the sea in their faces, the freshness of the wide open sky, the spring of the turf beneath the jingle's wheels, all spoke to them of their freedom. They were so happy that, had they dared, they would have sung aloud.

But Harkness now was conscious only of one thing, that Hesther Crispin, a black shawl over her head, only the outline of her figure to be seen against the blue night, was pressed close to him. Her hand touched his knee, the strands of her hair, escaping the shawl, blew close to his face, he could feel the beating of her heart. An ecstasy seized him at the sense of her closeness. Whatever was to come of that night, at least this he had—his perfect hour. The elder Crispin and his madness, the younger and his strangeness, the dim faded house, the jewels and the torn ' Orvieto,' the mad talk, all these vanished into unreality, and, curiously, this ride was joined directly to the dance around the town as though no other events had intervened.

Then he had won his freedom, this sanctified it. Then he had felt his common humanity with all life, now he knew his own passionate share in it.

He wanted nothing for himself but this, that, like Browning's strong peasant, he might serve his duchess, at the last receiving his white rose and watching her vanish into her own magical kingdom. A romantic, idealistic American, as has been already declared in this history; but ten hours ago both romance and idealism were theoretic, now they were pulsing, living things.

' Hesther's the one for my money,' Dunbar said, some of his happiness at their safety ringing through his voice. ' You should have seen her climb out of that window. She landed on the roof of that tool-house so lightly that not a mouse could have heard her. And then she swung down the pipe like a monkey. Tell me how you managed with friend Crispin.'

' It wasn't difficult,' Harkness answered. ' He went with me to that long room downstairs like a lamb. He told me that he had been wanting to speak with me to tell me that I was bothering his father and must keep away.'

' That you were bothering his father?'

' Yes. He—— Wait. Do you hear any one coming?'

They listened. The ramp-ramp of the sea was now very loud. They had come nearly two miles on the soft track across the Downs. They stayed listening, staring into the distance. There was no sound but the sea; then a bell ringing mournfully, regretfully, through the air.

' That's the Liddon,' said Dunbar. ' We must be nearly at our cottage. But I don't hear anything. Unless they saw the jingle they never would think of this. Our only danger was the younger Crispin going into Hesther's room after he left you. I believe we're safe.'

They stayed there listening. Very strange in that wide expanse, with only the bell for their company. They drove on a little way, and a building loomed up. This was a deserted cottage, simply the four walls standing.

' I'm to tie the pony to this,' Dunbar said. ' Jabez will fetch it in the morning.'

They climbed out of the jingle and waited while the pony was tied. Having done it, Dunbar raised his head, sniffing the air.

' I say, don't you think the mist's coming up a bit? It won't do if it gets too thick. We'll have difficulty in finding the Cove.'   .

It was true. The mist was spreading like very thin smoky glass. The pony was etherealised, the cottage a ghostly cottage.

' Well, come on,' Dunbar said. ' We haven't a great deal of time, but the Cove's only a step of the way. Along here to the right.'

He led, the others followed. Hesther had hitherto said nothing. Now she looked up at Harkness. ' Thank you for helping us. It was generous of you.'

He couldn't see her face. He touched her hand with his for a moment.

' I guess that was the least any one could do,' he said.

' Oh! I'm so glad it's over!' She gave a little shiver. ' To be out here free after those weeks, after that house—you don't know, you don't *know* what that was.'

' I can pretty well imagine,' Harkness answered grimly, ' from the hour or two I spent in your father-in-law's company. But don't let's talk about it just now. Afterwards we'll tell each other all our adventures.'

' Isn't it strange,' she said simply, ' we've only exchanged a word or two, we never knew one another before this evening, and yet we're like old friends? Isn't it pleasant?'

'Very pleasant,' he answered. 'We must always be friends.'

'Yes, always,' she said.

They were standing close to the broken wall of the cottage. It had a wonderfully romantic air in the night air. It was so lonely, and so independent as well. The storms that must beat around it on wild nights, the screams of the birds, the battering roar of the waves, and then to sink into that silence with only the voice of the bell for its company. But Dunbar was no poet—a ruined cottage was a ruined cottage to him.

'I don't like this mist,' he said. 'It's made me a little uncertain of my bearings. I wonder if you'd mind, Hesther, waiting here for five minutes while I go and see——'

'Oh no, we'll all stick together,' she interrupted. 'Why should we separate? Why, I'm more sure-footed than you are, David. You're trying to mother me again.'

'No, I'm not,' he answered doggedly; 'but I'm really not quite sure of the way down, and if we got in a mess half way it would be much worse your being there. Really these paths can be awfully nasty. I want to be *sure* of my way before you come—really, Hesther——'

She saw that it was important to him. She laughed.

'It's stupid, when I'm a better climber than you are. But if you like it—you're the commander of this expedition.'

She seated herself on a stone near the pony. The two men walked off. The sea mist was very faint, blowing in little wisps like tattered lawn, not obscuring anything but rendering the whole scene ethereal and unreal.

Suddenly, however, as though out of friendly interest, the stars, that had been quite obscured, again appeared, twinkling, humorous eyes looking down over the wall of heaven.

'We should be all right,' Dunbar said as the two men set off; 'we are up to time. The boat is bound to be there. It's lucky the fog hasn't come. That's a contingency I never thought of. The path down to the Cove is off here, to the right of the cottage somewhere. I've studied every inch of the country round here.'

The path appeared. 'Tell me, did you have a queer time with Crispin—the elder one, I mean?'

'I've never had so strange a conversation with any one,' said Harkness. 'Madness is a queer thing when you are in actual contact with it, because we have, every one of us, enough madness in ourselves to wonder whether some one else *is* so mad after all. He talked the most awful nonsense, and *dangerous* nonsense too, but there was a kind of theory behind it, something that almost held it all together; a sort of pathos too, so that you felt, in spite of yourself, sorry for the man.'

But Dunbar was no analyser of human motives. He despised fine shades, and was a man of action. 'Sorry for him! Just about as sorry as you are for a spider that is spinning a nest in your clothes cupboard. Sorry! He wants crushing under foot like a white slug, and that he'll get before I've finished with him. Why, man, he's murderous! He loves torture and slow fire, like the old Spaniards in the Inquisition. There's so little to catch on to— that's the trouble; but I bet that if he had caught us helping Hesther out of that house to-night there would be something to catch on to! Why, if we were to fall into his hands now! Ugh! it doesn't bear thinking of!'

'Oh yes, of course,' Harkness agreed, 'he's dangerously mad. He'll be in an asylum before many days are out. If ever I have been justified in any action of my life it has been this, in helping that poor girl out of the hands of those two men. All the same . . . oh! it's sad, Dunbar! There is something so tragic in madness, whether it's dangerous or no—something captive, like a bird in a cage, and something common to us all. . . .'

'Well, if you think that the kind of things that Crispin Senior is after are common to us all you must have a pretty low view of humanity. The beastly swine! Something pathetic? Why, you're a curious fellow, Harkness, to feel pathos in that situation.'

'You may hate it and detest it, you *must* confine it because it's dangerous to the community, but you can pity it all the same. His eyes—that longing to escape.'

But Dunbar had found the cleft. They were now right above the sea. Although there was so slight a wind, the waves were breaking noisily on the shore. The stars had gone again, but the edge of the cliff was clear, and far below it a thin line of ragged white leapt to the eye, vanished, and leapt again.

'Here's the path down,' said Dunbar. 'There isn't much light, but enough, I fancy. We'll both go down so that we can be sure of our way when we come back with Hesther, and we may be both needed to help her. The path's all right, though. It's

slippery after wet weather, but there's been no rain
for days.   Can you make it out clearly enough?'

'Yes,' Harkness said, but he felt anything but
happy.   Of all the things that he had done that
evening this was the one that he liked least.   He
had a very poor head for heights, growing dizzy
under any provocation; the angry snarl of the sea
bewildered him, and little breaths of vapour curled
about him changing from moment to moment the
form and shape of the scene.   He would have liked
to suggest to Dunbar that there was no need for
him to go down this first time, but, coward though
he might be, he had come down to Treliss to beat
that cowardice.

Certainly the adventures of that night were
giving him every opportunity.   He went to the edge
and looked over.   The sea banged up to him, and
the grey curved shadow of the Cove seemed to be
miles below him.   The little path ran on the edge
of the cliff between two precipitous slopes, and its
downward curve was sharp.

He pulled himself together, thinking of Hesther
waiting there by the cottage alone.   Dunbar had
already started; he followed.

When he had gone a little way his knees began
to wobble, his legs taking on a strange life of their
own.   His imagination had all his days been
dangerous for him in any crisis, because he always
saw more than was truly there: now the sea breeze
blew on either side of him, the path was so narrow
that there was not room to plant his two feet at the
same time, the dim shadow light confused his eyes,
and the roar of the sea leapt at him like a wild
animal.

However, he pressed forward, looking neither to

right nor to left, and with what thankfulness he felt
the wet sand yield beneath him and saw the boat
drawn up under an overhanging rock only a few
feet away from him!

'There it is,' said Dunbar, eyeing the boat with
intense satisfaction. 'Now I think we're all right.
I don't see what's going to stop us. We'll be
across there in half an hour and then have a
good hour before the train.' He held out his
hand.

'Harkness, I simply can't tell you what I think
of your doing all this for us. Coming down here
just to have a holiday, and then taking all these risks
for people you'd never seen before. It's fine of
you and I'll never forget it.'

'It's nothing at all,' said Harkness, blushing, as
he always did when he himself was at all in discussion.
'As a matter of fact, I've had what has been, I
suppose, the most interesting evening of my life,
and I daresay it isn't all over yet.'

'There's not much fear of their catching us
now,' said Dunbar; 'but you've been in more
real actual danger than you imagine. As I
said just now, anything might have happened to
us if he had caught us. You don't know how
remote that house is. He could do what he
pleased without any one being the wiser, and be
off in the morning leaving our corpses behind
him. The only servants in that house are those
two Japs.'

'There's Jabez,' said Harkness.

'Jabez is outside and is only temporary. He
wouldn't have stayed after to-morrow anyway. He
hates the man. Fine fellow, Jabez. I don't know
how I would have managed this affair without him.

He fell in love with Hesther. He'd do anything for her. And then like the rest of the neighbourhood he detested the Japanese.

'They are funny conservative people these Cornishmen. Whatever they may pretend, they've no use for foreigners, and especially foreigners like Crispin.'

They stood a moment listening to the sea.

'The tide's going out,' said Dunbar. 'I was a little anxious lest I'd pulled the boat up high enough this afternoon, and then, of course, some one might have come along and taken a fancy to it. However, I was pretty safe. No one ever comes down into this cove. But we've taken a lot of chances to-night and everything's come off. The Lord's on our side—as He well may be, considering the kind of characters the Crispins have.'

He looked at Harkness. 'Hullo, you're shivering. Are you cold?'

'No,' said Harkness, 'I suddenly got the creeps. Some one walking over my grave, I suppose. I feel as though Crispin had followed us and was listening to every word we were saying. I could swear I could see his horrid red head poking over that rock now. However, to tell you the exact truth, Dunbar, I didn't care overmuch for coming down that bit of rock just now. I'm not much at heights.'

'What! that path!' cried Dunbar. 'That's nothing. However, there's no need for both of us to go back. You can stay by the boat.'

But a sudden determination flamed up in Harkness that it should be he, and none other, that should fetch Hesther Crispin.

'No, I'll go. There's no need for you to come

though.   We'll be back here in ten minutes.   I'll
see that she gets down all right.'

'Very well,' said Dunbar.   'But look after
her.   She's not so good a climber as she thinks
she is.'

So Harkness started off.   He waved his hand
to Dunbar, who was now busied with the boat, and
began his climb.   He stumbled over the wet rocks,
nearly fell once or twice, and then came to the little
path.   His thought now was all of Hesther.   He
played with his imagination, picturing to himself
that he was going right out of the world to some
unknown heights where she awaited him, having
chosen him out of all the world, and there they
would live together, alone, happy always in one
another's company. . . .

What a fool he was when she was married, and,
even if she freed herself from that horrid en-
cumbrance, had that boy down there in the Cove
waiting for her.   But he could not help his own
state.   It did no harm.   He told no one.   It was
so new for him, this rich thrilling tingle of emotion
at the thought of some other human being, something
so different from his love for his sisters and his
admiration for his friends.   And to-night from
first to last there had been all the time this same
tingling of experience.   From his first getting into
the train until now he had seemed to be in direct
contact with life, contact with all the wrappers off,
with nothing in between him and it!

That he must never lose again.   After this
night he must never slip back to that old half-life
with its dilettante pleasures, its mild disappoint-
ments, its vague sense of exile.   He could not
have Hesther for himself, but, at least. he could live

the full life that she and her country had shown to him.

'Ours is a great wild country. . . .' Never back to the level plains again!

Full of these fine brave exulting thoughts, he had climbed a very considerable way when—suddenly the path was gone. There was no path, no rocks, no hillside, no Cove, no sea, no stars—nothing. He was standing on air. The fog in one second had crept upon him. Not the thin glassy mist of twenty minutes ago, but a thick, dense, blinding fog that hemmed in like walls of wadding on every side. In the sudden panic his legs gave way and he fell on to his knees and hands, clutching both sides of the narrow path, staring desperately before him. He heard the Liddon bell, as it seemed, quite close to his side, ringing down upon him.

4

His first thought was of Hesther—then of Dunbar. Here they were, all three of them, separated. The fog might last for hours.

He called, 'Dunbar! Dunbar! Dunbar!'

The bell echoed him, mocking him, 'Dunbar! Dunbar! Dunbar!'

Very cautiously he climbed upon his feet, steadying himself. The wind seemed completely to have died, and the sea sent up now only a faint rustle, like the mysterious movement of some hidden woman's dress, but the fog was so thick that it seemed to embrace Harkness ever more tightly—and it was cold with a bitter piercing chill. Harkness called again, 'Dunbar! Dunbar!' listened, and then, as there was no kind of answer, began to move slowly forward.

Once, many years before, when a small boy at his private school, there had been an hour that every week he had feared beforehand with a panic dread. This had been the time of the fire-escape practice, when the boys, from some second-floor window, were pushed down, feet foremost, into a long canvas funnel through which they slipped safely to the ground. The passing through this funnel was only of a moment's duration, but that moment to Harkness had been terrible in its nightmare stifling sense, pressing blinding confinement. Something of that he felt now. He seemed to be compelled to push against blankets of cold damp obstruction. The Fog assumed a personality, and it was a personality strangely connected in Harkness's confused brain with that little red-headed man who seemed now always to be pursuing him. He was somewhere there in the fog; it was part of his game that he was playing with Harkness, and he could hear that sweet melodious voice whispering: 'Pain, you know. Pain. That's the thing to teach you what life really means. You'll be thankful to me before I've done with you. You shouldn't have interfered with my plans, you know. I warned you not to.'

He tried to drive down his fancies and to control his body. That was his trouble—that every limb, every nerve, every muscle, seemed to be asserting its own independent life. His legs now—they belonged to him, but never would you have supposed it. His arms tugged away from him as though striving to be free. He was not trained for this kind of thing—a cultured American gentleman with two sisters who read papers to women's clubs in Oregon.

He beat down his imagination. He had been crawling on his hands and his knees, and now he put out one hand and touched space. His heart gave a sickening bound and lay still. Which way went the path, to right or to left? He tried to throw his memory back and recapture the shape of it. There had been a sharp curve somewhere as it bent out towards the sea, but he did not know how far now he had gone. He strained with his eyes but could see nothing but the wall of grey. Should he wait there until the fog cleared or Dunbar came to him: but the fog might be there for hours, and Dunbar might never come. No, he must not wait. The thought of Hesther alone in the fog, fearing every moment recapture by the Crispins, filled with every terror that her loneliness could breed in her, spurred him on. He *must* reach her, whatever the risk.

Stretching his arm at full length he touched the path again, but there was an interval. Had there been any break in the path when he came down it? He could not remember any. He felt backwards with his hand and found the curve, crept forward, then his foot slipped and his leg slid over the edge. He waited to stop the hammering of his heart, then, balancing himself, pulled it back, then forward again.

Lucky for him that there was no wind, but again not lucky, because had there been wind the fog might have been blown out of its course: as it was, with every instant it seemed to grow thicker and thicker.

Then he grew calmer. He must soon now be

reaching the top, and happiness came to him when he thought that for a time at least he would be Hesther's only protection. On him, until Dunbar reached them, she would have absolutely to rely. She would be cold and he must shelter her, and at the thought of her proximity to him, he with his arm around her, wrapping her with his coat, holding perhaps her hand in his, he was, himself, suddenly warm, and his body pulled together and was taut and strong.

He fancied that he might walk now. Very carefully he pulled himself up, stood on his feet, stepped forward—and fell.

5

He screamed, and as he did so the Fog seemed to put its clammy hand against his mouth, filling it with boneless fingers. This was the end—this death. All space was about him and a roar of air sweeping up to meet him.

Then dimly there came to his brain the message, thrown to him like a life-line, that he was not falling in space but was slipping down a slope. He lurched out with his hands, caught some thick tufts of grass, and held. His legs slid forward and then dangled. With all his forces—and the muscles of his arms were but weak—he pulled himself upward and then held himself there, his legs hanging over space.

While the tufts held, and so long as his arms had the strength, he could stay. How long might that be? Sickness attacked him, a kind of sea-sickness. Tears were in his eyes, and an intense self-pity seized him. What a shame that such an end should come to a man who had meant no harm to any one, whose life had yet such possibilities. He thought of his sisters. How they would miss him! He had been tiresome sometimes, and been restless at home, and pulled them up sharply when they had said things that he thought stupid, but now only his good points would be remembered. He had been kind to them; he had a warm heart. He—and here his brain, working it seemed through his aching, straining arms, began suddenly to whirl like a top, flinging in front of his eyes a succession of the most absurd pictures: days in spring woods gathering flowers, his mother and father laughing at something childish that he had said, a bar of music from some musical comedy, Erda appearing before Wotan in *Siegfried*, a night when he had come to a dinner party and had forgotten to wear a dress tie, the moment when once before an operation he had been wheeled into the operating theatre, the day when he had plucked up his courage and decided that he could buy the Whistler ' Little Mast,' the grave, anxious, kindly eyes of Strang as he leant across the etching table, a morning when he had run for an omnibus up Shaftesbury Avenue and missed it and the conductor had laughed, that hour with Maradick at the club, lights, scents, the cold fog drowning his mouth, his nose, his eyes—then chill space, a roaring wind and silence. . . .

How strange after that—and hours afterwards it seemed although it must have been seconds—to find that he was still living, that his arms were aching as though they were one extended toothache, and that he was still holding to those tufts of grass.

He had a kind of marvel at his endurance, and now, suddenly, a wonder as to why he was doing this. Was it worth while? How stupid this energy! How much better to let himself go and to sleep, to sleep. How delicious to sleep and be rid of the ache, the cold, the clammy fog!

With that, one of the grass tufts to which he was clinging lurched slightly, and his whole soul was active in its energy to preserve that life that but now he had thought to throw away. With a struggle to which he would have supposed he could not have risen, he drew his body up against the slope so that the earth to which he was clinging might the better restrain his weight. Then resting there, his fingers digging deep into the soil of the cliff, his head pressed against the rock, he uttered a prayer:

' O Lord, help me now. I have a life that has been of little use to the world, but I have, in this very day, seen better the uses to which I may put it. Help me from this, give me strength to live, and I will try to leave my idleness and my selfishness and meanness and be a worthier man. O Lord, I know not whether Thou dost exist or no, but, if Thou art near me, help me at least now to bear my death worthily, if it must be that, and to live my life to some real purpose if I am to have it back again. Amen.' Then he repeated the Lord's Prayer. After that he seemed to be quieted; a great comfort came to him so that he no longer had any anxiety, his heart beat tranquilly, and he only rested there, passive for the issue. ' If death comes,' he thought to himself, ' I believe that it will be very swift. I shall feel no more than I felt just now when I first tumbled. I shall not have so much pain as with a toothache. I am leaving no one in the whole world whose existence will be empty because I have gone. Hesther after to-night I shall never, in any case, see again, and I am fortunate because, before I die, I have been able to feel the reality of life, what love is, and caring for others more than myself.' He was quite tranquil. The tuft of grass tugged again. His legs were numb, and he had the curious fancy that one of his boots had slipped off, and that one foot, as light as a feather, was blowing loosely in the air.

Then it seemed to him—and now it was as though he were half asleep, working in a dream— that some one was, very gently, pushing him up-wards. At least he was rising. His hands, one by one, left their tufts of grass and caught higher refuge, first a projecting rock, then a thick hummock of soil, then a bunch of sea-pinks. In another while, his heart now beating again with a new excited anticipation, his head lurched forward on the earth into space. With a last frantic urge he pulled all his body together and lay huddled on the path safe once more.

He had now a new trouble because his body refused to move. He had no body, nothing that he could count upon for action. He tried to find his connection with it, endeavoured to rest upon his knees, but it was as though he had been all dissipated into the fog and was turned, himself now, into mist and vapour. Then this passed, and once more he crawled forward.

He turned a corner and met again the Liddon bell. It was strange how deeply this voice re-assured him. He had been all alone in a world utterly dead. He had not had, like Hardy's hero, the sight of the crustacean to connect him with eternal life. But this sudden, melancholy, lowing sound like a creature deserted, crying for its mate, brought him once more into reality. The bell was insistent and very loud. It swung through the fog up to him, ringing in his ear, then fading away again into distance. He spoke aloud as men do when they are in desperate straits: 'Well, old bell,' he cried, 'I'm not beaten yet, you see. They've done what they can to finish me, but I'm back again. You don't get rid of me so easily as all that, you know. You can come and look, if you like. Here I am, company for you after all.'

There was a little breeze blowing now in his eyes and this cheered him. If only the wind rose the fog would move and all might yet be well. His clothes were torn, his hands bleeding, his hat gone. He crawled into a sitting position, shook his fist in the air, and cried:

'You old devil, you're there, are you! It's your game all this. You're seeing whether you can finish me. But I'll be even with you yet.' And it did indeed seem to him that he could see through the mist that red head sticking out like a furze bush on fire. The hair, the damp pale face, the melancholy eyes, and then the voice:

'It's only a theory, of course, Mr. Harkness. My father, who was a most remarkable man. . . .'

The thought of Crispin enraged him, and the rage drove him on to his feet. He was standing up and moving forward quite briskly. He moved like a blind man, his hands before him as though he were expecting at every moment to strike some hard, sharp substance, but whereas before the fog had seemed to envelop him, strangling him, penetrating into his very heart and vitals, now it

retreated from before him like a moving wall.
The incline was now less sharp, and now less sharp
again. Little pebbles rolled from beneath his feet,
and he could hear them fall over down into distant
space, but he had no longer any fear. He was on
level ground. He knew that the down was spreading about him. He called out, ' Hesther! Hesther!'
not realising that this was the first time he had
spoken her name. He called it again, ' Hesther!
Hesther!' and again and again, always moving as
he fancied forward.

Then, as though it had been hurled at him
out of some gigantic distance, the rugged wall
of the cottage pierced the sky. He saw it, then
herself patiently seated beneath it. In another
moment he was kneeling beside her, both her
hands in his, his voice murmuring unintelligible
words.

6

She was so happy to see him. His face was
close to hers and for the first time he could really
see her, her large, grave, questioning eyes, her child's
face, half developed, nothing very beautiful in her
features, but to him something inexpressibly lovely
for which all his life he had been waiting.

She was damp with the fog, and the first thing
he did was to take off his coat and try to put it
around her. But she stood up resisting him.

' Oh no, I'm not cold. I'm not really. And
do you think I'll let you? Why, you! What
have you done? Your hands are all torn and your
face!'

She was very close to him. She put up her

hand and touched his face. It needed to muster everything that he had in him not to put his arms around her. He conquered himself. 'That's nothing,' he said; 'I had some trouble climbing up from the cliff. I was just half-way up when the fog came on. It wasn't much of a path in any case.'

She stood with her hand on his arm. 'Oh, what shall we do? We shall never find the boat now. The fog will clear and we will be caught. We can't move from here while it lasts.'

'No,' he said firmly, 'we can't move. This is the place where Dunbar will expect us. He'll turn up here at any moment. Meanwhile, we must just wait for him. Is the pony all right?'

'I don't know what I'd have done without the pony,' she said. 'When the fog came up I was terrified. I didn't know what I'd better do. I called your names, but, of course, you didn't hear. And then it got colder and colder and I kept thinking that I was seeing Them. His red hair. . . .'

She suddenly, shivering, put her hand on his arm. 'Oh, don't let them find us,' she said; 'I couldn't go back to that. I would rather kill myself. I *would* kill myself if I went back. What they are —oh! you don't know!'

He took her hand and held it firmly. 'Now see here, we don't know how long Dunbar will be, or how long the fog will last, or anything. We can't do anything but stay here, and it's no good if we stay here and think of all the terrible things that may happen. The fog can't last for ever. Dunbar may come any minute. What we have to do is to sit down on this stone here and imagine we are

sitting in front of our fire at home talking like old
friends about——oh well, anything you like——whatever old friends do talk about.   Can your imagination help you that far?'

He saw that she was at the very edge of her
nerves; a step further and she would topple over
into wild hysteria; he knew enough already about
her character to be sure that nothing would cause
her such self-scorn and regret as that loss of self-
control.   He was not very sure of his own control;
everything had piled up upon him pretty heavily
during the last hour; but she was such a child that
he had an immense sense of responsibility as though
he had been fifteen years older at least.

' I haven't very much imagination,' she said, in
a voice hovering between laughter and tears.
' Father always used to tell me that that was my
chief lack.   And we *are* old friends, as we said a
while ago, even though we have just met.'

' That's right,' he said.   ' Now we will have to
sit rather close together.   There's only one stone
and the grass is most awfully wet.   Every three
minutes or so I'll get up and shout Dunbar's name
in case he is wandering about quite close to us.'

He stood up and, putting his hands to his mouth,
shouted with all his might: ' Dunbar!   Dunbar!
Dunbar!'

He waited.   There was no answer.   Only the
fog seemed to grow closer.   He turned to her and
said:

' Don't you think the fog's clearing a little?'

She shook her head.   There was still a little
quaver in her voice: ' I'm afraid not.   You're
saying that to cheer me up.   You needn't.   I'm
not frightened.   Think how lucky I am to have

you with me. You mightn't have come back.
You might have missed your way for hours.'

When he thought of how nearly he had missed
his way for ever and ever he trembled. He mustn't
let his thoughts wander in those paths; he was here
to make her feel happy and safe until Dunbar came.
They sat down on the stone together, and he put
his arm around her to hold her there and to keep
her warm.

' Now what shall we talk about?' she asked him.

' Ourselves,' he answered her. ' We have a
splendid opportunity. Here we are, cut off by
the fog, away from every one in the world. We
know nothing about one another, or almost nothing.
We can scarcely see one another's faces. It is a
wonderful opportunity.'

' Well, you tell me about yourself first.'

' Ah! there's the trouble. I'm so terribly dull.
I've never been or thought or said anything interesting. I'm like thousands and thousands of people
in this world who are simply shadows to everybody
else.'

' Remember we're to tell the truth,' she said.
' No one ever honestly thinks that about themselves
—that they are just shadows of somebody else.
Every one has their own secret importance for
themselves—at least, every one in our village had.
People you would have supposed had *nothing* in
them, yet if you talked to them you soon saw that
they fancied that the world would end if they weren't
in it to make it go round.'

' Well, honestly, that isn't my opinion of myself,'
Harkness answered. ' I don't think that I help
the world to go round at all. Of course, I think
that there have to be all the ordinary people in it

like myself to appreciate all the doings and sayings of the others, the geniuses—to make the audience, you know. But I'm not even a very good audience. There are so many things I don't care for.'

'What *do* you care for?'

'Oh, different things at different times—not permanently for much. Pictures—especially etchings—music, travel. But never very deeply or urgently, except for the etchings. . . . Until to-night,' he suddenly added, lowering his voice.

'Until to-night?'

'Yes, ever since I left Paddington—let me see —how many hours ago? It's now about two o'clock, I suppose.' He looked at his watch. 'Ten minutes to two. Nearly nine hours. Ever since nine hours ago, I've felt a new kind of energy, a new spirit, the thrill, the excitement that all my life I've wanted to have but that never came until now. Being really *in* life instead of just watching it like a spectator.'

She put her hand on his. 'I am so glad you're here. Do you know I used to boast that I never could be frightened by anything? But these last weeks—all my courage has gone. Oh, why has this fog come? We were getting on so well, everything was all right—and now I know they'll find us, I know they'll find us. I'm sure he's just behind there, somewhere, hiding in the fog, listening to us. And perhaps David is killed. I can't bear it. I can't bear it!'

She suddenly clung to him, hiding her face in his cloak. He soothed her just as he would his own child, as though she had been his child all her life. 'Hesther! Hesther! You mustn't. You mustn't break down. Think how brave you've

been all this time.   The fog can clear in a moment
and then we'll still have time to catch the train.
Anyway the fog's a protection.   If Crispin were
after us he'd never find us in this.   Don't cry,
Hesther.   Don't be unhappy.   Let's just go on
talking as though we were at home.   You're quite
safe here.   No one can touch you.'

' Yes, I'm safe,' she whispered, ' so long as you're
here.'   His heart leapt up.   He forced himself to
speak very quietly:

' Now I'll tell you about *myself*.   It will be soon
over.   I grew up in a place called Baker in Oregon
in the United States.   It is a long way from anywhere, but all the big trains go through it on the
way out to the Pacific coast.   I grew up there with
my two sisters and my father.   I lost my mother
when I was very young.   We had a funny ramshackle old house under the mountains, full of
books.   We had very long winters and very hot
summers.   I went to a place called Andover to
school.   Then my father died and left me some
money, and since then—oh! since then I dare not
tell you what a waste I have made of my life, never
settling anywhere, longing for Europe and the old
beautiful things when I was in America, and longing
for the energy and vitality of America when I was
in Europe.   That's what it is to be really cosmopolitan—to have no home anywhere.

' The only intimate friends I have are the etchings, and I sometimes think that they also despise
me for the idle life I lead.'

He could see that she was interested.   She was
quietly sitting, her head against his shoulder, her
hand in his just as a little girl might listen to her
elder brother.

'And that's all?' she asked.

'Yes. Absolutely all. I'm ashamed to let you look at so miserable a picture. I have been like so many people in the world, especially since the war. Modern cleverness has taken one's beliefs away, modern stupidity has deprived one of the possibility of hero-worship. No God, no heroes any more. Only one's disappointing self. What is left to make life worth while? So you think while you are on the bank watching the stream of life pass by. It is different if some one or something pushes you in. Then you must fight for existence for your own or, better still, for some one else. They who care for something or some one more than themselves—some cause, some idea, some prophecy, some beauty, some person—they are the happy ones.' He laughed. 'Here I am sitting in the middle of this fog, a useless selfish creature who has suddenly discovered the meaning of life. Congratulate me.'

He felt that she was looking up at him. He looked down at her. Their eyes stared at one another. His heart beat riotously, and behind the beating there was a strange pain, a poignant longing, a deep, deep tenderness.

'I don't understand everything you say,' she replied at last. 'Except that I am sure you are doing an injustice to yourself when you give such an account. But what you say about unselfishness I don't agree with. How is one unselfish if one is doing things for people one loves? I wasn't unselfish because I worked for the boys. I had to. They needed it.'

'Tell me about your home,' he said.

She sighed, then drew herself a little away from

him, as though she were suddenly determined to
be independent, to owe no man anything.

' Mother died when I was very young,' she said.
' I only remember her as some one who was always
tired, but very, very kind. But she liked the boys
better. I remember I used to be silly and feel
hurt because she liked them better. But the day
before she died she told me to look after them, and
I was so proud, and promised. And I have tried.'

' Were they younger than you?'

' Yes. One was three years younger and the
other five. I think they cared for me, but never
as much as I did for them.'

She stopped as though she were listening. The
fog was now terribly thick and was in their eyes,
their nostrils, their mouths. They could see
nothing at all, and when he jumped to his feet and
called again, ' Dunbar! Dunbar! Dunbar!' he
knew that he vanished from her sight. He could
feel from the way that she caught his hand and held
it when he sat down again how, for a moment, she
had lost him.

' It's always that way, isn't it?' she went on, and
he could tell from an undertone in her voice that
this talking was an immense relief to her. She
had, he supposed, not talked to any one for weeks.

' Always what way?' he asked.

' That if you love some one very much they
don't love you so much. And then the same the
other way.'

' Very often,' he agreed.

' I'm sure that's what I did wrong at home.
Showed them that I cared for them too much.
The boys were very good, but they were boys, you
know, and took everything for granted as men do.'

She said this with a very old world-wise air. ' They were dear boys—they were and are. But it was better before they went to school, when they needed me always. Afterwards when they had been to school they despised girls and thought it silly to let girls do things for them. And then they didn't like being at home—because father drank.'

She dropped her voice here and came very close to him.

' Do you know what it is to hate and love the same person? I was like that with father. When he had drunk too much and broke all the things— when we had so few anyway—and hit the boys, and did things—oh, dreadful things that men do when they're drunk—then I hated him. I didn't love him. I didn't want to help him—I just wanted to get away. And before—before he drank so much he was so good and so sweet and so clever. Do you know that my father was one of the cleverest doctors in the whole of England? He was. If he hadn't drunk he might have been anywhere and done anything. But sometimes when he *was* drunk and the boys were away at school, and the house was in such a mess, and the servant wouldn't stay because of father, I felt I couldn't go on—I *couldn't*!—and that I'd run down the road leaving everything as it was, into the town and hide so that they'd never find me. . . . And now,' she suddenly broke out, ' I have run away—and see what I've made of it!'

' It isn't over yet,' he said to her quietly. ' Life's just beginning for you.'

' Well, anyway,' she answered, with a sudden resolute calm that made her seem ever so much older and more mature, ' I've helped the boys to start in life, and I won't have to go back to all that

again—that's something. It's fine to love some
one and work for them as you said just now, but if
it's always dirty, and there's never enough money,
and the servants are always in a bad temper, and
you never have enough clothes, and all the people
in the village laugh at you because your father
drinks, then you want to stop loving for a little and
to escape anywhere, anywhere to anybody where it
isn't dirty. Love isn't enough—no, it isn't—if
you're so tired with work that you haven't any
energy to think whether you love or not.'

She hesitated there, looking away from him,
and said so softly that he with difficulty caught her
words: ' I will tell you one thing that you won't
believe, but it's true. I wanted to go to Crispin.'

He turned to look at her in amazement.

' You *wanted* to go?'

' Yes. I know you thought that I went for the
boys and father. I know that David thinks that
too. Of course that was true a little. He promised
me that they should have everything. It was a
relief to me that I needn't think of them any more.
But it wasn't only that. I wanted to go. I wanted
to be free.'

' To be free!' Harkness cried. ' My God!
What freedom! I can understand your wanting to
escape, but with *such* men. . . .'

She turned round upon him eagerly. ' You
don't know what he can be like—the elder Crispin,
I mean. And to a girl, an ignorant, conceited girl.
Yes, I was conceited, that was the cause of every-
thing. Father had all sorts of books in his room.
I used to read everything I could see—French and
German in a kind of way—and secretly I was very
proud of myself. I thought that I was more learned

than any one I knew, and I used to smile to myself secretly when I overheard people saying how good I was to the boys, and how unselfish, and I would think, " That's not what I am at all.   If you only knew how much I know, and the kind of things, you'd be surprised."

' I was always thinking of the day when I would escape and marry.   I fancied I knew everything about marriage from the books that I had read and from the things that father said when he was drunk. I hadn't a nice idea of marriage at all.   I thought it was old-fashioned to fall in love, but through marriage I could reach some fine position where I could do great things in the world, and always in my mind I saw myself coming one day back to my village and every one saying: " Why, I had not an idea she was like *that*.   Fancy all the time she was with us we never knew she was clever like *this*." '

She laughed like a child, a little maliciously, very simply and confidingly.   He saw that she had for the moment forgotten her danger, and was sitting there in the middle of a dense fog on a lonely moor at a quarter past two in the morning with an almost complete stranger as though she were giving him afternoon tea in the placid security of a London suburb.   He was glad; he did not wish to bring back her earlier terror, but for himself now, with every moment that passed, he was increasingly anxious.   Time was flying; now they could never catch that train.   And above all, what could have happened to Dunbar?   He must surely have found them by now had some accident not come to him. Perhaps he had slipped as Harkness had done and was now lying smashed to pieces at the bottom of that cliff.   But what could he, Harkness, do better

than this? While the fog was so dense it was
madness to move off in search of any one. And if
the fog lasted, were they to sit there until morning
and be caught like mice in a kitchen?

And beneath his anxiety, as his arm held the
child at his side, there was that strange mixture of
triumph and pain, of some odd piercing loneliness
and a deep burning satisfaction. Meanwhile her
hand rested in his, soft and warm like the touch
of a bird's breast.

'When Mr. Crispin came—the elder, the father
—and talked to me I was flattered. No one before
had ever talked to me as he did about his travels
and his collections and the grand people he knew,
just as though I were as old as he was. And then
David—Mr. Dunbar—was always asking me to
marry him. I'd known him all my life, and I liked
him better than any one else in the whole world;
but just because I'd always known him he wasn't
exciting. He was the last person I wanted to marry.
Then Mr. Crispin made father drink, and I hated
him for that, and I hated father for letting him do
it. I went up to Mr. Crispin's house and told him
what I thought of him, and he talked and talked
and talked, all about having power over people for
their good and hurting them first and loving them
all afterwards. I didn't understand most of it, but
the end of it was that he said that if I would marry
his son he would leave father alone and would give
me everything. I should see the world and all
life, and that his son loved me and would be kind
to me.

'After that it was the strangest thing. I don't
say that he hypnotised me. I knew that he was
bad. Every one in the place was speaking about

him. He had done some cruel thing to a horse,
and there was a story, too, about some woman in
the village. But I thought that I knew better than
all of them, that I would save father and the boys
and be grand myself—and then I would show David
that he wasn't the only one who cared for me.

'And so—I consented. From that moment I
promised I was terrified. I knew that I had done
a terrible thing. But it was too late. I was already
a prisoner. That is a hysterical thing to say, but
it is true. They never let me out of their sight.
I was married very quickly after that. I won't
say anything about the first week of my marriage
except that I didn't need books any more to teach
me. I knew the sin I'd committed. But I was
proud—I was as proud as I was frightened. I wasn't
going to let any one know what a terrible position
I was in—and especially David. When we went
to Treliss, David came too and waited. In my
heart I was so glad he was there.

'You don't know what went on in that house.
The younger Crispin wasn't unkind. He was
simply indifferent. He thought of nothing and
nobody but his father. His father mocked him,
despised him, scorned him, but he didn't care. He
follows his father like a dog. At first you know
I thought I could make a job of it, carry it through.
And then I began to understand.

'First one little thing, then another. The elder
Crispin was always talking, floods of it. He was
always looking at me and smiling at me. After
two days in the house with him I hated him as I
hadn't known I could hate any one. When he
touched me I trembled all over. It became a kind
of duel between us. He was always talking

nonsense about making me love him through pain
—and his eyes never said what his mouth said.
They were like the eyes of another person caught
there by mistake.

'Then one day I came into the library upstairs
and found him with a dog. A little fox-terrier.
He had tied it to the leg of the table and was flicking
it with a whip. He would give it a flick, then
stand back and look at it, then give it another flick.
The awful thing was that the dog was too frightened
to howl, too terrified to know that it was being hurt
at all. He was smiling, watching the dog very
carefully, but his eyes were sad and unhappy.
After that there were many signs. I knew then
two things, that he was raving crazy mad and that
I was a prisoner in that house. They watched me
night and day. I had no money. My only hope
of escape was through David, who was always getting
word to me, begging me to let him help me. But
I still had my pride, although it was nearly beaten.
I wouldn't yield until—until the night before you
came; then something happened, something he tried
to do; the younger Crispin stopped him that time,
but another time—well, there mightn't be any one
there. That settled it all. I let David know
through you that I would go. I *had* to go. I
couldn't risk another moment. I couldn't risk
another moment, I tell you.' She suddenly sprang
up, caught at Harkness's hands in an agony, crying:

'Don't stay here! Don't stay here! They can
find us here! We're going to be caught again.
Oh, please come! Please! Please!'

She was suddenly crazy with terror. Had he
not held her with all his force she would have
rushed off into the fog. She struggled in his arms,

pulling and straining, crying, not knowing what she said. Then suddenly she relaxed, would have tumbled had he not held her, and murmuring, ' I can't any more—oh, I can't any more!' collapsed, so that he knew she had fainted.

7

He sat down on the stone, laying her in his arms as though she were his child. He was, himself, not strongly built, but she was so slight in his hold that he could not believe that she was a woman. He murmured words to her, stroked her forehead with his hand; she stirred, turning towards him, and resting her head more securely on his breast. Then her hand moved to his cheek and lay against it.

At last after a long while she raised her head, looked about her, stared up at him as though she had just awoken, turned, and kissed him on the cheek. She murmured something—he could not catch the words—then nestled down into his arms as though she would sleep.

There began for him then, sitting there, staring out into the unblinking fog, his hardest test. As surely as never before in his life had he known what love truly was, so did he know it now. This child in her ignorance, her courage, her hard history, her contact with the worst elements in human nature, her purity, had found her way into the innermost recesses of his heart. He saw as he sat there, with a strange, almost divine clarity of vision, both into her soul and into his own. He knew that when she faced life again he would be the first to whom she would turn. He knew that

with one word, one look, he could win her love.
He knew that she had also never felt what love was.
He knew that the circumstances of this night had
turned her towards him as she would never have
been turned in ordinary conditions. Yes, he knew
this too—that had they met in everyday life she
would never have loved him, would not indeed
have thought of him twice.

He was not a man about whom any one thought
twice. With the exception of his sisters no woman
had ever loved him; this child, driven to terrified
desperation by the horrors of the last weeks, had
been wakened to full womanhood by those same
horrors, and he had happened to be there at the
awakening. That was all. And yet he knew that
so honest was she, and good and true, that did she
once go to him she would stay with him. He saw
steadily into the future. He saw her freedom from
the madman to whom she was married, then her
union with himself. His happiness, and her gradual
discovery of the kind of man that he was. Not
bad—oh no—but older, far older than herself in
many other ways than years, tired so easily, caring
nothing for all the young things in life, above all
a man in the middle state, solitary from some
elemental loneliness of soul. It was true that
to-night had shown him a new energy of living, a
new happiness, a new vigour, and he would perhaps
after to-night never be the same man as he was
before. But it was not enough. No, not enough
for this young girl just beginning life, so ignorant
of it, so trustful of him that she would follow the
path that he pointed out. And for himself! How
often he had felt like Nejdanov in *Virgin Soil* that
' everything that he had said or done during the day

seemed to him so utterly false, such useless nonsense, and the thing that ought to be done was nowhere to be found . . . unattainable . . . in the depths of a bottomless pit.' Well, of to-night that was not true. What he had done was useful, was well done. But to-morrow how would he regard it? Would it not seem like senseless melodrama, the mad Crispins, his fall from the cliff, this eternal fog? How like his history that the most conclusive and eternal acts of his life should take place in a fog! And this girl whom he loved so dearly, if he married her and kept her for himself would not his conscience, that eternal tiresome conscience of his, would it not for ever reproach him, telling him that he had spoilt her life, and would not he be for ever watching to catch that moment when she would realise how dull, how old, how negative he was? No, he could not . . . he could not . . .

Then there swept over him all the fire of the other impulse. Why should he not, at long last, be happy? Could any man in the world be better to her than he would be? After all he was not so old. Had he not known when he shared in that dance round the town that he could be part of life, could feel with the common pulse of humanity? Did young Dunbar know life better than he? With him she had lived always and yet did not love him.

And then he knew with a flash like lightning through the fog that at this moment, when she was waking to life and was trusting him, he could, by only a few words, lead her to love Dunbar. She had always seen him in a commonplace, homely, familiar light, but he, Harkness, if he liked, could show her quite another light, could turn all this fresh romantic impulse that was now flowing towards himself into another channel.

But why should he? Was that not simply sentimental idealism? Dunbar was no friend of his, he had never seen him before yesterday, why should he give up to him the only real thing that his life had yet known?

But it was not sentimental, it was not false. Youth to youth. In years he was not so old, but in his hesitating, Quixotic, undetermined character there were elements of analysis, self-questioning, regret, that would make any human being with whom he was intimately related unhappy.

Sitting there, staring out into the fog, he knew the truth—that he was a man doomed to be alone all his days. That did not mean that he could not make much of his life, have many friends, much good fortune—but in the last intimacy he could go to no one and no one could go to him.

He bent down and kissed her forehead. She stirred, moved, sat up, resting back against him, her feet on the ground.

'Where am I?' she whispered. 'Oh yes.' She clung to his arm. 'No one has come? We are still alone?'

'No,' he answered her gently, 'no one has come. We are still alone.'

8

'What time is it?' she asked.

He looked at his watch. 'Half-past two.'

'We have missed that train now.'

'I don't know. And anyway there's probably another.'

' And David?'

' He's lost his way in the fog. He'll turn up at any moment.' He stood up and shouted once again:

' Dunbar! Dunbar! Dunbar!'

No answer.

He stood over her looking down at her as she sat with drooping head. She looked up at him. ' I'm ashamed at the way I've behaved,' she said, ' fainting and crying. But you needn't be afraid any more. I shan't give in again.'

Indeed, he seemed to see in her altogether a new spirit, something finer and more secure. She put out her hand to him.

' Come and sit down on the stone again as we were before. It's better for us to talk and then we don't frighten ourselves with possibilities. After all, we can't *do* anything, can we, so long as this horrid fog lasts? We must just sit here and wait for David.'

He sat down, put his arm around her as he had done before. The moment had come. He had only now to speak and the result was certain—the whole of his future life and hers. He knew so exactly what he would say. The words were forming on his lips.

' Hesther dear, I've known you so short a time, but nevertheless I love you with all my heart and being. When you are rid of this horrible man will you marry me? I will spend all my life in making you happy——'

And she, oh, without an instant's doubt, would say ' Yes,' would hide in his arms, and rest there as though secure, yes, utterly secure for life. But the battle was over. He would not begin it again.

He clipped the words back and sat silent, one hand clenched on his knee.

It was as though she were waiting for him to speak. Their silence was packed with anticipation. At last she said:

'What is the matter? Is there something you're afraid of that you don't like to tell me? You needn't mind. I'm through my fear.'

'No, there's nothing,' he answered. At last he said: 'There *is* one thing I'd like to say to you. I suppose I've no right to speak of it, seeing how recently I've known you, but I guess this night has made us friends as months of ordinary living never would have made us.'

'Yes, you're right in that,' she answered. He knew what she was expecting him to say.

'Well, it's about Dunbar.' He could feel her hand jump in his. 'He loves you so much—so terribly. He isn't a man, I should think, to say very much about his feelings. I've only known him for an hour or two, and he wouldn't have said anything to me if he hadn't *had* to. But from the little he did say I could see what he feels. You're in luck to have a man like that in love with you.'

She took her hand out of his, then, very quietly but very stiffly, answered:

'But I've known him all my life, you know.'

'That's just why I'm speaking about him,' Harkness answered.

'It's rather strange to have the friend of your life explained to you by some one who has known him only for an hour or two.' She laughed a little angrily.

'But that's just why I'm speaking,' he answered. 'When you've known some one all your life you

can't see them clearly. That's why one's own
family always knows so little about one. You
can't see the wood for the trees. In the first
minutes a stranger sees more. I don't say that
I know Dunbar as *well* as you do—I only say
that I probably see things in him that you don't
see.'

They had been so close to one another during
this last hour that he felt as though he could see,
as through clear water, deep into her mind.

He knew that, during those last minutes, she
had been struggling desperately. She came up
to him victorious and, smiling and putting her hand
into his, said:

' Tell me what *you* think about him.'

' Simply that he seems to me a wonderful fellow.
He seems to you, I expect, a little dull. You've
always laughed at him a bit, and for that very reason,
and because he's loved you for so long, he's tongue-
tied when you're there and shy of showing you what
he really thinks about things. He has immense
qualities of character—fidelity, honesty, devotion,
courage—things simply beyond price, and if you
loved him and showed him that you did you'd
probably see quite new things—fun and spontaneity and imagination—things that he had always
been afraid to show you until now.'

Her hand trembled in his.

' You speak,' she said, ' as though you thought
that you were so much older than both of us. I
don't feel that you are. Can't you——?' she broke
off. He knew what she would say.

' My dear,' and his voice was eloquently paternal,
' I *am* older than both of you—years and years older.
Not physically, perhaps, so much, but in every other

kind of way. I am an old fogey, nothing else.
You've both of you been kind to me to-night, but
in the morning, when ordinary life begins again,
you'll soon see what a stuffy old thing I am. No,
no. Think of me as your uncle. But don't miss—
oh, don't miss!—the love of a man like Dunbar.
There's so little of that unselfish devoted love in
the world, and when it comes to you it's a crime to
miss it.'

'But you can't force yourself to love any one!'
she cried sharply.

'No, you can't *force* yourself, but it's strange
what seeing new qualities in some one, looking at
some one from another angle, will do. Try and
look at him as though you'd met him for the first
time, forget that you've known him always. I tell
you that he's one in a million!'

'Yes, he's good,' she answered softly. 'He's
been wonderful to me always. If he'd been less
wonderful perhaps—I don't know, perhaps I'd have
loved him more. But why are we talking about it?
Aren't I married as it is?'

'Oh, that!' He made a little gesture of re-
pulsion. 'We must get rid of that at once.'

'It won't be very difficult,' she answered,
dropping her voice to a whisper. 'He hasn't been
faithful to me—even during these weeks.'

He put his arm round her and held her close
as though he were most truly her father. 'Poor
child!' he said, ' poor child!'

She trembled in his arms.

'You——' she began. 'You——? Don't
you——?' She could say no more.

'I'm your friend,' he answered, 'to the end of
life. Your old avuncular friend. That's my job.

Think of your *young* friend freshly. See what a
fellow he is.   I tell you that's a man!'

She did not answer him, but stayed there hiding
her head in his coat.

There was a long silence, then, stroking her hair,
he said:

'Hesther dear, I'm going to try once again.'
He got up and, putting his hands trumpet-wise to
his mouth, shouted through the fog:

'Dunbar! Dunbar! Dunbar!'

This time there was an answer, clear and definite.
'Hallo! Hallo! Hallo!' He turned excitedly to
her. She also sprang to her feet. 'He's there!
I can hear him!'

'Dunbar! Dunbar!'

The answer came more clearly: 'Hallo! Hallo!
Hallo!'

They continued to exchange cries. Sometimes
the reply was faint. Once it seemed to be lost
altogether. Then suddenly it was close at hand.
A ghostly figure was shadowed.

Dunbar came running.

9

He caught their hands in his. He was breathless. He sank down on the stone beside them.

'Give me a minute. . . . I'm done. Lord!
this filthy fog. . . . Where haven't I been?' He
panted, staring up at them with wide distracted
eyes.

'Do you realise? I've failed. It's no use our
crossing in that boat now even if we could find it.
We've missed that train. We're done.'

'Nonsense,' Harkness broke in. 'Why, man, what's happened to you? This isn't like you to lose your courage. We're not done or anything like it. In the first place, we're all together again. That's something in a fog like this. Besides, so long as we stick together we're out of their power. They can't force us, all of us, back into that house again. So long as we're out of that house we're safe.'

'Oh, are we?' said Dunbar. 'Little you know that man. I tell you we're not safe—or Hesther's not safe—until we're at least a hundred miles away. But forgive me,' he looked up at them both, smiling, 'you're quite right, Harkness. I haven't any right to talk like this. But you don't know what a time I've had in that fog.'

'I had a little bit of a time myself,' said Harkness.

'Well, in the first place,' went on Dunbar, 'I was terrified about you. I knew that you didn't know these cliffs well. When the fog started I called to you to come back, but you didn't hear me, of course. I was an idiot to let you start out at all.

'And then, when it came to myself climbing them I wasn't very successful. I was nearly over the edge fifty times at least. But at last when I *did* get to the top the ridiculous thing was that I started off in the wrong direction. There I was only five minutes from the cottage and the pony and Hesther; I know the place like my own hand, and yet I went in the wrong direction.

'God knows where I got to. I was nearly over into the sea twice at least. I kept calling your names, but the only thing I heard in answer was that beastly bell. I never went very far, I imagine, because when I heard your voice at last, Harkness, I was quite close to it. But just to think of it! Every other contingency in the world I'd considered except just this one! It simply never entered my head.'

' Well, now,' said Harkness, ' let's face the facts. It's too late for that train. Is there any other that we can catch?'

' There's one at six, but I don't see ourselves hanging about here for another three hours, nor, if the fog doesn't lift, can Hesther get down into that cove. I'm not especially anxious to try it myself, as a matter of fact.'

' No, nor I,' said Harkness, smiling. ' Then we count the boat out. There aren't many other things we can do. We can take the pony and follow him. He'll lead us straight back to Treliss to whatever stables he came from—a little too close to the Crispin family, I fancy. Secondly, we can wait here until the fog clears; that *may* be in three minutes' time, it may be to-morrow. You both know more about these sea-fogs down here than I do, but, from the look of it, it's solid till Christmas.'

' A heat fog this time of year,' said Dunbar, ' within three miles of the sea can last for twenty-four hours or longer—not as thick as this though— this is one of the thickest I've ever seen.'

' Well, then,' continued Harkness, ' it isn't much good to wait until it clears. The only thing remaining for us is to walk off somewhere. The question is, where? Is there any garage within a mile or two or any friend with a car? It isn't three o'clock yet. We still have time.'

' Yes,' said Dunbar, ' there is. I've had it in

my mind all along as an alternative. Indeed it was the first thing of all that I thought of. Three miles from here there's a village, Cranach. The rector of Cranach is a sporting old man called Banting. During the last week or two we've made friends. He's sixty or so, a bachelor, and he's got a car. Not much of a car, but still it's something. I believe if we go and appeal to him—we'll have to wake him up, of course—he'll help us. I know that he disapproves strongly of the Crispins. I thought of him before, as I say, but I didn't want to involve him in a row with Crispin. However, now, as things have gone, it's got to be. I can think of no other alternative.'

'Good,' said Harkness, 'that settles it. Our only remaining difficulty is to find our way there through this fog.'

'I can start straight,' said Dunbar. 'Left from the cottage and then straight ahead. Soon we ought to leave the Downs and strike some trees. After that it's across the fields. I don't think I can miss it.'

'What about the pony?' asked Hesther.

'We'll have to leave him. He must be there for Jabez in the morning or Jabez will have to pay for both the pony and the cart.'

They started off. The character of the fog seemed now slightly to have changed. It was certainly thicker in some places than in others. Here it was an impenetrable wall, but there it seemed to be only a gauze covering hanging before a multitude of changing scenes and persons. Now it was a multitude of armed men advancing, and you could be sure that you heard the clang of shield on shield and a thousand muffled steps. Now it was horses wheeling, their manes tossing, their tails flying, now secret furtive figures that moved and peered, stopped, bending forward and listening, then moved on again.

All the world was stirring. A breeze ran along the ground rustling the short thin grass. Seagulls were circling the mist crying. A ship at sea was sounding its horn. Figures seemed to press in on every side.

They linked arms as they went, stumbling over the tussocks at every step. It was strange how the sudden vanishing of the cottage left them forlorn. It had been their one sure substantial hold on life. They were in their own world while they could touch those ruined stones, but now they walked in air.

Nevertheless Dunbar walked forward confidently. He thought that he recognised this landmark and that. 'Now we veer a bit to the left,' he said. 'We should be off the moor in another step.'

They walked forward. Suddenly Hesther pulled back, crying, 'Look out! Look out!' Another instant and they would have walked forward into space. The mist here twisted up into thinning spirals as though to show them what they had escaped; they could just see the sharp black line of the cliff. Far, far beneath them the sea purred like a cat.

They stopped where they were as though fixed like images into the wall of the fog.

Dunbar whispered: 'That's awful. Another moment. . . .'

It was Hesther who pulled them together again. ' Let's turn sharp about,' she said, ' and walk straight in front of us. At least we escape the sea.'

They turned as she had said and then walked forward, but in the minds of all of them there was the same thought. Some one was playing with them, some one like an evil Will-o'-the-wisp was leading them, now here, now there. Almost they could see his red poll gleaming through the fog and could hear his silvery voice running like music up and down the scale of the mist.

They were, three of them, worn with the events of the night. They were beginning to walk somnambulistically. Harkness found in himself now a strange kind of intimacy with the Fog.

Yes, spell it with a capital letter. The Fog. The FOG. Some emanation of himself, rolling out of him, friendly and also hostile. He and Crispin were of the Fog together. They had both created it, and as they were the good and the evil of the Fog so was all Life, shapeless, rolling hither and thither, but having in its elements Good and Evil in eternal friendship and eternal enmity.

Every part of his body was aching. His legs were so weary that they dragged with him, protesting; his eyes were for ever closing, his head nodding. He stumbled as he walked, and at his side, step with step in time, the Fog accompanied him, a mountainous grey-swathed giant.

He was talking, words were for ever pouring from him, words mixed with fog, so that they were damp and thick before ever they were free. ' In life there are not, you know, enough moments of clear understanding. Between nations, between individuals, those moments are too often confused by winds that, blowing from nowhere in particular, ruffle the clear water where peace of mind and love

of soul for soul are reflected. . . . Now the waters
are clear.   Let us look down.'

Yes, he had read that somewhere. In one of
Galleon's books perhaps?   No matter.   It meant
nothing.   'A fine sentiment.   What it means.
. . . Well, no matter.   Don't you smell roses?
Roses out here on the moor.   If it wasn't for the
fog you'd smell them—ever so many.'   And so he
tore the ' Orvieto ' into shreds.   Little scraps flying
in the air like goose feathers.   What a pity!   Such
a beautiful thing. . . .

'Hold up,' cried Dunbar. 'You're asleep,
Harkness.   You'll have us all down.'

He pulled together with a start, and opening
his eyes wide and staring about him saw only the
disgusting fog.

'This fog is too much of a good thing.   Don't
you think so?   I guess we could blow it away if
we all tried hard enough.   You think Americans
always say "I guess," don't you?   The English
books always make them.   But don't you believe
it.   We only do it to please the English.   They
like it.   It satisfies their vanity.'

He seemed to be climbing an enormous endless
staircase.   He mounted another step, two, and
suddenly was wide awake.

'What nonsense I'm talking!   I've been half
asleep.   This fog gets into your brain.'   He felt
Hesther's arm within his.   He patted her hand
encouragingly.   'It's all right, Hesther.   We'll be
out of this soon.   Just another minute or two.'

'By Jove, you're right,' Dunbar cried; 'these
are trees.'

And they were.   A whole row of them.   Crusoe
was not more glad to see the footprint on the sand

than were those three to see those trees. 'Now I
know where we are!' Dunbar cried triumphantly.
'Here's the bridge and here's the lane. What luck
to have found it!'

The trees seemed to step forward and greet
them, each one tall and dignified, welcoming them
to a happier country. They were on a road and had
no longer the turf beneath their feet. The fog
here was truly thinner, so that very dimly they
could see the mark of the hedge like a clothes-line
in mid-air.

They moved now much more rapidly, and in their
hearts was an intense, an eager relief. The fog
thinned until it was a wall of silver. Nothing was
distant, but it was a world of tangible reality. They
could kick pebbles with their feet, could hear sheep
moving on the farther side of the hedge.

'This is better,' said Dunbar. 'We'll get out
of this yet. Cranach is only a mile or so from here.
I know this lane well. And the fog's going to lift
at last.'

Even as he spoke it swept up, thick and grey,
deeper than before. The trees disappeared, the
hedges. They had once more to grope for one
another's hands and walk close.

Harkness could feel from the way that Hesther
leaned against him, and the drag of her feet, that she
was near the end of her endurance. She said
nothing. Only walked on and on.

They were all now silent. They must have
walked, it seemed to them, for miles. An endless
walk that had no beginning and no end. And
then Harkness was strangely aware—how, he never
knew—that Dunbar and Hesther were drawing
closer together.

He felt that new relation that he had in a way created beginning to grow between them. She drew away from Harkness ever so slightly. Then suddenly he knew that Dunbar had put his arm around her and was holding her up. She was so weary that she did not know what she was doing— but for that quiet, resolute, determined boy it must have been a moment of great triumph, the first time in their two lives that she had in any way surrendered to him or allowed him to care for her. Harkness was once more alone.

They walked and walked and walked. They did not know where they were walking, but in their minds they were sure it was straight to Cranach.

Suddenly, after, as it seemed, hours of silence in a dead world, Dunbar cried:

' We're there. Oh, thank God! we're there. This is the rectory wall.'

A wall was before them and an open gate. They walked through the gate, only dimly seen, stumbled where the lawn rose from the gravel, then forward again, down on to the gravel again. The door was open.

Like somnambulists they walked forward. The door closed behind them.

Like somnambulists awakened they saw lights, a dim hall where flags waved.

For Harkness there was something familiar— quite close to him, the chatter-chatter of a clock, like a coughing dog. Familiar? He stared.

Some one was standing, looking at him and smiling.

With sudden agony in his voice, as a man cries in a terrible dream, Harkness shouted:

'Out, Dunbar! Back! Back! Run for your life!'

But it was too late.

That voice of exquisite melody greeted them:

'I had no idea that of your own free will you would return. My son only a quarter of an hour ago departed in search of you. I welcome you back.'

PART IV
THE TOWER

PART IV

THE TOWER

I

WITH an instinctive movement both Harkness and Dunbar closed in upon Hesther.

The three stood just in front of the heavy locked door facing the dim hall. On the bottom stair was Crispin Senior, and on the floor below him, one on either side, the two Japanese servants.

A glittering candelabra, hanging high up, was fully lit, but it seemed to give a very feeble illumination, as though the fog had penetrated here also.

Crispin was wearing white silk pyjamas, brown leather slippers, and a dressing-gown of a rich bronze-coloured silk flowered with gold buds and leaves. His eyes were half-closed, as though the light, dim though it was, was too strong for him. His face wore a look of petulant, rather childish melancholy. The two servants were statues indeed, no sign of life proceeding from them. There was, however, very little movement anywhere, the flags moving in the draught the chief.

Hesther's face was white, and her breath came in little sharp pants, but she held her body rigid. Harkness after that first cry was silent, but Dunbar stepped forward shouting:

'You damned hound—you let us go or you shall have this place about your ears!' The hall echoed the words, which, to tell the truth, sounded very empty and theatrical. They were made to sound the more so by the quietness of Crispin's reply.

'There is no need,' he said, ' for all those words, Mr. Dunbar. It is your own fault that you interfered and must pay for your interference. I warned you weeks ago not to annoy me. Unfortunately you wouldn't take advice. You *have* annoyed me—sadly, and must suffer the consequences.'

'If you touch a hair of her head——' he burst out.

'As to my daughter-in-law,' Crispin said, stepping down on to the floor, and suddenly smiling, ' I can assure you that she is in the best possible hands. She knows that herself, I'm sure. What induced you, Hesther,' he said, addressing her directly, ' to climb out of your window like the heroine of a cinematograph and career about on the sea-shore with these two gentlemen is best known only to yourself. At least you saw the error of your ways and are in time, after all, to go abroad with us to-day.'

He advanced a step towards them. ' And you, Mr. Harkness, don't you think that you have rather violated the decencies of hospitality? I think you will admit that I showed you nothing but courtesy as host. I invited you to dinner, then to my house, showed you my few poor things, and how have you repaid me? Is this the famous American courtesy? And may I ask, while we are on the question, what business this was of yours?'

'It was anybody's business,' said Harkness

firmly, ' to rescue a helpless girl from such a house as this.'

' Indeed?' asked Crispin. ' And what is the matter with this house?'

Here Hesther broke in: ' Look back two nights ago,' she cried, ' and ask yourself then what is the matter with this house and whether it is a place for a woman to remain in.'

' For myself,' said Crispin, ' I think it is a very nice house, and I am quite sorry that we are leaving it to-day. That is, some of us—not all,' he added softly.

' If you are going to murder us,' Dunbar cried, ' get done with it. We don't fear you, you know, whatever colour your hair may be. But whether you murder us or no I can tell you one thing, that your own time has come—not many more hours of liberty for *you*.'

' All the more reason to make the most of those I *have* got,' said Crispin. ' Murder you? No. But you *have* fallen in very opportunely for the testing of certain theories of mine. I look forward to a very interesting hour or two. It is now just four o'clock. We leave this house at eight—or, at least, some of us do. I can promise all of us a very interesting four hours with no time for sleep at all. I have no doubt you are all tired, wandering about in the fog for so long must be fatiguing, but I don't see any of you sleeping—not for an hour or two, at least.'

Hesther said then: ' Mr. Crispin, I believe that I am chiefly concerned in this. If I promise to go quietly with you abroad I hope that you will free these two gentlemen. I give you that promise and I shall keep it.'

'No, no,' Dunbar cried, springing forward. 'You shan't go with him anywhere, Hesther, by heaven you shan't. Not while there's any breath in my body——'

'And when there isn't any breath in your body, Mr. Dunbar,' said Crispin, 'what then?'

'A very good line for an Adelphi melodrama, Mr. Crispin,' said Harkness, 'but it seems to me that we've stayed here talking long enough. I warn you that I am an American citizen and am not to be kept here against my will——'

'Aren't you indeed, Mr. Harkness?' said Crispin. 'Well, that's a line of Adelphi drama, if you like. How many times in a secret service play has the hero declared that he's an American citizen? Which only goes to show, I suppose, how near real life is to the theatre—or rather how much more theatrical real life is than the theatre can ever hope to be. But you're all right, Mr. Harkness—I won't forget that you're an American citizen. You shall have special privileges. That I promise you.'

Dunbar then did a foolish thing. He made a dash for the farther end of the hall. What he had in mind no one knows—in all probability to find a window, hurl himself through it, and escape to give the alarm. But the alarm to whom? That was, as far as things had yet gone, the foolishness of their position. A policeman arriving at the house would find nothing out of order, only that there two gentlemen had broken in, barbarously, at a midnight hour to abduct the married lady of the family.

Dunbar's effort was foolish in any case; its issue was that, in a moment of time, without noise or a word spoken, the two Japanese servants had him held, one hand on either arm. He looked stupid enough, there in the middle of the hall, his eyes dim with tears of rage, his body straining ineffectively against that apparently light and casual hold.

But it was strange to perceive how that movement of Dunbar's had altered all the situation. Before that the three were at least the semblance of visitors demanding of their host that they should be allowed to go; now they were prisoners and knew it. Although Hesther and Harkness were still untouched they were as conscious as was Dunbar of a sudden helplessness—and of a new fear.

Harkness watched Crispin, who had walked forward and now stood only a pace or two from Dunbar. Harkness saw that his excitement was almost uncontrollable. His legs, set widely apart, were quivering, his nostrils panting, his eyes quite closed so that he seemed a blind man scenting out his enemy.

'You miserable fellow,' he said—and his voice was scarcely more than a whisper. 'You fool—to think that you could interfere. I told you . . . I warned you . . . and now am I not justified? Yes—a thousand times. Within the next hour you shall know what pain is, and I shall watch you realise it.'

Then his body trembled with a sort of passionate rhythm as though he were swaying to the run of some murmured tune. With his eyes closed and the shivering it was like the performance of some devotional rite. At least Dunbar showed no fear.

'You can do what you damn well please,' he shouted. 'I'm not afraid of you, mad though you are.'

'Mad? Mad?' said Crispin, suddenly opening his eyes. 'That depends. Yes, that depends. Is a man mad who acts at last when given a perfectly just and honourable opportunity for a pleasure from which he has restrained himself because the opportunity hitherto was *not* honourable? And madness? A matter of taste, my friends, decides that. I like olives—you do not. Are you therefore mad? Surely not. Be broad-minded, my friend. You have much to learn and but little time in which to learn it.'

Harkness perceived that the man was savouring every moment of this situation. His anticipations of what was to come were so ardent that the present scene was coloured deep with them. He looked from one to another, tasting them, and his plans for them on his tongue. His madness—for never before had his eyes, his hands, his whole attitude of body more highly proclaimed him mad—had in it all the preoccupation with some secret life that leads to such a climax. For months, for years, grains of insanity, like coins in a miser's hoard, had been heaping up to make this grand total. And now that the moment was come he was afraid to touch the hoard lest it should melt under his fingers.

He approached Harkness.

'Mr. Harkness,' he said quite gently, 'believe me I am sorry to see this. You took me in last evening, you did indeed. I felt that you had a real interest in the beautiful things of art, and we had that in common. All the time you were nothing but a dirty spy—a mean and dirty spy. What right had you to interfere in the private life of a private gentleman who, twenty-four hours ago, was quite unknown to you, simply on the word of a crazy braggart boy? Have you so little to do that you must be poking your fingers into every one else's business? I liked you, Mr. Harkness. As I told you quite honestly last evening, I don't know where I have met a stranger to whom I took more warmly. But you have disappointed me. You have only yourself to thank for this—only yourself to thank.'

Harkness replied firmly. 'Mr. Crispin, I had every right to act as I have done, and I only wish to God that it had been successful. It is true that when I came down to Cornwall yesterday I had no knowledge of you or your affairs, but, in the Treliss hotel, quite inadvertently, I overheard a conversation that showed me quite plainly that it was some one's place to interfere. What I have seen of you since that time, if you will forgive the personality, has only strengthened my conviction that interference—immediate and drastic—was most urgently necessary.

' Thanks to the fog we have failed. For Dunbar and myself we are for the moment in your power. Do what you like with us, but at least have some pity on this child here who has done you no wrong.'

'Very fine, very fine,' said Crispin. 'Mr. Harkness, you have a style—an excellent style—and I congratulate you on having lost almost completely your American accent—a relief for all of us. But come, come, this has lasted long enough. I would point out to you two gentlemen that, as one of you has already discovered, any sort of resistance is quite useless. We will go upstairs. One of my servants first—you two gentlemen next, my other servant following, then my daughter-in-law and myself. Please, gentlemen.'

He said something in a foreign tongue. One Japanese started upstairs, Harkness and Dunbar followed. There was nothing else at that moment to be done. Only at the top of the stairs Dunbar turned and cried: 'Buck up, Hesther. It will be all right.' And she cried back in a voice marvellously clear and brave: 'I'm not frightened, David; don't worry.'

Harkness had a momentary impulse to turn, dash down the stairs again, and run for the window as Dunbar had done; but as though he knew his thought the Japanese behind him laid his hand on his arm; the thin fingers pressed like steel. At the upper floor Dunbar was led one way, himself another. One Japanese, his hand still on his arm, opened a door and bowed. Harkness entered. The door closed. He found himself in total obscurity.

2

He did not attempt to move about the room, but simply sank down on to the floor where he was. He was in a state of extreme physical weariness— his body ached from head to foot—but his brain was active and urgent. This was the first time to himself that he had had—with the exception of his cliff climbing—since his leaving the hotel last evening, and he was glad of the loneliness. The darkness seemed to help him; he felt that he could think here more clearly; he sat there, huddled up, his back against the wall, and let his brain go.

At first it would do little more than force him to ask over and over again: 'Why? Why? Why? Why did we do this imbecile thing? Why, when

we had all the world to choose from, did we find
our way back into this horrible house? It was a
temptation to call the thing magic and to have done
with it, really to suggest that the older Crispin had
wizard powers, or at least hypnotic, and had willed
them back. But he forced himself to look at the
whole thing clearly as a piece of real life as true and
as actual as the ham-and-eggs and buttered toast
that in another hour or two all the world around
him would be eating. Yes, as real and actual as a
toothbrush, that was what this thing was; there
was nothing wizard about Crispin; he was a
dangerous lunatic, and there were hundreds like him
in any asylum in the country. As for their return,
he knew well enough that in a fog people either
walked round and round in a circle or returned to
the place that they had started from.

At this point in his thoughts a tremor shook
his body. He knew where *that* was from, and the
anticipation that lying, like a chained animal, deep
in the recesses of his brain, must soon be loosed
and then bravely faced. But not yet, oh no, not
yet! Let his mind stay with the past as long as
it might.

In the past was Crispin. He looked back over
that first meeting with him, the actual moment
when he had asked him for a match, the dinner,
the return to the hotel when, influenced then by
all that Dunbar had told him, he had seen him
standing there, the polite gestures, the hospitable
words, the drive in the motor. . . . His mind
stopped abruptly *there*. The door swung to, the
lock was turned.

In that earlier Crispin there had been something
deeply pathetic—and, when he dared to look forward,

he would see that in the later Crispin there was the same. So with a sudden flash of lightening revelation that seemed to flare through the whole dark room he saw that it was not the real Crispin with whom they—Hesther, Dunbar, and he—were dealing at all.

No more than the ravings of fever were the real patient, the wicked cancerous growth the real body, the broken glass the real picture that seemed to be shattered beneath it.

They were dealing with a wild and dangerous animal, and in the grip of that animal, pitiably, was the true struggling, suffering soul of Crispin. Not struggling now perhaps any more; the disease had gone too far, growing through a thousand tiny, almost unnoticed stages to this horrible possession.

He knew now—yes, as he had never, never known it, and would perhaps never have known it had it not been for the sudden love for and tenderness towards human nature that had come to him that night—what, in the old world, they had meant by the possession of evil spirits. What it was that Christ had cast out in His ministry. What it was from which David had delivered King Saul.

Quick on this came the further question. If this were so, might he not perhaps when the crisis came—as come he knew it would—appeal to the real Crispin and so rescue both themselves and him? He did not know. It had all gone so far. The animal with its beastly claws deep in the flesh had so tight a hold. He realised that it was in all probability the personality of Hesther herself that had urged it to such extremes. There was something in her clear-sighted, simple defiance of him that had made Crispin's fear of his powerlessness—

the fear that had always contributed to his most dangerous excesses—climb to its utmost height. He had decided perhaps that this was to be the real final test of his power, that this girl should submit to him utterly. Her escape had stirred his sense of failure as nothing else could do. And then their return, all the nervous excitement of that night, the constant alarm of the neighbourhoods in which they had stayed, so that, as the younger Crispin had said, they had been driven ' from pillar to post,' all these things had filled the bowl of insanity to overflowing. *Could* he rescue Crispin as well as themselves?

Once more a tremor ran through his body. Because if he could not—— Once more he thrust the anticipation back, pulling himself up from the floor and beginning slowly, feeling the wall with his hand like a blind man, to walk round the room.

His eyes now were better accustomed to the light, but he could make out but little of where he was. He supposed that he was on the second floor, where were the rooms of Hesther and the younger Crispin. The place seemed empty, there was no sound from the house. He might have been in his grave. Fantastic stories came to his mind, Poe-like stories of walls and ceilings growing closer and closer, of floors opening beneath the foot into watery dungeons, of fiery eyes seen through the darkness. He repeated then aloud:

' I am Charles Percy Harkness. I am thirty-five years of age. I was born at Baker, Oregon, in the United States of America. I am in sound mind and in excellent health. I came down to Cornwall yesterday afternoon for a holiday, recommended to do so by Sir James Maradick, Bart.'

This gave him some little satisfaction; to himself he continued, still walking and touching the wall-paper with his hand: ' I am shut up in a dark room in a strange house at four in the morning for no other reason than that I meddled in other people's affairs. And I am glad that I meddled. I am in love, and whatever comes out of this I do not regret it. I would do over again exactly what I have done, except that I should hope to do it better next time.'

He felt then seized with an intense weariness. He had known that he was, long ago, physically tired, but excitement had kept that at bay. Now quite instantly, as though a spring in the middle of his back had broken, he collapsed. He sank down there on the floor where he was, and all huddled up, his head hanging forward into his knees, he slept. He had a moment of conscious subjective rebellion when something cried to him: ' Don't surrender. Keep awake. It is part of his plan that you should sleep here. You are sur-rendering to *him*.'

And from long, misty distances he seemed to hear himself reply:

' I don't care what happens any more. They can do what they like. . . . They can do what they like. . . .'

And almost at once he was conscious that they were summoning him. A tall thin figure, like an old German drawing, with wild hair, set mouth, menacing eye like Baldung's ' Saturnus,' stood before him and pointed the way into vague misty space. Other figures were moving about him, and he could see, as his eyes grew stronger, that a vast multitude of naked persons were sliding forward like pale lava from a volcano down a steep precipitous slope.

As they moved there came from them a shuddering cry like the tremor of the ground beneath his feet.

'Not there! Not there!' Harkness cried, and Saturnus answered, 'Not yet! You have not been judged.'

Almost instantly judgement followed—judgement in a narrow dark passage that rocked backward and forward like the motion of a boat at sea. The passage was dark, but on either side of its shaking walls were cries and shouts and groans and piteous wails, and clouds of smoke poured through, as into a tunnel, blinding the eyes and filling the nostrils with a horrible stench.

No figure could be seen, but a voice, strong and menacing, could be heard, and Harkness knew that it was himself the voice was addressing. His naked body, slippery with sweat, the acrid smoke blinding him, the voices deafening him, the rocking of the floor bewildering him, he felt desperately that he must clear his mind to answer the charges brought against him.

The voice was clear and calm: 'On February 2, 1905, your friend Richard Hentley was accused in the company of many people, during his absence, of having ill-treated his wife while in Florence. You knew that this was totally untrue and could have given evidence to that effect, but from cowardice you let the moment pass and your friend's position was seriously damaged. What have you to say in your defence?'

The thick smoke rolled on. The walls tottered. The cries gathered in anguish.

' On March 13, 1911, you wired to your sisters in America that you were ill in bed when you were in perfect health, because you wished to stay for a week longer in London in order to attend some races.   What have you to say in your defence?

' On October 3, 1906, you grievously added to the unhappiness of Mrs. Harrington-Adams by asserting in mixed company that no one in New York would receive her and that all Americans were astonished that she should be received at all in London.'

Here at any rate was an opportunity.   Through the smoke he cried:

' There at least I am innocent.   I have never known Mrs. Harrington-Adams.   I have never even seen her.'

' No,' the voice replied.   ' But you spoke to Mrs. Phillops, who spoke to Miss Cator, who then cut Mrs. Adams.   Other people followed Miss Cator's example, and you were quoted as an authority. Mrs. Adams' London life was ruined.   She had never done you any harm.

' On December 14, 1912, you told your sisters that you hated the sight of them and their stuffy ways, that their attempts at culture were ridiculous, and that, like all American women, they were absurdly spoilt.'

Through the smoke Harkness shouted: ' I am sure I never said——'

The voice replied: ' I am quoting your exact words.'

' In a moment of pique I lost my temper.   Of course I didn't mean——'

' On June 3, 1913, you went secretly into the library of a friend and stole his book of Rembrandt

drawings. You knew in your heart that you had
no intention of returning it to him, and when,
some months later, he spoke of it, wishing to lend
it to you, and wondered why he could not find it, you
said nothing to him about your own possession of it.'

Harkness blushed through the rolling smoke.
' Yes, that was shameful,' he cried. ' But I knew
that he didn't care about the book and I——'

' What have you to say against these charges?'

' They are all little things,' Harkness cried,
' small things. Every one does them. . . .'

' Judgement! Judgement! Judgement!' cried
the voice, and suddenly he felt himself moving in
the vast waters of human nudity that were slipping
down the incline. He tried to stay himself; he
flung out his hands and touched nothing but cold
slimy flesh.

Faster and faster and faster. Colder and colder
and colder. Darker and darker and darker. Despair seized him. He called on his friends. Others
were calling on every side of him. Thousands
and thousands of names mingled in the air. The
smoke came up to meet them—vast billowing clouds
of it. He knew with a horrible consciousness that
below him a sea of upturned swords were waiting
to receive them. Soon they would be impaled.
. . . With a shriek of agony he awoke.

He had not been asleep for more, perhaps, than
ten minutes, but the dream had unnerved him.
When he rose from the ground he tottered and
stood trembling. He knew now why it was that
his enemy had designed that he should sleep; he
knew *now* that he could no longer ward off the
animal that on padded feet had been approaching
him—the pain! The pain! The pain!

The sweat beaded his forehead, his knees gave way, and he sank yet again upon the floor. He was murmuring: ' Anything but that. Anything but that. I can't stand pain. I can't *stand* pain, I tell you. Don't you know that I have always funked it all my life long? That I've always prayed that whatever else I got it wouldn't be *that*. That I've never been able to bear to see the tiniest thing hurt, and that in all my thought about going to the war, although I didn't try to escape it, it was even more the pain that I would see than the pain that I would feel.

'And now to wait for it like this, to know that it may be torture of the worst kind, that I am in the power of a man who can reason no longer, who is himself in the power of something stronger and more evil than any of us.'

Then dimly it came through to him that he had been given three tests to-night, and, as it always is in life, the three tests especially suited to his character, his strength and weakness, his past history. The dance had stripped him of his aloofness and drawn him into life, his love for Hesther that he had surrendered had taken from him his selfishness —and now he must lose his fear of pain.

But that? How could he lose it? It was part of the very fibre of his body, his nerves throbbed with it, his heart beat with it. He could not remember a time when it had not been part of him. When he had been five or six his father had decided that he must be beaten for some little crime. His father was the gentlest of human beings, and the beating would be very little, but at the sight of the whip something had cracked inside his brain.

He was not a coward; he had stood up to the

beating without a tear, but the sense of the coming pain had been more awful than anything that he could have imagined. It was the same afterwards at school. He was no coward there either, shared in the roughest games, stood up to bullies, ventured into the most dangerous places.

But one night earache had attacked him. It was a new pain for him and he thought that he had never known anything so terrible. Worse than all else were the intermissions between the attacks and the warnings that a new attack was soon to begin. That approach was what he feared, that terrible and fearful approach. He had said very little, had only lain there white and trembling, but the memory of all those awful hours stayed with him always.

Any thought of suffering in others—of poor women in childbirth, of rabbits caught in traps, of dogs poisoned, of children run over or accidentally wounded—these things, if he knew of them, produced an odd sort of sympathetic pain in himself. The strangest thing had been that the war, with all its horrors, had not driven him crazy as he might have expected from his earlier history. On so terrible a scale, was it that his senses soon became numbed? He did the work that he was given to do, and heard of the rest like cries beyond the wall. Again and again he had tried to mingle, himself, in it; he had always been prevented.

A dog run over by a motor car struck him more terribly than all the agonies of Ypres.

But these things, what had they to do with his present case? He could not think at all. His brain literally reeled, as though it shook, tried to steady itself, could not, and then turned right over. His body was alive, standing up with all its nerves on tiptoe. How was he to endure these hours that were coming to him?

' I must get out of this!' some one, not himself, cried. It seemed to him that he could hear the strange voice in the room. ' I must get out of this. How dare they keep me if I demand to be let out? I am an American citizen. Let me out of this. Can't you hear? Bring me a light and let me out. I have had enough of this dark room. What do you mean by keeping me here? You think that you are stronger than I. Try it and see. Let me out, I say! Let me out!'

He tottered to his feet and ran across the room, although he could not see his way, blundering against the opposite wall. He beat upon it with his hands.

' Let me out, do you hear! Let me out!'

He was not himself, Harkness. He could no longer repeat those earlier words. He was nobody, nothing, nothing at all. They could not hurt him then. Try as they might they could not hurt him, Harkness, when he was not Harkness. He laughed, stroking the wall gently with his hand as though it were his friend.

' It's all right, do you see? You can't hurt me because you can't find me. I'm hiding. *I* don't know where to find myself, so that it isn't likely you will find me. You can't hurt nothing, you know. You can't indeed.'

He laughed and laughed and laughed—gently enjoying his own joke. There was a sudden knocking on the door.

' Come in!' he said in a whisper. ' Come in!'

His heart stood still with fear.

The door opened, splashing into the darkness a shower of light like water flung from a bucket. In the centre of this the two Japanese were standing.

' Master says please come. If you ready he ready.'

At sight of the Japanese a marvellous thing had happened. All his fear had on the instant left him, his beastly physical fear. It fell from him like an old suit of clothes, discarded. He was himself, clear-headed, cool, collected, and, in some strange new way, happy.

Harkness followed them.

3

Harkness followed, conscious only of one thing, his sudden marvellous and happy deliverance from fear. He could not analyse it—he did not wish to. He did not consider the probable length of its duration. Enough that for the present Crispin might cut him into small pieces, skin him alive, boil him in a large pot like a lobster, and he would not care. He followed the sleek servants like a school-boy.

The Tower? Then at last he was to see the interior of this mysterious place. It had exercised, all through this adventure, a strange influence over him, standing up in his imagination white and pure and apart, washed by the sea, guarded by the woods behind it, having a spirit altogether of its own and quite separate from the man who for the moment occupied it. This would be perhaps the last build-ing on this world that would see his bones move and have their being; he had a sense that it knew and sympathised with him and wished him luck.

Meanwhile he walked quietly. His chance would still come and with Dunbar beside him. Or was he never to see Dunbar again? Some of his new-found courage trembled. The worst of this present moment was his loneliness. Was the final crisis to be fought out by himself with no friends at hand? Was he never to see Hesther again? He had an impulse to throw himself forward, attack the servants, and let come what will. The silence of the house was terrible—only their footsteps soft on the thick carpet—and if he could wring a cry or two from his enemies that would be something. No, he must wait. The happiness of others was involved with his own.

The men stopped before a dark-wooded door.

They went through and were met by a white circular staircase. Up this they passed, paused before another door, and crossed the threshold into a high circular brilliantly lit room. For the moment Harkness, his eyes dimmed a little by the shadows of the staircase, could see nothing but the gayness and brightness of the place, papered with a wonderful Chinese pattern of green and purple birds, cherry-coloured pagodas, and crimson temples. The carpet was a soft heavy purple, and there were a number of little gilt chairs, and, in front of the narrow barred window, a gilt cage with a green and crimson macaw.

All this, standing by the door shading his eyes from the dazzling crystal candelabra, he took in; then suddenly saw something that swept away the rest—Hesther and Dunbar standing together, hand in hand, by the window. He gave a cry of joy, hurrying towards them. It was as though he had not seen them for years; they caught his hand in theirs. Crispin was there watching them like a benevolent father with his beloved children.

'That's right,' he said. 'Make the most of your time together. I want you to have a last talk.'

He sat down on one of the gilt chairs.

'Won't you sit down? In a moment I shall leave you alone together for a little while—in case you have any last words. . . .' Then he leaned forward in that fashion so familiar now to Harkness, huddled together, his red hair and little eyes and pale white soft hands alone alive. 'Well, and so—in my power, are you not? The three of you. You can laugh at my ugliness and my stupidity and my bad character, but now you are in my hands completely. I can do whatever I like with you. Whatever . . . the last shame, the last indignity, the uttermost pain. I, ludicrous creature that I am, have absolute power over three fine young things like you, so strong, so beautiful. And then more power and then more and then more. And over many finer, grander, more beautiful than you. I can say crawl and you will crawl, dance and you will dance . . . I who am so ugly that every one has always laughed at me. I am a little God, and perhaps not so little, and soon God Himself . . .'

He broke off, making the movement of music in the air with his hands.

'You a little overestimate the situation,' said Harkness quietly. 'For the moment you can do what you like with our bodies because you happen to have two servants who, with their Jiu-Jitsu and the rest of their tricks, are stronger than we are. It is not you who are stronger, but your servants whom your money is able to buy. I guess if I had

you tied to a pillar and myself with a gun in my
hand I could make you look pretty small.   And in
any case it is only our bodies that you can do anything with.   Ourselves—our real selves—you can't
touch.'

   ' Is that so?' said Crispin.   ' But I have not
begun.   The fun is all to come.   We will see
whether I can touch you or no.   And for my
daughter-in-law '—he looked at Hesther—' there is
plenty of time—many years perhaps.'

   Nothing in all his life would ever appeal more
to Harkness than Hesther then.   From the first
moment of his sight of her what had attracted him
had been the exquisite mingling of the child and
of the woman.   She had been for him at first some
sort of deserted waif who had experienced all the
cruelty and harshness of life so desperately early
that she had known life upside down, and this had
given her a woman's endurance and fortitude.   She
was like a child who has dressed up in her mother's
clothes for a party and then finds that she must take
her mother's place

   And now when she must, after this terrible night,
be physically beyond all her resources she seemed,
in her shabby ill-made dress, her hair disordered,
her face pale, her eyes ringed with grey, to have a
new courage that must be similar to that which he
had himself been given.   She kept her hand in
Dunbar's, and with a strange, dim, unexpected pain
Harkness realised that that new relation between
the two of which he had made the foundation had
grown through danger and anxiety the one for
another already to a fine height.   Then he was
conscious that Hesther was speaking.   She had
come forward quite close to Crispin and stood in

front of him looking him calmly and clearly in the
eyes.

'Please let me say something. After all I am
the principal person in this. If it hadn't been for
me there would not have been any of this trouble.
I married your son. I married him, not because
I loved him, but because I wanted things that I
thought that you could give me. I see now how
wrong that was and that I must pay for doing such
a thing. I am ready to do right by your son. I
never would have tried to run away if it had not
been for you—the other night. After that I was
right to do everything I could to get away. I
begged your son first—and he refused. You have
had me watched during the last three weeks—every
step that I have taken. What could I do but try
to escape?

'We've failed, and because we've failed and
because it has been all my fault I want you to punish
me in any way you like but to let my two friends go.
I was not wrong to try to escape.' She threw up
her head proudly, 'I was right after the way you
had behaved to me, but now it is different. I have
brought them into this. They have done nothing
wrong. You must let them go.'

'You must let all of us go,' Dunbar broke in
hotly, starting forward to Hesther's side. 'Do
you think we're afraid of you, you old play-acting
red-haired monkey? You just let us free or it will
be the worse for you. Do you know where you'll be
this time to-morrow? Beating your fancy-coloured
hair against a padded cell, and that's where you
should have been years ago.'

'No, no,' Hesther broke in. 'No, no, David.
That's not the way. You don't understand. Don't

listen to him.   I'm the only one in this; I tell you—
can't you hear me?—that I will stay.   I won't try
to run away, you can do anything to me you like.
I'll obey you—I will indeed.   Please, please—
Don't listen to him.   He doesn't understand.   But
I do.   Let them go.   They've done no harm.
They only wanted to help me.   They didn't mean
anything against you.   They didn't truly.   Oh!
let them go!   Let them go!'

In spite of her struggle for self-control her
terror was rising, her terror never for herself but
now only for them.   She knew, more than they, of
what he was.   She saw perhaps in his face more
than they would ever see.

But Harkness saw enough.   He saw rising into
Crispin's eyes the soul of that strange hairy fetid-
smelling animal between whose paws Crispin's own
soul was now lying.   That animal looked out of
Crispin's eyes.   And behind that gaze was Crispin's
own terror.

Crispin said:

' This is very comforting for me.   I have waited
for this moment.'

Then Harkness came over to him and stood very
close to him.

' Crispin, listen to me.   It isn't the three of us
who matter in this, it is yourself.   Whatever you
do to us we are safe.   Whatever you think or hope
you can't touch the real part of us, but for yourself
to-night this is a matter of life or death.

' I may know nothing about medicine and yet
know enough to tell you that you're a sick man—
badly sick—and if you let this animal that has his
grip on you get the better of you in the next two
hours you're finished, you're dead.   You know

that as well as I.   You know that you're possessed
of an evil spirit as surely as the man with the spirits
that cleared the Gadarene swine into the sea.   It
isn't for our sakes that I ask you to let us go to-night.
Let us go.   You'll never hear from any of us again.
In the morning, in the decent daylight, you'll know
that you've won a victory more important than any
you've ever won in your life.

'You talk about mastering us, man.   Master
your own evil spirit.   You know that you loathe it,
that you've loathed it for years, that you are miserable and wretched under it.   It is life or death for
you to-night, I tell you.   You know that as well
as I.'

For one moment, a brief flashing moment,
Harkness met for the first and for the last time
the real Crispin.   No one else saw that meeting.   Straight into the eyes, gazing out of them
exactly as a prisoner gazes from behind iron bars,
jumped the real Crispin, something sad, starved, and
dying.   One instant of recognition and he was gone.

'That is very kind of you, Mr. Harkness,'
Crispin said.   'I knew that I should enjoy this
quarter of an hour's chat with you all, and truly I
am enjoying it.   My friend Dunbar shows himself
to be quite frankly the young ruffian he is.   It will
be interesting to see whether in—say an hour's
time from now—he is still in the same mind.   I
doubt it; quite frankly I doubt it very much.   It
is these robust natures that break the easiest.   But
you other two—really how charming.   All altruism
and unselfishness.   This lady has no thought for
anything but her friends, and Mr. Harkness, like
all Americans, is full of fine idealism.   And you
are all standing round me as though you were my

children listening to a fairy story. Such a pretty picture!'

'And when you come to think of it here, I am quite alone, all defenceless, one to three. Why don't you attack me? Such an admirable opportunity! Can it be fear? Fear of an old fat ugly man like me, a man at whom every one laughs!'

Dunbar made a movement. Harkness cried: 'Don't move, Dunbar. Don't touch him. That's what he wants.'

Crispin got up. They were now all standing in a little group close together. Crispin gathered his dressing-gown around him.

'The time is nearly up,' he said. 'I am going to leave you alone together for a little last talk. You'll never see one another again after this, so you had best make the most of it. You see that I am not really unkind.'

'It is hopeless.' Harkness turned round to the window. 'God help us all.'

'Yes, it is hopeless,' Crispin said gently. 'At last my time has come. Do you know how long I have waited for it? Do you know what you represent to me? You have done me wrong, the two of you, broken my hospitality, betrayed my bread and salt, invaded my home. I have justice if I punish you for that. But you stand also for all the others, for all who have insulted me and laughed at me and mocked at me. I have power at last. I shall prick you and you shall bleed. I shall spit on you and you shall bow your heads, and then when you are at my feet stung with a thousand wounds I will raise you and care for you and love you, and you shall share my power——'

He jumped suddenly from his gilt chair and

strutted, waving his hands as though he were commanding an army, towards the macaw, who was asleep with his head under his crimson wing. ' I shall be king in my own right, king of men, emperor of mankind, then one with the gods, and at the last I will shower my gifts. . . .'

He broke off, looking up at a red-lacquer clock that stood on a little round gilt table. ' Time— time—time nearly up!' He swung round upon the three of them.

Dunbar burst out:

' Don't flatter yourself that you'll get away to-morrow. When we're missed———'

' You won't be missed,' Crispin answered with a sigh, as though he deeply regretted the fact. ' The hotel will receive a note in the morning saying that Mr. Harkness has gone for a coast walk, will return in a week, and will the hotel kindly keep his things until his return? Of course the hotel most kindly will. For Mr. Dunbar—well, I believe there is only an aunt in Gloucester, is there not? It will be, I imagine, a month at least before she makes any inquiry. Possibly a year. Possibly never. Who knows? Aunts are often extra-ordinarily careless about their nephews' safety. And in a week. Where can one not be in a week in these modern days? Very far indeed. Then there is the sea. Anything dropped from the garden over the cliff so completely vanishes, and their faces are so often—well, spoilt beyond recognition. . . .'

' If you do this,' Hesther cried, ' I will———'

' I regret to say,' interrupted Crispin, ' that after eight this morning you will not see your father-in-law of whom you are so fond for six months at least. Ah, that is good news for you, I am sure.

That is not to say you will never see him again.
Dear me, no. But not immediately. Not immediately!'

Harkness caught Hesther's hand. He saw that
she was about to make some desperate movement.
'Wait,' he said; 'wait. We can do nothing now.'

For answer she drew him to her and flung out
her hand to Dunbar. 'We three. We love one
another,' she cried. 'Do your worst.'

Crispin looked once more at the clock. 'Melodrama,' he said. 'I, too, will be melodramatic.
I give you twenty minutes by that clock—a situation
familiar to every theatre-goer. When that clock
strikes six I shall, I'm afraid, want the company of
both of you gentlemen. Make your adieus then
to the lady. Your eternal adieus.'

He smiled and gently tip-toed from the room.

4

'And so the curtain falls on Act Three of this
pleasant little drama,' said Dunbar huskily, turning
towards the window. 'There will be a twenty minutes'
interval. But the last act will be played *in camera*.
If only one wasn't so beastly tired—and if only it
wasn't all my fault. . . .' His voice broke.

Harkness went up to him, put his arm around
him and drew him to him. 'Look here. I'm
older than both of you. I might almost be your
father, so you've got to obey my orders. I'll be
best man at your wedding yet, David, yours and
Hesther's. There's nobody to blame. Nothing
but the fog. But don't let's cheat ourselves either.
We're shut up here at half-past five in the morning

miles from any help, no way out, no telephone, and
two damn Japs who are stronger than we are, in
the power of a man who's as mad as a hatter and as
bloodthirsty as a tiger.

'It's going to be all right; I tell you. I know
it. I feel it in my bones. But we've got to behave
for these twenty minutes—only seventeen of them
now—as though it won't be. It's of no use for us
to make any plan. We'll have to do something
on the spur of the moment when we see what the
old devil has up his sleeve for us——

'Meanwhile, as I say, make the best of these
minutes.'

He put out his arm and drew Hesther in.

'I tell you that I love you both. I've only
known you a day, but I love you as I've never loved
any one in my life before. I love you as father and
brother and comrade. It's the best thing that has
happened to me in all my life.'

The three, body to body, stood looking out
through the gilded bars at the sky, silver grey, and
washed with shifting shadows.

'After all,' he went on, 'if our luck doesn't
hold, and we are going to die in the next hour or
so, what is it? It's only what millions of fellows
passed through in the war and under much more
terrible conditions. Imagination is the worst part
of that I fancy, and I suggest that we don't think
of what is going to happen when this time is over—
whether it goes well or ill—we'll fill these twenty
minutes with every decent thought we've got, we'll
think of every fine thing that we know of, and every
beautiful thing, and everything that is of good
report.'

'All I pray,' said Dunbar, 'is that I may have

one last dash at that lunatic before good-bye. He can have a hundred Japs around him but I'll get at him somehow. Harkness, you're a brick. I brought you into this. I had no right to, but I'm not going to apologise. We're here. The thing's done, and if it hadn't been for that rotten fog——— But you're right, Harkness. We'll think of all the ripping things we know. With me it's simple enough. Because the beginning and the middle and the end of it is Hesther. Hesther first and Hesther second and Hesther all the time.'

He didn't look at her, but stared out of the window.

'By Jove, the sun's coming. It's been up round the corner ever so long. It will just about hit the window in another ten minutes. It seems kind of stupid to stand here doing nothing.'

He stepped forward and felt the bars. 'Take hours to get through that, and then there's a drop of hundreds of feet. No, you're about right, Harkness. There's nothing to be done here but to say good-bye as decently as possible."

He sighed. 'I didn't want to kick the bucket just yet, but there it is, it can happen to anybody. A fellow can be as strong as a horse, forget to change his socks and next day be finished. This is better than pneumonia anyway! All the same I can't help feeling we missed our chance just now when we had him alone in here———'

'No,' said Harkness, 'I was watching him. That's what he wanted, for us to go for him. I am sure that he had the Japs handy somewhere, and I think he wanted to hurt us in front of Hesther. But his brain works queerly. He's formulated a kind of book of rules for himself. If we take such and such a step, then he will take such and such another. A sort of insane sense of justice. He's worked it all out to the minute. Half the fun for him has been the planning of it, and then the deliberate slowness of it, watching us, calculating what we'll do. Really a cat with mice. There's nothing for deliberate consecutive thinking like a madman's brain.'

Hesther broke in:

'We're wasting time. I know—I feel as you do—that it's going to be all right, but however he fails with you he *can* carry me off somewhere, and so it *is* very likely that I don't see either of you again for some time. And if that's so—*if* that's so, I just want to say that you've been the finest men in the world to me.

'And I want you to know that whatever turns up for me now—yes, whatever it is—it *can't* be as bad as it was before yesterday. I can't ever again be as unhappy as I was now that I've known both of you as I've known you this night.

'I didn't realise, David, how I felt about you until Mr. Harkness showed me. I've been so selfish all these years, and I suppose I shall go on being selfish, because one doesn't change all in a minute, but at least I've got the two best friends a woman ever had.'

'Hesther,' Dunbar said, turning towards her, 'if we get free of this and you can get rid of that man—I ask you as I've asked you every week for the last ten years—will you marry me?'

'Yes,' she said. But for the moment she turned to Harkness. He was looking through the bars out to the sky, where the mist was now very faintly rose like the coloured smoke of far-distant fire. She put her hand on his shoulder, keeping her other hand in Dunbar's.

'I don't know why you said you were so much older than we are. You're not. Do you promise to be the friend of both of us always?'

'Yes,' he said. Something mockingly repeated in his brain, 'It is a far far better thing that I do——'

He burst out laughing. The macaw awoke, put up his head and screamed.

'You are both younger by centuries than I,' he said. 'I was born old. I was born with the Old Man of Europe singing in my ears. I was born to the inheritance of borrowed culture. The gifts that the fairies gave me at my cradle were Michael Angelo's "David," Rembrandt's "Goldweigher's Field," the Temples at Paestum, the Da Vinci "Last Supper," the Breughels at Vienna, the view of the Jungfrau from Mürren, the Grand Canal at dawn, Hogarth's prints, and the Quintet of the *Meistersinger*. Yes, the gifts were piled up all right. But just as they were all showered upon me in stepped the Wicked Fairy and said that I should have them all—on condition that I didn't touch! Never touch—never. At least I've known that they were there, at least I've bent the knee, but—until last night—until last night . . .'

He suddenly took Hesther's face between his two hands, kissed her on the forehead, on the eyes, on the mouth:

'I don't know what's coming in a quarter of an hour. I don't like to think. To tell you the truth, I'm in the devil of a funk. But I love you, I love you, I love you. Like an uncle you know, or at least like a brother. You've taken a match and set fire to this old tinder-box that's been dry and dusty so long, and now it's alight—such a pretty blaze!'

He broke away from them both with a smile that suddenly made him look young as they'd never seen him:

' I've danced the town, I've climbed rocks, I've dared the devil, I've fallen in love, and I know at last that there's such a hunger for beauty in my soul that it must go on and on and on.   Why should it be there?   My parents hadn't it, my sisters haven't it, no one tried to give it to me.   I've done nothing with it until last night, but now when I've needed it it's come to my help.   I've touched life at last. I'm alive.   I never can die any more!'

The macaw screamed again and again, beating at the cage with its wings.

' Hesther, never lose courage.   Remember that he can't touch you, that no one can touch you. You're your own immortal mistress.'

The red-lacquered clock struck the quarter, and at the same moment the sun hit the window. Strange to see how instantly that room with the coloured pagodas, the fantastic temples, the gilt chairs, and the purple carpet shivered into tinsel. The dust floated on the ladder of the sun: the blue of the early morning sky was coloured faintly like a bird's wing.

The sun flooded the room, wrapping them all in its mantle.

' Let's sit down,' said Dunbar, pulling three of the gilt chairs into the centre of the room, where the sun shone brightest.   ' I've a kind of idea that we'll need all the strength we've got in a few minutes. That's fine what you said, Harkness, about being alive, although I didn't follow you altogether.

'I'm not very artistic.   A man who's been on
the sea since he was a small kid doesn't go to many
picture galleries and he doesn't read books much
either.   To tell you the truth, there's always such
a lot to do, and when I've finished the *Daily Mail*
there doesn't seem time for much more, except a
shocker sometimes.   The sort of mess we're in now
wouldn't make a bad shocker, would it?   Only
you'd never be able to make Crispin convincing.
All I know is, if I wrote a book about him I'd have
him tortured at the end with little red devils and
plenty of pincers.   However, I get what you mean,
Harkness, about being alive.

'I felt something of the same thing in the war
sometimes.   At Jutland, although I was in the
devil of a funk all the time, I was sort of pleased with
myself too.   Life's always seemed a bit unreal
since the armistice, until last night.   And it's a
funny thing, but when I was helping Hesther climb
out of that window and expecting Crispin Junior to
poke his head up any minute I had just that same
pleased-all-over feeling that I had at Jutland.   So
that's about the same as you feel, Harkness, only
different, of course, because of your education. . . .
Hesther, if we win out of this and you marry me
I'll be so good to you—so good to you—that——'

He beat his hands desperately on his knees.

'Here's the time slipping and we don't seem to
be doing anything with it.   It's always been my
trouble that I've never been able to say what I
mean—couldn't find words, you know.   I can't
now, but it's simple enough what I mean——'

Hesther said: 'If we only have ten minutes
like this it's so hard to choose what you would say,
but I'd like you to know, David, that I remember

everything we've ever done together—the time I
missed the train at Truro and was so frightened
about father, and you said you'd come in with me,
and father hadn't even noticed I'd been away; and
the time you brought me the pink fan from Madrid;
and the time I had that fever and you sat up all
night outside my room, those two days father was
away; and the day Billy fell over the Bring Rock
and you climbed down after him; and the time you
brought me that Sealyham and father wouldn't let
me have him; and the time just before you went off
to South Africa and I wouldn't say good-bye.   I've
hurt you so many times and you've never been
angry with me once—or only that once.   Do you
remember the day I struck you in the face because
you said I was more like a boy than a girl?   I thought
you were laughing at me because I was so untidy
and dirty and so I hit you.   And do you remember
you sprang on me like a tiger, and for a moment I
thought you were going to kill me?   You said no
one had ever struck you without getting it back.
Then suddenly you pulled yourself in—just like
going inside and shutting your door.

'I've never seen you until to-night, David.
I've been blind to you.   You've been too close to
me for me to see you.   It will be all right.   We'll
come out of this and then we'll have such times—
such wonderful times——'

She came up to him, drew his head to her breast.
He knelt on the floor at her feet, his arms round her,
his head on her bosom.   She stroked his hair,
looking out beyond him to the blue of the sky.

Harkness felt a mad wildness of impatience.
He went to the window and tugged at the bars.
In despair his hands fell to his side.

' The only chance, Dunbar, is to go straight for
him the moment we're out of this room, even if
those damned Japs are with him. We can't do
much, but we may smash him up a bit first. Then
there's Jabez. We've forgotten Jabez. Where's
he been all this time?'

Dunbar looked up. ' I expect he went home
after we went off.'

' No,' said Harkness, ' he was to be there till six.
He told me. What's happened to him? At any
rate he'll give the alarm if we don't turn up.'

' No, he'll think we got safely off.'

' Yes, I suppose he will. My God, it's five to
six. Look here, stand up a moment.'

They stood up.

' Let's take hands. Let's swear this. Whatever happens to us now, whether some of us survive
or none, whether we die now or live happily ever
afterwards, we'll be friends for ever, nothing shall
ever separate us, for better or worse we're together
for always.'

They swore it.

' And see here. If I don't come out of this
don't have any regrets either of you. Don't think
you brought me into this against my will. Don't
think that whichever way it goes I regret a moment
of it. You've given me the finest time.'

Dunbar laughed. ' I sort of feel we're going
to have a chance yet. After all, he's been probably
playing with us, trying to frighten us. There'll
be nothing in it, you see. Anyway I'll get a crack
at his skull, and now that I've got you, Hesther, I
wouldn't give up this night for all the wealth of the
Indies. I don't know about life or death. I've
never thought much about it, to tell you the honest

truth, but I bet that any one who's as fond of any
one as I am of you can't be very far away, whatever
happens to their body.'

'There goes six.'

The red-lacquer clock struck. Hesther flung
her arms around Harkness and kissed him, then
Dunbar.

They all stood listening. Just as the clock
ceased there was a knock at the door.

5

Harkness went to the door and opened it; not
Crispin, as he had expected, but one of the Japanese.
For the first time he spoke:

'Beg your pardon, sir. The master would be
glad you see him upstairs.' Harkness did not look
back. He knew that Dunbar and Hesther were
clasped tightly in one another's arms. He walked
out, closing the door behind him. He stood with
the Japanese in the small space waiting. It was a
dim, subdued light out here. You could only see the
thick stone steps of the circular staircase winding
upwards out of sight. Harkness's brain was working now with feverish activity. Whatever Crispin's
devilish plan might be he would be there to watch
the climax of it. If Harkness and Dunbar were
quick enough they could surely have Crispin
throttled before the Japanese were in time; without
Crispin it was likely enough that the Japanese would
be passive. This was no affair of theirs. They
simply obeyed their master's orders.

He wondered why he had not attempted something in that room just now—why, indeed, he had

prevented Dunbar; but some instinct had told him then that Crispin was longing to shame them in some way before Hesther. He had then an almost overpowering impulse to turn back, run into that room, fling his arms about Hesther and hold her until those devils pulled them apart. It was an impulse that rose blinding his eyes, deafening his ears, stunning his brain. He half turned. The door opened and Dunbar came out. Harkness sighed with relief. At the sight of Dunbar the temptation left him.

They mounted the stairs, one Japanese in front of them, the other behind. At the next break in the flight the Japanese turned and opened a door on the left.

'In here, gentlemen, if you please,' he said, bowing.

They entered a small room with no windows, quite dark save for one dim electric light in the ceiling, and without furniture save for two wicker chairs.

They stood there waiting. 'The master,' said the Japanese, 'he much obliged if you gentlemen will kindly take your clothes off.'

For a moment there was silence. They had not realised the words. Then Dunbar broke out: 'No, by God, no! Strip for that swine! Harkness, come on! You go for that fellow, I'll take this one!' and instantly he had hurled himself on the Japanese nearest the door.

Harkness flung at the one who had spoken. He was conscious of his fingers clutching at the thin cotton stuff of the clothes, and, beneath the clothes, the cold hard steel of the limbs. His arms gripped upwards, caught the cloth of the shirt, tore it, slipped on the smooth, hairless chest. Then in his left forearm there was a pain, sharp as though some ravenous animal had bitten him there, then an agony in the middle of his back, then in his left thigh.

Against his will he cried out; the pain was terrible—awful. Every nerve in his body was rebelling so that he had neither strength nor force. He slipped to the floor, writhing involuntarily with the agony of the twisted muscle and, even as he slipped, he saw sliding down over him, impervious, motionless, fixed like a shining mask, the face of the Japanese.

He lay on the floor; panic flooded him. His helplessness, the terror of what was coming next, the fright of the dark—it was all he could do at that moment not to burst into tears and cry like a child.

He was lying on the floor, and the Japanese, kneeling beside him, had one arm under him as though to make his position more comfortable.

'Very sorry,' the Japanese murmured in his ear; 'the master's orders.'

As the pain withdrew he felt only an intense relief and thankfulness. He did not care about what had gone before nor mind what followed. All he wished was to be left like that until the wild beating of his heart softened and his pulse was again tranquil.

Then he thought of Dunbar. He turned his head and saw that Dunbar also was lying on the floor, on his side. Not a sound came from him. The other Japanese was bending over him.

'Dunbar!' Harkness cried in a voice that to his own surprise was only a whisper, 'wait. It's no

good with these fellows. We'll have our chance
later.'

Dunbar replied, the words gritted from between
his teeth: 'No—it's no good—with these devils.
It's all right, though. I'm cheery.'

Harkness saw then that the Japanese had been
stripping Dunbar, and he noticed with a curious
little wonder that his clothes had been arranged in
a neat, tidy pile—his socks, his collar, his braces, on
his shirt and trousers. He saw the Japanese move
forward as though to help Dunbar to his feet; there
was a movement as though Dunbar were pushing
him away. He rose to his feet, naked, strong,
his head up, swung out his arms, pushed out his
chest.

'No bones broken with their monkey tricks.
Hurry up, Harkness. We may as well go into
the sea together. I bet the water's cold.'

But no. The Japanese said something. Dunbar
broke out:

'I'm damned if I will.' Then, turning to
Harkness: 'He says I've got to go on by myself.
It seems they're going to separate us. Rotten luck,
but there's no fighting these two fellows here.
Well, cheerio, Harkness. You've been a mighty
fine pal, if we don't meet again. Only that rotten
fog did us in.'

Harkness struggled to his knees. 'No, no,
Dunbar. They shan't separate us. They shan't
——' but there was a touch of a hand on his arm
and instantly, as though to save at all costs another
pressure of that nerve, he sank back.

Dunbar went out, one of the Japanese following
him. The door closed.

Now indeed Harkness needed all his fortitude.

He had never felt such loneliness as this. From the beginning of the adventure there had been an element so fantastic, so improbable, that except at certain moments he had never believed in the final reality of it. There was something laughable, ludicrous about Crispin himself; he had been like a child playing with his toys. Now absolutely Harkness was face to face with reality.

Crispin did mean all that he had threatened. And what that might be———!

The Japanese was beginning to take off his clothes, very lightly and gently pulling his coat from under him. Harkness sat up and assisted him. This did not matter. Of what significance was it whether he had clothes or no? What mattered was that he should be out of this horrible room where there was neither space nor light nor company. Anything anywhere was better. The Japanese' cool hard fingers slipped about his body. He himself undid his collar and mechanically dropped his collar-stud into the right-hand pocket of his waistcoat, where he always put it when he was undressing. He bent forward and took off his shoes.

The Japanese gravely thanked him. There was a small hole in his right sock and he slipped it off quickly, covering it with his other hand. He was ashamed for the Japanese to see it.

His clothes were piled as neatly as Dunbar's. He stood up feeling freshened and cool.

Then the Japanese, bowing, moved to the door. Harkness followed him.

They climbed the stairs once more, the stone striking cold under Harkness's bare feet. They must now be reaching the very top of the Tower.

There was a sense of space and height about them and a stronger light.

The Japanese paused, pushed back a door and sharply jerked Harkness forward. Harkness nearly fell, but was caught by some one else, closed his eyes involuntarily against a flood of light into which he seemed, with a curious sensation as though he had dived from a great height, to be sinking ever deeper and deeper, then to be struggling up through bursting bubbles of colour. His eyes were still closed against the sun that pressed like a warm palm upon the lids.

He felt hands moving about him; then that he was held back against something cold; then that he was being bound, gently, smoothly; the bands did not hurt his flesh. There was a pause. He still kept his eyes closed. Was this death then? The sun beat upon his body, warm and strong. The cool of the pillar to which he was bound was pleasant against his back. There were boards beneath his feet, and on their dry, friendly surface his toes curled. A delicious soft lethargy wrapped him round. Was this death? One sharp pang like the pressure of an aching tooth and then nothing, sinking into dark silence through this shaft of deep and burning sunlight. . . .

He opened his eyes. He cried aloud with astonishment. He was in what was plainly the top room of the Tower, a high white place with a round ceiling softly primrose. One high window went the length from floor to ceiling, and this window, which was without bars, blazed with sun and shone with the colours of the early morning blue. The room was white—pure virgin white—round, and bare of furniture. Only—and this was what had

caught the cry from Harkness—three pillars supported the ceiling, and to these three pillars were
bound by white cord, first himself, then Dunbar,
then, naked as they, Jabez.

The fisherman stood there facing Harkness—a
gigantic figure. Yesterday afternoon on the hill,
last night in the garden, Harkness had not recognised the man's huge proportions under his
clothes. Now, bound there, with his black hair
and beard, his great chest, the muscle of his arms
and thighs, the sunlight bathing him, he was
mighty to see.

His eyes were mild and puzzled like the eyes
of a dog who has been chained against reason. He
was making a strange restless motion from side to
side as though he were testing the white cords that
held him. His face above his beard, his neck,
the upper part of his chest, his hands, his legs beneath the knees, were a deep russet brown, the rest
of him a fair white, striking strangely with the jet
blackness of his hair.

He smiled as he saw Harkness's astonishment.

'Aye, sir,' he said. 'It wasn't me you was
expectin' to see here, and it wasn't myself that was
expectin' to be here neither.'

They were alone—no Japanese, no Crispin.

'I've been in here half an hour before you come,'
he went on. 'And I can tell you, sir, I was mighty
sorry to see them bringin' both you gentlemen in.
Whatever happens to me, I said, they've got clear
away. It never kind of struck me that the fog was
going to worry you.'

'Why didn't you get away yourself, Jabez?'
Harkness asked him.

'They was down on me about an hour after.

The fog had come on pretty thick and I was walkin' up and down out there thinkin'. I hadn't no more than another hour of it and pleasin' myself to think how mad that old devil would be when he'd found out what had happened and me safe in my own house with the mother, when all of a sudden I hear the car snortin'. "Somethin' up," I says, and three seconds later, as you might say, they was on me. If it hadn't been for that fog I might of got clear, but they was on me before I knew it. I had a bit of a struggle with they dirty stinkin' foreigners, but they got a lot of dirty tricks an Englishman would be ashamed of using. Anyway they had me down on the ground pretty quick and hurt me too.

‘ They trussed me up like a fowl, carried me into the hall, and didn't the old red-headed devil spit and curse? You've never seen nothing like it, sir. Sure raving mad he was that time all right. And he came and kicked me on the face and pulled my beard and spat in my eyes. I don't know what's coming to us right now, but I pray the Almighty Father to give me just one turn with my fist. I'll land him.

‘ Then, sir, they carried me upstairs and tumbled me into a dark room. There I was for I wouldn't like to say how long. Then they came in and took my things off me, the dirty foreigners. It's only a foreigner would think of a thing like that. I struggled a bit, but what's the use? They put their thumb in your back and they've got you. Then they tied me up here. I had to laugh, I did really. Did you ever see such a comic picture as all three of us without a stitch between us tied up here at six in the morning?

‘ When I tell mother about it she'll laugh all

right.   Like the show down to St. Ives when they
have the boxing.   I suppose we'll be getting out
of this all serene, sir, won't we?'

'Of course we will,' said Dunbar.   'Don't
you worry, Jabez.   He's been doing all this to
frighten us.   He daren't touch us really.   Why,
he'll have the county about his ears as it is.   Don't
you worry.'

'Thank you, sir,' said Jabez, still moving from
side to side within the bands, 'because you see, sir,
I wouldn't like anything to happen to me just now.
Mother's expectin' an addition to the family in a
month or so and there's six on 'em already, an' it
needs a bit of doing looking after them all.   I
wouldn't have been working for this dirty blackguard here if it hadn't been for there being so many
of us—not that I'd have one of them away, if you
understand me, sir.'

'You needn't be afraid, Jabez,' Dunbar said.
'When we get out of this Mr. Harkness and I
will see that you never have any anxiety again.
You've been a wonderful friend to us to-night and
we're not likely to forget it.'

'Oh, don't you mistake me, sir,' said Jabez.
'It wasn't no help I was asking for.   I'm doing
very well with the boat and the potatoes.   It was
only I was thinking I wouldn't like nothing exactly
to happen to me along of this crazy lunatic here, if
you understand me, sir. . . . I'm not so sure if
they give me time I couldn't get through these bits
of rope here.   I'm pretty strong in the arm, or used
to be—not so dusty even now.   If I could work
at them a bit——'

The door opened and Crispin came in.

He appeared to Harkness as he stepped in,

quietly closing the door behind him, like some strange creature of a dream. He seemed himself, in the way that he moved with his eyes nearly closed, somnambulistic. He was wearing now only his white silk pyjamas, and of these the sleeves were rolled up, showing his fat white arms. His red hair stood on end like an ill-fitting wig. In one hand he carried a curved knife with a handle of worked gold.

In the room, blazing with sunlight, he was like a creature straight from the boards of some neighbouring theatre, even to the white powder that lay in dry flakes upon his face.

He opened his eyes, staring at the sunlight, and in their depths Harkness saw the strangest mingling of terror, pathos, eager lust, and a bewildered amazement, as though he were tranced. The gaze with which he turned to Harkness had in it a sudden appeal; then that appeal sank like light quenched by water.

He was wrung up on the instant to intensest excitement. His whole body trembled. His mouth opened as though he would speak, then closed again.

He came close to Harkness. He put out his hand and touched his neck.

'We are alone,' he said, in his soft, beautiful voice. He stroked Harkness's neck. The soft, boneless fingers! Harkness looked at him, and, strangely, at that moment their eyes were very close to one another. They looked at one another gently. In Harkness's eyes were no malice; in Crispin's that strange mingling of lust and unhappiness.

Harkness only said: 'Crispin, whatever you

do to us, leave that girl alone.   I beg you leave
her. . . .'

He closed his eyes then.   God helping him he
would not speak another word.   But a triumphant
exultation surged through him because he knew
that he was not afraid.

There was no fear in him.   It was as though the
warm sun beating on his body gave him courage.

Standing behind the safeguard of his closed eyes
his real soul seemed to slip away, to run down the
circular staircase into the hall and pass happily into
the garden, down the road to the sea.

His soul was free and Crispin's was imprisoned.

He heard Crispin's voice: ' Will you admit now
that I have you in my hand?   If I touch you here
how you will bleed—bleed to death if I do not
prevent it.   Do you remember Shylock and his
pound of flesh?   "Oh! upright Judge!"   But there
is no judge here to stay me!'

The knife touched him.   He felt it as though it
had been a wasp's sting—a small cut it must be—
and suddenly there was the cool trickle of blood
down his skin.   Then his right shoulder—a prick!
Now a cut again on his arm.   Stings—nothing
more.   But the end had really come then at last?
His hands beneath the bonds moved suddenly of
their own impulse.   It was not natural not to strive
to be free, to fight for his life.

He opened his eyes.   He was bleeding from
five or six little cuts.   Crispin was standing away
from him.   He saw that Dunbar, crimson in the
face, was struggling frantically with his cords and
was shouting.   Jabez, too, was calling out.   The
room, hitherto so quiet, was alive with movement.
Crispin now stood back from him watching him.

The sight of blood had completed what these weeks had been preparing.

With that first touch of the knife on Harkness's body Crispin's soul had died. The battle was over. There was an animal here clothed fantastically in human clothes like a monkey or a dog at a music-hall show. The animal capered, stood on its hind legs, mowed in the air with its hands. It crept up to Harkness and, whining like a dog, pricked him with the knife point now here, now there, in a hundred places.

Harkness looked out once more at the great window with its splash of glorious sky, then ceased to struggle with his cords. His lips moved in some prayer perhaps, and once more, surely now for the last time, he closed his eyes. He had a strange vision of all the moving world beyond that window. At that moment at the hotel the maids would be sweeping the corridors, people would be stirring and rubbing their eyes and looking at their watches; in the town, family breakfasts would be preparing, men would be sauntering down the narrow streets to their work, the connection with the London train would be running in with the London papers, already the men and women would be in the fields, the women would be waiting perhaps for the fishing-fleet to come in, Mrs. Jabez would be at the cottage door looking up the road for her husband. . . .

His heart pounded into his mouth; with a mighty impulse he drove it back. Crispin was laughing. The knife was raised. His face was wrinkled. He was running round the room, round and round, making with the knife strange movements in the air. He was whispering to

himself. Round and round and round he ran,
words pouring from his mouth in a thick unending
stream. They were not words, they were sounds,
and once and again a strange sigh like a catch of
the breath, like a choke in the throat. He ran,
bending, not looking at the three men, bending low
as though as he ran he were looking for something
on the floor.

Then quite suddenly he straightened himself,
and with a growl and a snarl, the knife raised in
one hand, hurled himself at Jabez.

All followed then quickly. The knife flashed
in the sunlight. It seemed that the hands caught
at Jabez's eyes, first one and then another; but there
had been more than the hands, because suddenly blood
poured from those eyes, spouting over, covering
the face, mingling with the beard.

With a great cry Jabez put forth his strength.
Stung by agony to a power that he had never known
until then his body seemed to rise from the ground,
to become something superhuman, immortal. The
great head towered, the limbs spread out, it seemed
for a moment as though the pillar itself would fall.

The cord that tied him to the pillar snapped
and his hands were free. He tottered, the blood
pouring from his face. He moved, blindly, stagger-
ing. Not a sound had come from him since that
first cry.

His hands flung out, and in another moment
Crispin was caught into his arms. He raised him.
The little fat hands fluttered. The knife flashed
loosely and fell to the ground. The giant swung
into the middle of the room, blinded, but holding
to himself ever tighter and ever tighter the short
fat body.

Crispin, his head tossed back, his legs flung out in an agony now of terror, screamed with a strange, shrill cry like a rabbit entrapped.

Jabez turned, and now he had Crispin's soft chest against his bleeding face, the arms fluttering above his head. As he turned his shoulder touched the glass of the window. He pushed backward with his arm and the window swung open, some of the broken glass tinkling to the ground. There was a great rush of air.

That strange thing, like no human body, the white silk, the brown slippers, the red hair, swung. For one second of a time, suspended as it were on the thread of that long animal scream, so shrill and yet so thin and distant, the white face, its little eyes staring, the painted mouth open, hung towards Harkness. Then into the air, like a coloured bundle of worthless junk; for a moment a dark shadow across the steeple of sunlight, and then down, down, into fathomless depths of air, leaving the space of sky stainless, the morning blue without taint. . . .

Jabez stood for a moment facing them, his chest heaving in convulsive pants. Then crying ' My eyes! My eyes!' crumpled to the floor.

6

First Harkness was conscious of a wonderful silence. Then into the silence, borne in on the back of the sea breeze, he heard the wild chattering of a multitude of birds. The room was filled with their chatter, up from the trees, crowding the room with their life.

Straight past the window, like an arrow shot

from a bow, flashed a sea-gull. Then another more
slowly wheeled down, curving against the blue like
a wave released into air.

He recognised all these things, and then once
again that wonderful blessed stillness. All was
peace, all repose. He might rest for ever.

After, it seemed, an infinity of time, and from
a vast distance, he caught Dunbar's voice :

' . . . Jabez! Jabez! Jabez, old fellow! The
man's fainted. Harkness, are you all right? Did
he hurt you?'

' No,' Harkness quietly answered. ' He didn't
hurt me. He meant to, though. . . .' Then a
green curtain of dark thick cloth swept through the
heaven and caught him into its folds. He knew
nothing more. The last thing he heard was the
glorious happy chattering of the birds.

7

He slowly climbed an infinity of stairs, up and
up and up. The stairs were hard to climb, but he
knew that at their summit there would be a glorious
view, and, for that view, he would undergo any
hardship. But oh! he was tired, desperately tired.
He could hardly raise one foot above another.

He had been walking with his eyes closed,
because it was cooler that way. Then a bee stung
him. Then another. On the chest. Now on
the arm. Now a whole flight. He cried out.
He opened his eyes.

He was lying on a bed. People were about him.
He had been climbing those stairs naked. It
would never do that those strangers should see him.

He must speak of it. His hand touched cloth.
He was wearing trousers. His chest was bare, and
some one was bending over him touching places
here and there on his body with something that
stung. Not bees after all. He looked up with
mildly wondering eyes and saw a face bending over
him—a kindly bearded face, a face that he could
trust. Not like—not like—that strange mask face
of the Japanese. . . . That other . . .

He struggled on to his elbow, crying: 'No, no.
I can't any more. I've had enough. He's mad,
I tell you——'

A kind rough voice said to him: 'That's all
right, my friend. That's all over. No harm
done——'

My friend! That sounded good. He looked
round him and in the distance saw Dunbar. He
broke into smiles, holding out his hand.

'Dunbar, old man! That's fine. So you're all
right?'

Dunbar came over and sat on his bed, putting
his arm around him.

'All right? I should think so. So are we all.
Even Jabez isn't much the worse. That devil
missed his eyes, thank heaven. He'll have two
scars to the end of his time to remind him, though.'

Harkness sat up. He knew now where he was,
on a sofa in the hall—in the hall with the tattered
banners and the clock that coughed like a dog.
He looked at the clock—just a quarter to seven!
Only three-quarters of an hour since that awful
knock on the door.

Then he saw Hesther.

'Oh, thank God!' he whispered to himself.
'*Nunc dimittis* . . .'

She came to him.   The three sat together on the sofa, the bearded man (the doctor from the village under the cliff, Harkness afterwards found) standing back, looking at them, smiling.

' Now tell me,' Harkness said, looking at Dunbar, ' the rest that I don't know.'

' There isn't much to tell.   We were only there another ten minutes.   When you fainted off I felt a bit queer myself, but I just kept together, and then heard some one running up the stairs.

' I thought it was one of the Japs returning, but there was a great banging on the door and then shouting in a good old Cornish accent.   I called back that I was tied up in there and that they must break in the door.   That they did and burst in— two fishermen and old Possiter the policeman from Duntrent.   He's somewhere about the house now with two of the Treliss policemen.   Well, it seems that a fellow, Jack Curtis, was going up the hill to his morning work in the Creppit fields above the wood here when he heard a strange cry, and, turning the corner of the road, finds on the path above the rocks, Crispin—pretty smashed up, you know.   He ran—only a yard or two—to the Possiter's cottage.   Possiter was having his break-fast and was up here in no time.   They got into the house through a window and saw the two Japanese clearing off up the back garden.   Curtis chased them, but they beat him and vanished into the wood.   They stopped two other men who were passing, and then came on Hesther tied up in the library.   She sent them to the Tower.'

' Well—and then?' said Harkness.

' There isn't much more.   Except this.   They got up the doctor, had poor old Jabez's face looked to and cleared him off down to his cottage, were examining your cuts—all this down here. Suddenly a car comes up to the door and in there bursts— young Crispin! The two Treliss policemen had turned up three minutes earlier in *their* car and were here alone except for Possiter examining Crispin Senior—who was pretty well smashed to pieces I can tell you.

' Crispin Junior breaks through, gives one look at his father, shouts out some words that no one can understand, puts a revolver to his temple, and blows the top of his head off before any one can stop him. Topples right over his father's body. The end of the house of Crispin!

' I saw all this from the staircase. I was just coming down after looking at you. I heard the shot, saw old Possiter jump back, and got down in time to help them clear it all up.

' No one knows where he'd been. To Truro, I imagine, looking for all of us. He must have cared for that madman, cared for him or been hypnotised by him—*I* don't know. At least he didn't hesitate——'

' And now, sir, would you mind telling me . . .?' said the stout red-faced Treliss policeman, advancing towards them.

8

He was free; it was, from the moment that the red-faced policeman, smiling upon him benevolently, had informed him that, for the moment, he had had from him all that he needed, his one burning and determined impulse—to get away from that hall, that garden, that house, with the utmost possible urgency.

He had not wished even to stay with Hesther and Dunbar. He would see them later in the day —would see them, please God, many many times in the years to come.

What he wanted was to be alone—absolutely alone.

The cuts on the upper part of his body were nothing—a little iodine would heal them soon; it seemed that there had come to him no physical harm—only an amazing all-invading weariness. It was not like any weariness that he had ever before known. He imagined—he had had no positive experience—that it resembled the conditions of some happy doped trance, some dream-state in which the world was a vision and oneself a disembodied spirit. It was as though his body, stricken with an agony of weariness, was waiting for his descent, but his soul remained high in air in a bell of crystal glass beyond whose surface the colours of the world floated about him.

He left them all—the doctor, the policeman, Dunbar, and Hesther. He did not even stop at Jabez's cottage to inquire. That was for later. As half-past seven struck from the church tower below the hill he flung the gate behind him, crossed the road, and struck off on to the Downs above the sea.

By a kind of second sight he knew exactly where he would go. There was a path that crossed the Down that ran slipping into a little cove, across whose breast a stream trickled, then up on to the Down again, pushing up over fields of corn, past the cottage gardens up to the very gate of the hotel.

It was all mapped in his mind in bright, clear-painted colours.

The world was indeed as though it had only

that morning been painted in green and blue and gold. While the fog hung, under its canopy the master-artist had been at work. Now from the shoulder of the Down a shimmer of mist tempered the splendour of the day. Harkness could see it all. The long line of sea on whose blue surface three white sails hovered, the bend of the Down where it turned to deeper green, the dip of the hill out of whose hollow the church spire like a spear steel-tipped gesticulated, the rising hill with the wood and the tall white tower, the green downs far to the right where tiny sheep like flowers quivered in the early morning haze.

All was peace. The rustling whisper of the sea, the breeze moving through the taller grasses, the hum of tiny insects, a lark singing, two dogs barking in rivalry, a scent of herb and salt and fashioned soil—all these things were peace.

Harkness moved a free man as he had never been in all his life as yet. He was his own master, and God's servant too. Life might be a dream— it seemed to him that it was—but it was a dream with a meaning, and the events of that night had given him the key.

His egotism was gone. He wanted nothing for himself any more. He was, and would always be, himself, but also he had lost himself in the common life of man. He was himself because his contact with beauty was his own. Beauty belonged to all men in common, and it was through beauty that they came to God, but each man found beauty in his own way, and, having found it, joined his portion of it to the common stock.

He had been shy of man and was shy no longer; he had been in love, was in love now, but had surrendered it; he had been afraid of physical pain and was afraid no longer; he had looked his enemy in the eyes and borne him no ill-will.

But he was conscious of none of these things—only of the freshness of the morning, of the scents that came to him from every side, and of this strange disembodied state, so that he seemed to float, like gossamer, on air.

He went down the path to the little cove. He watched the ripple of water advance and retreat. The stream of fresh water that ran through it was crystal clear, and he bent down, made a cup with his hands, and drank. He could see the pebbles, brown and red and green like jewels, and thin spires of green weed swaying to and fro.

He buried his face in the water, letting it wash his eyes, his forehead, his nostrils, his mouth.

He stood up and drank in the silence. The ripple of the sea was like the touch on his arm of a friend. He kneeled down and let the fine sand run, hot, through his fingers. Then he moved on.

He climbed the hill: a flock of sheep passed him, huddling together, crying, nosing the hedge. The sun touched the outline of their fleece to shining light. He cried out to the shepherd:

' A fine morning!'

' Aye, a beautiful morning!'

' A nasty fog last night.'

' Aye, aye—all cleared off now, though. It'll be a warm day.'

The dog, his tongue out, his eyes shining, ran barking hither, thither. They passed over the hill, the sheep like a cloud against the green.

He pushed up, the breeze blowing more strongly now on his forehead.

He reached the cottage gardens, and the smell of roses was once more thick in his nostrils. The chimneys were sending silver skeins of smoke into the blue air. Bacon smells and scent of fresh bread came to him.

He was at the hotel gates. Oh! but he was weary now! Weary and happy. He stumbled up the path, smelling the roses again. Into the hall. The gong was ringing for breakfast. Children, crying out and laughing, raced down the stairs, past him. He reached his room. He opened the door. How quiet it was! Just as he had left it.

Ah! there was the tree of the ' St. Gilles,' and there the grave friendly eyes of Strang leaning over the etching-table to greet him.

Just as they were—but he!—not as he had been! He caught his face in the glass, smiling idiotically.

He staggered to his bed, flung himself down, still smiling. His eyes closed. There floated up to him a face—a little white face crowned with red hair, but not evil now, not animal—friendly, lonely, asking for something. . . .

He smiled, promising something. Lifted his hand. Then his hand fell, and he sank deep, deep, deep into happy, blissful slumber.

THE END